My Phantom

The Memoir of Christine Daaé

Anstance Tamplin

Straight Up Press

Pacific Northwest USA

My Phantom is a publication of Straight Up Press

ISBN 978-0-9824579-0-0

Cover photo copyright 2009 © by Krzysztof Nieciecki. Image from BigStockPhoto.com

Printed in the United States of America

For Nellie
still brainy, beautiful and beguiling

1

*G*ASTON LEROUX WAS WRONG about many things. The falling chandelier. The deaths of Joseph Buquet and Philippe de Chagny. Most of all, the opera ghost, who was not a terrifying monster but a mesmerizing man. Yet I can't blame the novelist for his fevered imaginings at my expense. Even Raoul, my husband of thirty-seven years, went to his grave without learning how close the Phantom of the opera came to winning my hand. He will always have my heart.

That Sunday morning I had the streets of Paris to myself. Neither the steady drizzle from the low clouds nor the cold breeze from the Seine discouraged me. Others could spend the 26th day of September toasting themselves beside the first fire of autumn, nose-deep in *Le Temps* or snoozing on the divan. Mine would be spent on a quest to find another friend. A real friend, one I could see and touch.

To fully understand, picture those same streets on a fine afternoon, crowded with *flâneurs* at the café tables who pause over their cards to exchange speculative glances with a giggling flock of opera dancers as they pass by. Watch their eyes narrow at the young woman following the *coryphées* – blonde, pretty enough, the same theatrical posture – but unaccompanied by friends or family. Alone. Now see the dancers' elegant protectors watching from the wings of the stage just beyond the place where the opera chorus awaits its entrance cue. Observe how the men inspect the cluster of young singers, measuring with their eyes and noting the girl standing a few steps to the side. Apart. Always alone. Always apart.

Today there were few passersby to notice me as I strode toward Rue Réaumur. Raindrops spotted the long blue apron of a bread delivery woman who wheeled her wicker basket into a café near the Palais de la Bourse. Tourists braving the showers ignored me as they turned up Rue Saint Denis to admire the triumphal arch on the site of an ancient city gate. But outside the Conservatoire des Arts et Métiers the coachmen eyed me from their seats atop the parked broughams, likely judging the hour too early and me too well-dressed to be a street walker. I focused my gaze on their carriage horses, drawing from one a friendly whicker as a reward, and made sure to keep my pace brisk.

Searching stares and vulgar asides no longer shocked me. Six years at the Paris opera had finally steeled me to the city's lusty ways. I had been so innocent when I arrived at Charles Garnier's lavish new opera house – a country girl of thirteen, newly-orphaned, and already overwhelmed by the city's tumult. On the front steps that first day I'd been transfixed by the sight of Carpeaux's naked dancers, voluptuous and joyful and very much alive though imprisoned in stone. Inside the Palais

Garnier my astonishment turned to wonder at this strange new world where bare-breasted sirens cavorted across the ceiling of the grand staircase, trumpeted golden horns beneath the auditorium's glowing chandelier and flanked the box once meant for France's final emperor. And the music! All I'd known of opera came from a single visit to the theater in Rennes for a Meyerbeer opera, a history pageant with rousing hymns extolling the greatness of God. I had never heard the sorrowful final duet of Aida and Radames in their tomb beneath the temple of Vulcan. Or the heartbreaking aria of mad Lucia di Lammermoor after she murdered her bridegroom. And the ecstasy of Leonore and Florestan – "After great sufferings! Oh, delight past utterance!" – when she rescued him from the deepest dungeon. Such passion thrilled me. And every inch of the opera house fairly throbbed with it. In the private boxes where couples disappeared behind crimson curtains. In the gilded dancers' foyer where the ballerinas flirted with their callers. In the prima donna's dressing room where wealthy suitors thronged with their extravagant gifts. In the street beside the stage door where a shabbier crowd of hopefuls waited with empty hands and lovesick hearts. Inside the opera and out, Paris pursued the pleasures of the flesh.

Though I soon ripened into a young woman whose face and figure matched the preference of the day, I remained alone and apart. Sometimes I studied myself in the mirror, leaning close to scrutinize my face and then moving backward to see myself full length, searching for the flaw that must exist. How else to explain my solitude? On the sidewalks of the city I often drew unwanted attention, but in the opera house I was a tribe of one. From the start, the ballet students scorned me as they did all singers. But the other singing students also kept a polite distance. In a pleasure palace overflowing with ardent admirers in the grip of *l'amour*, I alone remained unclaimed. Even a pudgy contralto with smallpox scars on her face had attracted the attentions of an apprentice carpenter from the set shop.

Still, my heart was light that morning as I neared the Marché St. Martin. Over the past six months my life had been remade. Suddenly a happier destiny beckoned, a future I would affirm by visiting the bird market. This time I didn't stop to admire the brightly-colored parrots or to check the latest fashion in cages. Instead, I proceeded through a chirping chorus of bird song directly to the stall of Henri Auguste, an opera buff who'd recognized me on my first visit to the Sunday *marché aux oiseaux* several years before.

Today the old man gave me a smile as I approached. "Mademoiselle Daaé! Come to admire my canaries?"

I grinned back at him. "To admire, and also to buy. I've been given my own dressing room." His smile widened and he cocked his head, inviting me to continue. "And I'm to sing Siebel in Gounod's *Faust*!"

"A trouser role, but a good one. Soon you'll be a brilliant Marguerite." He pulled the felt hat from his head, leaving white wisps of hair in disarray, and held it over his heart. "I knew this day would come!"

I reached out and touched the shoulder of his blue cotton jacket. "Mine is the smallest dressing room, and the farthest from the stage. In fact, the only thing to recommend it is an enormous mirror. But I am pleased to have a room of my own, and I'm looking for a little friend to share it."

At that, M. Auguste showed me his birds, moving ceremoniously from cage to cage and explaining the finer points of the Spanish Timbrado. With a wave of his hand he dismissed those with dusty blue feathers – "Only a golden singer will do for you" – and finally settled on a sleek male with lively eyes. As for the cage, the bird seller insisted I take the only one he judged fine enough to adorn even the smallest dressing room at Garnier's opera house: a tall rectangle of gold-finished wire with a cherub at each corner of the footed base.

He transferred my bird into his new home and set about wrapping the cage with paper and string for our trip to the opera house. "So, Mademoiselle Christine, how do you account for this good fortune?"

"I have a new teacher. A genius, monsieur." I dipped my head, hiding from the curiosity in his eyes. "I have not sung so well since my father died."

I busied myself with my change purse, counting out francs and centimes. Hoping to distract him, I came up with a question of my own. "Papageno! Perhaps that's what I'll name him. What do you think?"

M. Auguste carefully gathered the strings and knotted them atop the bird cage. "I like it. Mozart's bird catcher always makes me laugh."

I poured the coins into his hand. "Me too."

Before I could grasp the ring he'd left unwrapped at the top of the cage, M. Auguste swept my parcel into his arms. "I'll help you to a cab."

As we walked between the market stalls to the cab stand on the corner, his thoughts returned to opera. "What's this I hear about a ghost at the Palais Garnier? There was another report yesterday in *Le Figaro*."

I lifted a hand to signal the first carriage in line and turned back to the bird seller as the *fiacre* rolled slowly toward us. "Lately the dancers talk of nothing else. Every mishap large or small is blamed on the ghost. When a flat collapses on the stage, the ghost knocked it over. When a hair ribbon goes missing, the ghost carried it off."

The cab driver climbed down from his seat and opened the door of the carriage. M. Auguste passed Papageno's wrapped cage to him and then took my hand to help me inside. "Seems to me a theater so new scarcely has enough history to have engendered a phantom."

He gave my hand a farewell squeeze and then settled the bird cage on the seat beside me. "But, as we know, adding a ghost rarely harms the libretto."

At the opera house, the Sunday porter showed no surprise at my early-morning appearance. By then all the porters were accustomed to my odd hours and grateful for my generous tips. As he carried Papageno's cage off to my dressing room, I drifted through the streets of the theater toward the apron of the stage. In a few weeks time, when the season began, backstage would be jammed with props and sets, swarmed by dressers and stage hands, but today I had the space and the time to contemplate the great void in front of the stage. The ghost light glowed from the boards downstage center, a theatrical superstition that provided the practical benefit of allowing me to safely find my way. The lamp wasn't bright enough to strike gold sparks along the auditorium's gilded edges or reveal the contrasting crimson on the walls and floor. The cavernous theater swallowed the light, leaving the boxes shadowed and the stalls in gloom.

I stopped before the hood of the prompter's box and looked out into the dim auditorium. Italian singers call the spot *in bocca al luppo* – in the mouth of the wolf. And I suppose those rows of boxes did look like devouring teeth to performers who lacked confidence. I'd never seen it that way. Such irony! Since joining the opera, the stage was the only place where I was never alone. Being one singer among many in the chorus had freed me from anxiety about performing. But soon I would take the stage by myself as Siebel, alone in the spotlight with all eyes upon me while I sang of my secret love. I searched my feelings, probing for fear, and found only exhilaration. After my father's death, the development of my voice had faltered. From sorrow, or adolescence, or loneliness, I never knew. In time I gave up the dream that was his only bequest – to become principal soprano in the greatest opera company in the world – and resigned myself to the chorus. Now, with both my life and my voice remade, I dared to dream again.

My reverie broke when something – a sound? a movement? – drew my attention to the first ring of boxes. The grand tier. A frisson of unease ran through me. "Box 5 belongs to the ghost." The recollection of Meg Giry's voice whispered through my mind. "That's one of my mother's boxes." She'd led a pack of dancers down the stairs from the common dressing rooms as I passed alone on my way up. "She hears him in there." At that, Cecile

Jammes' blue eyes went round as marbles. "And she gives him his program." I'd swept by the dancers without a word, torn by an inner contradiction. How could I deny the existence of their silly ghost when I myself was personally acquainted with an angel?

That paradox shadowed my steps as I turned my back on the empty auditorium and made my way through the depths of the stage to my new dressing room. The porter had lit the gas lamps that bracketed the mirror above the dressing table and placed Papageno's cage, still swathed in brown paper and string, on the scratched top. I unpinned my hat and left it beside the birdcage. Then I slipped out of my coat, shook off the raindrops and hung it inside the doorless wardrobe that stood next to a tall wall mirror framed in elaborately-carved mahogany. I didn't mind the worn and mismatched furniture, or the scuff marks on the bare white walls. Until last week, this room had been used for storage. Now it was mine, and Papageno was the first step toward making it my own.

"Time to come out and see your new home." I lifted the strings hanging from the top of the cage and started to untie the knot. "There are many fine singers here. That should make you feel welcome."

I wound the loose string around one hand as I untied the birdcage, quietly singing the comic song of his namesake from the first act of *Die Zauberflöte*. "A net for maidens I should like to catch the pretty dears by dozens."

Carefully, so as not to alarm the canary inside, I pulled the paper from the cage and let it drift to the floor. "At home I'd shut them up safely and never from me would they roam."

From his perch in the middle of the cage, Papageno seemed to study me, his tiny black eyes vivid against his golden feathers. But after a moment, the canary tilted his head and seemed to look past me. A second later, he lost all interest in me and sidestepped down his perch. Just then a thread of stale air brushed my neck.

I turned into it, expecting that the door to my dressing room had swung open. Instead, I found a strange man standing beside the carved mirror. A mirror which now gaped from the wall, revealing a dim passage beyond. For a moment, everything seemed to freeze in place with only the hiss of the gaslight to show me that this wasn't a waxwork tableau.

He was tall. Broad-shouldered. A silky fringe of dark hair brushed the white wings of his collar. Rain drops sparkled on his finely-tailored cape and the broad-brimmed hat that shadowed his face. Slowly he raised a hand encased in a black leather glove and lifted the hat from his head.

Light fell on his face. At first, I saw only his eyes – dark as pitch but flashing with an emotion I couldn't name. Before I could solve that mystery, another drew my attention. A crease slanted across the pale skin of his face. From the right eye, across the tip of the nose and the plane of the cheek, to the left ear. Then I saw that the crease was really the edge of a mask that fit as snugly as a second skin. And for the first time since discovering the strange man standing in my dressing room, a stab of fear pierced me.

As if sensing my feelings, he held out his free hand in supplication. "Don't be frightened, Christine. You're not in danger."

At the sound of his voice, my fear vanished as quickly as a wave melts into the sand. The man before me was indeed a stranger. But from the day I arrived at the Paris opera, his voice had been my only friend.

2

*L*ONG BEFORE I heard his voice, I knew his story. Or, at least, I thought I did. My father filled my childhood with stories. When we lived in Sweden, where I was born, he explained the beauties of the world with Norse myths like that of the valkyries, the virgin warriors whose armor casts the flickering light of the aurora borealis as they ride out to select dead heroes to fill Valhalla. When we lived in Brittany, where my father died, he explained the dangers of the world with Breton legends like the *korrigans*, the malicious fairies who steal and enslave human children after replacing them with changelings. But no matter where we found ourselves, my father's favorite stories – and mine – were about the Angel of Music.

My parents were peasants who struggled to wrest a living from the tired soil of our small farm near Uppsala. I have no memory of my mother, just impressions – a lilac scent, a throaty laugh, a gentle touch. After her death, my father sold the farm and took to the road with his violin and his only child. He was never much of a farmer, but he was famous for his fiddling across Sweden, where his music was in great demand for weddings and festivals. We traveled the countryside from fair to fair, where he drew crowds with his Scandinavian melodies. Often I sang, and when our performance ended, people dropped coins in the hat he left on the ground before us. Like a squirrel collecting acorns to last through the winter, my father hoarded our earnings in summer to sustain us through the dark months to come. And so we slept wherever a bed could be made – under the stars in the soft grass of a meadow when the weather was fine and in the hay loft of a friendly farmer's barn when storm winds blew.

One warm night we lay side by side atop our blankets under a shimmering sky in a field that smelled sweetly of new-mown hay. I rose up on an elbow and turned toward my father. "Papa, why don't the stars sing? They're so beautiful. They must be full of joy."

"They are, child. Full of joy and resounding with beautiful music." His eyes gleamed in the starlight. "But only the Angel of Music can hear their song."

Another night rain drummed on the barn roof above us while below a small herd of milk cows lowed in their stalls. "Can cattle make music, Papa? Like a Sunday choir?"

"There is music in everything, Christine. In the rain and the wind. In the animals on the land and the fishes in the sea. In the trees rooted in the earth and the stars sailing across the sky."

He smoothed the blanket under my chin. "Everything in the world makes music, but only the Angel of Music can hear it all. And because he alone hears all the music of the world, the Angel of Music inspires the greatest music we make. He visits the greatest singers and composers and musicians. Sometimes he comes to their cradle with celestial harmonies and produces a wondrous prodigy like Mozart. Sometimes he brings to a schoolroom a divine voice and produces a rare nightingale like Jenny Lind. There is no genius who hasn't been visited at least once by the Angel of Music."

"People say you're a genius with the violin, Papa. Has the Angel of Music visited you?"

In the darkness, I couldn't see my father's smile, but I heard it in his voice. "Perhaps. And perhaps one day he'll visit you, Christine."

Weeks later at a fair in Ljimby I thought I spotted the Angel of Music at the edge of the crowd. The thin-faced old man in a black frock coat stood very still as my father played his violin, his blue eyes narrowed and his mouth a stern line. That afternoon my father's music soared, pulsing with emotion as his fingers danced up and down the neck of his violin even as the bow became a blur of speed. The intensity of the gaze the old man fixed upon my father frightened me, and when the time came for me to sing, I tugged my father's sleeve and begged off, claiming a stomach ache from the candy I'd eaten after lunch. The next day the old man returned, accompanied by a fashionably-dressed woman with a stylish straw hat perched atop her gray chignon. Again my father played with rare emotion, each note as clear as the chime of a bell yet all combining fluidly like pearls of music on a single strand of sound. As he played song after song, a smile slowly spread across the woman's face and she whispered to the old man beside her. Her smile gave me courage, and when my turn came to sing, I stepped forward without hesitation.

13

Like my father, my voice that day seemed inspired, surpassing childhood charm and suggesting for the first time that I might possess a rare talent. By the time I finished, the old man's smile matched that of his companion.

My father had scooped the coins out of his old blue hat and was counting them into the leather pouch I held open when the pair approached us. The old man removed his top hat and bowed first to me and then to my father. "Please allow me to introduce myself." An unfamiliar accent colored his speech. "I am Professor Valérius of the music conservatory in Paris." He touched the elbow of the woman beside him. "And this is my wife."

When my father introduced me, the professor and Madame Valérius in turn took my hand. She greeted me kindly in unaccented Swedish, which reassured me. As the men spoke together, she led me a few steps away to a wooden bench in the shade of an oak tree.

"A professor! Thank goodness." I sank down beside Madame Valérius and carefully smoothed my skirt just as she'd done. "I thought he was the Angel of Music come to take Papa away."

She tilted her head as she looked down on my face. "And why would he do that, my dear?"

"Because Papa is a genius and the Angel of Music visits them all."

Her smile warmed me. "And has this angel visited you, Christine?"

A blush heated my cheeks. "I thought the professor....You see, I've never sung so well."

Her laughter came light and merry. "Perhaps my husband is an angel of music. He thinks your father may be the first violin of the world and says that you have the makings of a great artist. He wants you both to come with us to Paris."

Looking back now, I can only marvel at how readily my father agreed to Professor Valérius' plan. To leave everyone and everything he'd known to satisfy the whim of a stranger seems like a reckless gamble. Some may suspect the music professor's praise swelled my father's head and fueled an unwarranted ambition. A country fiddler the first violin of the world! Others may suppose his aspirations centered on me. Parents' dreams for their children often exceed their youngster's talents.

At the time, I didn't question his decision because Papa was the hero of my eight-year-old's world. By the time I'd grown up enough to become curious about his choice, he was gone.

In France, my father and I became students. Our new home was a large house in the old village of Auteuil west of Paris. I spent the morning in lessons with Madame Valérius in the attic schoolroom, perfecting my penmanship, dabbling in history and literature, and studying a multitude of new languages – Italian, German, English – in addition to French. Three mornings a week my father practiced his violin in the music room downstairs while I studied above. After lunch on those days, Professor Valérius instructed us both in music theory and composition for two hours, and then moved to the piano for my voice lessons for another hour or two. My father and the professor spent Tuesdays and Thursdays at the conservatory in the city. On those afternoons Madame Valérius taught me the womanly arts – painting and embroidery, cooking and cleaning, dancing and dressing.

From the start, I took to all my studies. In Sweden my education had been haphazard – a few years of church school when my mother was alive, a few months of dame school in the winters after she died. Before her marriage, Madame Valérius had been a teacher, and she was a gifted educator. Even more, she was a devoted friend who cared for me with a mother's love. The professor was more like an affectionate uncle, but he, too, could make learning an adventure. The first time I held a sheet of music in my hand he told me to think of the notes as graceful long-necked swans that fly up the scale and glide back down. "Your voice, Christine, will help them take flight and then ease them back to earth." To this day, in my mind's eye, I see my voice as swans soaring free.

As a student, my father struggled. To him, the black notes on the staff were like carrion birds aligned on telegraph wires, waiting to swoop down and wrench the joy from his music. A self-taught violinist who played only by ear, he rebelled against melodies pasted on a page and harmonies unalterably fixed by a composer. Professor Valérius had hoped to find him a spot in an orchestra, where he could earn his keep and gain renown for his virtuosity. Time and again, at first hearing my father's violin, conductors responded with enthusiasm. Even my father's inability to read music proved little impediment because of his knack for grasping a tune after a single hearing. But soon Papa's fiddle would begin to diverge from the rest of the violins – holding a note an extra beat here or dropping an octave there – and he would be let go. Finally, he found a position that suited him at a *café-concert* in Boulevard Rochechouart where he performed

16

Scandinavian folk tunes to an audience of drinkers and dancers very much like the wedding revelers who'd acclaimed his fiddling back home in Sweden. Soon he stopped joining me for the professor's lessons on music theory and composition, and he stopped going to the conservatory two days each week. But he still joined us for my voice lessons, and when Professor Valérius fell ill, Papa took charge of my instruction.

All of our lives changed forever in the summer of 1870. After many weeks of hot and dry weather, the sky darkened with smoke from the burning forest at Fontainebleau. In Auteuil, the faithful paraded through the narrow streets, carrying Christian relics and chanting prayers for rain. And an outbreak of smallpox spread from Paris into our home, where the professor fell gravely ill. Madame Valérius nursed him through the crisis, but afterwards his recovery stalled, leaving him weak and trembling. In late July, she closed up the house and moved us all to a cottage in the village of Perros-Guirec in Brittany, where she hoped the sea air would restore her husband's vigor. There I found the first true friend of my childhood, a lively boy from Paris named Raoul who came to my father for violin lessons.

Then, with the suddenness of a summer squall, the world turned topsy-turvy. Before the month was out, France declared war on Prussia. By September the emperor surrendered the army and abdicated the throne. The defiant people of Paris proclaimed the Third Republic even as their new government scurried to safety at Versailles. For the next five months, the Germans besieged the rebellious city, starving the citizens by day and bombarding them by night. Not long after the siege was lifted, the laborers who had suffered for *liberté* formed their own city government – the Paris Commune – with dreams of a worker's paradise. In May 1871 the commune was crushed in a short but bloody civil war that left Paris ablaze. When the smoke cleared, the Palais des Tuileries, the Hôtel de Ville and the Palais d'Orsay lay in ruins.

Through it all, we remained in Brittany, where the wretched fate of Paris weighed heavily on us all. Raoul stayed through that winter as well, and his high spirits served as welcome tonic during those anxious months. Professor Valérius remained an invalid. He spent his good days in a chair by a window overlooking the sea with a blanket covering his legs. On his bad days he lacked the strength to leave his bed. And so the Breton sojourn that had already stretched to months was prolonged into years as the music professor's health continued its gentle decline. By the time we buried him in the autumn of 1873, Raoul had long-since returned to Paris, the Auteuil house had been sold, and my father in turn had fallen sick. Through the bleak winter, Papa withered before my eyes. He lost interest in his violin and no longer told his stories. But on the night he died, his thoughts returned to the Angel of Music.

"Christine." In the halo of light cast by the oil lamp, his frail hand rose from the quilt and I covered it with my own. "Child, I am going."

I leaned forward and, with my free hand, stroked his forehead. His face was bloodless and his skin cold. "I love you, Papa."

His eyes closed, and I hoped he'd fallen back into a restless sleep. Though I treasured each word

18

and each moment of consciousness, I wanted even more to spare him this agony. A few minutes later, he roused again and our eyes met for the last time, his serene and mine brimming. "When I reach heaven, Christine, I will send the Angel of Music to you."

"Oh, Papa." I bowed my head until my cheek rested against his. "I love you."

We buried him in the graveyard of the ancient church at Perros-Guirec, where he'd liked to sit and watch the sun sink into the wild Breton sea. Then in the late summer of 1874 Madame Valérius and I finally returned to Paris. A place had been found for me at the singing school at the new opera house. She took a small flat nearby in the Rue Notre Dame des Victoires and kept a little room under the eaves for me. With both her husband and his great musical discovery dead, Madame Valérius transferred all her affection and faith to me. How could I tell her that our hopes were in vain? With my father's death, everything was lost – my happiness, my voice, my soul. My enthusiasm for music vanished, and I did not distinguish myself in my studies. I was just thirteen, burdened by the dreams of the dead but determined not to disappoint my living benefactress. And so I hid from her and the rest of the world the utter misery of my life in M. Garnier's opulent opera house.

An opera house is no place for a child, especially a new theater in the throes of readying works for its first season. The rest of the company – soloists and principal dancers, choir and corps de ballet – were a seasoned troupe who'd performed together for years in the old opera house. In the hubbub of settling into their dressings rooms, learning the idiosyncrasies of their stage and mastering the acoustics of their auditorium, it was easy to overlook the new girl from Brittany. When I wasn't in class or rehearsal, I explored every meter of my new home, from the rooftop where an enormous Apollo raised his lyre over the heart of Paris to the cavernous stone cellar where few others ventured. When grief overtook me, I would descend into the bowels of the theater to my hideaway, an out-of-the-way niche where I thought I could hide my tears.

But no one can hide from an angel.

"Why are you crying?"

His voice was captivating, as dark as the finest chocolate and as rich as a thundering chord. Huddled in my niche, wet cheek against my upraised knees, I blurted out the truth. "I miss my papa."

"Old Daaé? The violinist?"

"Then you've seen him?" I raised my head and peered into the cellar's gloom. "He promised you would. He told me he'd send the Angel of Music from heaven."

For a moment, he didn't reply, and I feared he'd slipped away. When he spoke again, the words seemed to whisper in my ear. "And here I am."

3

LIGHT POOLED around us from the lantern in one of his hands as we walked through the dark passage that opened behind the mirror in my dressing room. His other hand held mine gently, the leather of his glove cool and smooth against my skin. He led me into an underworld I hadn't discovered in my explorations of the opera's vast stone cellars. This was not the first basement, the precinct of workshops, wardrobes or lighting studio, inhabited by carpenters and dressers, gasmen and scene shifters, or the hushed and deserted second basement that held my secret refuge. Those places we avoided, descending little-known staircases tucked in remote corners and moving along the shadowed edges of vast caverns whose massive stone columns supported masonry ceilings laced with pipes for water and gas. He didn't speak during our journey, and neither did I. The air freshened on the final set of stairs, which spiraled tightly toward a bluish light. The narrow steps ended on a gaslit landing at the edge of an underground lake. We stopped beside a small rowboat tied to an iron ring.

"Where are we?" I watched him hang the lantern in the bow of the boat. "Where are you taking me?"

"This is the *cuve* beneath the stage." He offered his hand to help me into the boat. "We're going to my house across the lake."

The tank. I knew of it, of course. All of the opera people did. No doubt at one time most of Paris knew of it as well. The *cuve* had been news in 1861 when work began on the emperor's grand opera house in the center of the new boulevards being created in the heart of the Right Bank. Almost as soon as it began, work stopped when excavators discovered a subterranean branch of the Seine running through the middle of the work site on Boulevard des Capucines. M. Garnier's ingenious solution was to build a double foundation with an artificial lake to control the water and keep moisture from undermining the building above. Nineteen years later, only intimates of the opera house remembered the underground lake in the deepest cellar twelve meters below the ground. In my years at Garnier's opera, I'd never heard of anyone who'd actually seen it.

I allowed him to steady me as I stepped into the row boat and seated myself in the stern. I tightened my fingers around his gloved hand and looked up at him. "You're the opera ghost."

"The opera ghost. The phantom." For the first time, he gave me one of the smiles that I would soon learn were very rare. "The Angel of Music."

I held onto his hand and his attention. "What should I call you?"

"The Phantom. It suits me." He shrugged slightly. "I have no other name."

22

And so the Angel of Music who was my teacher became my Phantom. When I first came to know him, as a lonely young girl ensnared by a captivating voice, he'd spurned the role of teacher. "In time, perhaps," he'd told me. "For now, you have Gabriel, the chorus master. And also the Maestro." He became my friend instead.

Imagine my delight on my fourteenth birthday when a messenger arrived at the singing school carrying a box from the finest patisserie in Paris and presented it to me. How I'd dreaded that day. Not only would I endure my first birthday without my father, but compounding that heartache would be my classmate's scorn for failing to provide the obligatory treat on my special day. The boys wouldn't care, but the girls would be indignant, making me even more of an outcast. A few weeks before, as we savored an orange and almond sponge cake glazed with apricots, a girl named Sybil, who bullied us all, had gone around the classroom, pointing to each of us in turn and demanding that we name our birthday. After my truthful reply, the delicious cake turned to lead in my belly. I had no money to buy a cake, and I couldn't ask Madame Valérius, who existed in genteel poverty and failing health. And so I'd counted down the days to September 15 with growing apprehension that I shared with my angel and braced myself for the sneers of my classmates. But he turned that dreaded birthday into a triumph with an enormous chocolate cake iced in coffee cream and topped by a Renaissance angel with flowing robes and flowing hair and his head lifted in song. Hours later, at my hideaway, I found another gift: a tiny pear-shaped sapphire strung on a fine gold chain. "Sapphires are your birthstone," he told me when I thanked him. "And they protect from envy and harm."

I didn't question his friendship. My father had promised me an angel, not a tutor. And his arrival in a sorrowful hour confirmed that mystic pledge. Nor had I felt uncertainty when he finally did become my teacher just six months ago. By that time my secret friend was also my trusted guide, one who'd helped me survive within the competitive and impersonal world of the opera. As he predicted, his voice lessons had enabled me to thrive there as well. Every morning at 8 o'clock I made my way to the unused dressing room that was now my own to study with the Angel of Music, and six months later, I was to sing Gounod's Siebel. Why would I question?

Yet sitting in that boat while he rowed us across the dark water of the underground lake, I finally did. "Why did you speak to me that day? The first day?"

The lantern in the bow silhouetted him, leaving his face in darkness. "You were lonely and sad, and I'd known desolation, too."

"Are you desolate still?"

At that, the steady rhythm of his rowing stopped. The silence spun out between us, broken only by the drip, drip, drip from the blades of the oars he held above the water. At last the oars dipped back into the black lake. "No. Not for a long time."

A few minutes later the rowboat glided to a stop. The lantern light revealed only a wide ledge backed by a blank stone wall. Yet when he reached into the shadows and brushed his hand along that blank wall, with a click and a whir the stone gave way and a door appeared. He pushed it wide and swept an arm in invitation. "Please come in."

The house by the lake reminded me of an artist's studio in Montparnasse or Les Batignolles – one large room with each corner devoted to a separate pursuit: a library of leather-bound books, a music room with piano and organ, a workshop for oil and pastels, a dining alcove hung with canvases large and small. And like those studios, light flooded this space, not pouring through the glass walls of an atelier but from gas glowing in large bronze torchieres bracketed to walls of stone. Somehow that stone and bronze also brought to mind a cathedral, deceptively simple yet irrevocably permanent, with an austere elegance shared by the man himself.

While I stood silently just inside the door, he peeled off his gloves, tossed them along with his hat onto a settee upholstered in a burgundy Utrecht velvet and topped them with his cape. Except for the gold silk of his cravat and white linen of his shirt, he wore black, clothes so well-made he might have been one of the aristocratic habitués of the dance foyer in the opera house overhead. But for all the elegance of his attire, he was no fop. The fine wool of his frock coat and brocade waistcoat enclosed a powerfully-built frame that narrowed sharply from wide shoulders to trim waist. When I asked the obvious question – "How did you come by this house?" – the muscles in his arms bulged as he acted out his response. "I built it." He mimed the struggle to set a heavy load into place above his head. "Raised every cursed stone."

He lifted a hand toward a door amidst the library bookcases. "Your bedroom is there. Your bath as well."

A wave of panic washed over me. "My bedroom? What on earth—"

He turned toward me, his face unreadable beneath the mask. But in his eyes I detected surprise. "We have much work to do. Now and then, when I can find the time, you will come to me here for intensive training."

"But what about them?" I pointed at the stone ceiling. "Gabriel? And Maestro?"

He waved away my objection. "They've been informed."

I staggered in surprise as I took a step toward him. "And Madame Valérius will be so—"

He coolly reached out a hand to steady me and then shrugged. "By now she has received my note. Her mind will be at ease."

At that moment, my mind was anything but easy. Since my father's death I'd made my own way in the world. The friendship and counsel of Madame Valérius and the Angel of Music had helped, it is true, but all of the decisions had been mine alone. Now my invisible friend and tutor had suddenly become flesh in the guise of a masked stranger, taking control of my life, commanding where I would sleep and when I would work. God alone knew what other surprises lay in store for me at his bizarre house by the lake.

He'd turned away from me and walked into the music room, shrugging out of his frock coat as he went. But I stood transfixed, looking from the place where the front door had melted back into a stone wall to the man lifting the keyboard cover on the grand piano. I fought the panic bubbling inside me. He was my teacher. He was my friend. He was the Angel of Music my father had promised me.

"We'll begin with the duet from *Otello*." He sat on the piano bench and placed his hands on the keys. "You've learned Desdemona as I instructed?"

I didn't reply, and he glanced over his shoulder to discover me still standing by the door. He swung around on the piano bench to face me. "Christine, forgive me. Of course you need refreshment before we begin."

Once again his words disarmed me. Hadn't I told the bird seller of the genius of my new teacher? And wasn't he the very incarnation of genius? Abrupt? Single-minded? Yet he was a caring genius as well. One who had known desolation. One who was instantly contrite to find me ill at ease.

"I'm fine. We can start immediately." He turned back to the keyboard without seeing my teasing smile. "I hope you will find my Desdemona superior to La Carlotta's."

For an instant, his hands hovered over the keyboard – "I should hope so!" – and then he sounded the first note for my warm up. Like most voice teachers, the Phantom directed me to begin by humming the scales he played – four notes up and three notes down – as we moved through all three octaves of my range.

He played with one hand and studied me as I stood beside the piano, with my feet slightly apart, my arms loose at my sides and my posture erect but relaxed. The notes buzzed in my ears and cheeks and chest as he talked about the work ahead. "Today you must try to let Christine dissolve

27

and Desdemona emerge. Her emotion must become yours."

With one hand he played "do" while the other swooped in midair to signal a two-octave glide that began in the middle of my chest voice, dropped lower still before soaring into my head voice and then falling back into my chest. The sung notes felt smoother, chiming in my highest head voice and gonging in my deepest chest voice. "If you open yourself to the music, you open yourself to the emotion. Don't think, just feel."

He signaled for me to begin singing staccato arpeggios – "do, mi, sol, si, sol, mi, do" – then touched his free hand to his chin to signal me to loosen my jaw. Each note flew free like an individual bird, and I felt like a human harp plucked by an invisible hand. "Let the emotion in. Let the music invade your soul and you will feel in it your bones."

When he sensed my readiness, he segued smoothly from the routine scales of the schoolroom to the howling thunderstorm that inflames the hatred and terror of the tragic lovers. Gioachino Rossini combined elements of two Shakespeare tragedies to create his Otello and Desdemona. From *Romeo and Juliet* he took the secret marriage, endless duels and family betrayal, and from *Othello* he took the evil schemer, murderous jealousy and political ambition. In the Act III finale, a thunderclap wakes Desdemona, who sees by the flashes of lightning that her jealous husband has slipped into her bedroom and hovers by the bed with a dagger in his hand.

"*Indegna!*" A single word – dishonorable – but how the Phantom colored it with anger. "*La tradisti, o crudel*!" With what purity of tone and perfect intonation he denounced his cruel betrayer.

At that moment, as I took my place beside his right shoulder, I thought he must truly be an angel because his voice was genuinely divine. I'd never heard him sing, and the unearthly beauty of his song terrified me. If his voice set the standard, I feared mine would never live up to his aspirations. Still, I knew I must try.

"*Sono innocente.*" I poured emotion into the notes as they floated from me, weighing them with the anguish of an innocent unjustly denounced. "*Uccidimi, se vuoi, perfido, ingrato!*" The defiance of the unjustly accused. "*Sfoga il tuo reo furore, intrepida morrò.*" The terror and despair of the condemned.

Like many other composers of opera, Rossini liked to mirror the stormy emotions of his characters with weather effects on stage, creating a barrage of hail by shaking a metal box filled with small rocks or a howling wind by twirling a long thin board between two ropes. But even without stage dressing, the growing storm fanned our confrontation. Rossini's music clamored with disorienting bolts of lightning and frightening roars of thunder.

"Cruel storm. With your lightning and your horrible thunder, you increase my fury." The wild intensity of the Phantom's voice pulled me like a magnet, drawing me into the dream that opera conjures for the audience.

"Cruel storm. With your lightning and your horrible thunder, you increase my fear and horror." I responded to him with a passion and conviction I'd never before achieved.

Beyond Act III's heavenly music, the greatest gift of Rossini's *Otello* is the ending: the murder of Desdemona and the suicide of Otello. Before its premier at Teatro del Fondo in Naples in 1816, all opera *seria* – serious opera – had to have the same happy ending as opera buffa – comic opera. With tragic endings now in fashion, I would have to learn to die convincingly to become a principal singer at the Paris opera. But our first duet in the Phantom's house by the lake ended without the acting lessons that would later become routine. His hands simply fell still on the keyboard, leaving no sound to distract from the rough sob with which he punctuated the duet's last words: "The vendetta is complete."

When the final note died away, I closed my eyes, gulped the air and let my shoulders slump. At that moment I realized that I didn't yet have the necessary stamina for a leading role. To become an opera diva, a pretty voice was just the start.

When he took my hand, I opened my eyes and found that his glowed with satisfaction. "That's how you must always sing – with all your heart – and soon you will become Desdemona."

He gave my fingers a quick squeeze before releasing my hand. "Remember, every performance will be the first for someone in the audience and the last for someone else. You must be sure to make each one special."

His words brought me a hot flush of pleasure, and I turned away, not wanting him to see such a girlish response. On the wall beside the piano hung a violin very much like my father's. The pipes and console of the organ occupied the rest of the music room.

"An organ." Ever so lightly, I drew my hand across the uppermost of the four keyboards.

He came up behind me. "My first instrument."

"And this?" I lifted the small gilt frame with a fragment of black satin enclosed under glass.

"The gift of a dear friend." He reached over my shoulder and, with one lean finger, traced the outline on the glass. "My first mask."

4

*T*HE MASK. So much has been made of the mask. In his novel, M. Leroux depicted me angrily trying to snatch it from the Phantom's face that first day in his house by the lake. Later the novelist described an uncontrollable urge that drove me to successfully unmask my teacher. I laughed out loud when I read that scene, and my outburst drew the attention of Raoul in his chair beside the fireplace of the little salon. My husband's upraised eyebrow invited an explanation, one I waved away with a flick of my wrist. "Just a bit of Colette's nonsense, my dear." He smiled and nodded and disappeared again behind his newspaper. I smoothed the dust jacket of *La Vagabonde*, which hid Leroux's novel, and continued reading. Raoul had decreed *Le Fantóme de l'opéra* an outrage and banned it from our home. But, of course, I couldn't resist a book which pretended to tell my own story.

In truth, I found M. Leroux's portrayal of me insulting. When had I ever been so headstrong, so thoughtless, so ill-mannered? For a well-bred young lady to attack anyone, let alone her teacher, was unimaginable. Though my parents had been peasants, their daughter was genteel: Mme. Valéri-us made sure of that. By the age of twenty, I had the polish needed to survive among the aristocrats of the Faubourg St. Germain, whose world I would one day join.

Still, I wondered, as anyone would, why the Phantom wore a mask? That curiosity must have shown in my eyes when I turned to face him as we stood together at the organ that first day. I lifted the framed mask in my hand, but before I could ask, he gently pressed a finger against my lips.

"We won't speak of it." Such anguish in his eyes, such torment in his voice. "Never."

Have you ever happened on an injured animal and found yourself torn by conflicting emotions, on the one hand pity for the creature's suffering and on the other apprehension that the beast will strike? So it was with me. Though invisible, I knew his wounds were real. Why else would he choose to live shut away underground? The world above the sidewalks must have seemed very bleak indeed to one who preferred to inhabit that man-made cavern. Of course, I sympathized with his pain. But a note of dread underscored my compassion. What kind of man shunned all others that way? In my years at the opera, I had always stood alone and apart. Yet my loneliness paled beside the Phantom's solitude. His isolation frightened me. Thus my response to him seesawed that first day and for many days to come. Weeks and months would pass before my emotions about the Phantom found firm ground.

In that time I discovered new dimensions to my consoling angel. He was a passionate singer. He was a caring friend. He was a commanding impre-

33

sario. But first and foremost, he was a demanding teacher. And because I was determined to please my teacher, I overcame my fear of the man.

He drew me back to the piano but didn't take a seat on the bench. Instead he maneuvered my body as if it belonged to one of the mannequins at Maison du Bon Marché. His firm but impersonal hands gently pulled my shoulders back and straightened my arms at my sides before coming to rest at my waist – one lightly spanning my belly, the other placed against my spine. "Breathe in. Slowly."

I followed his instructions, letting the air spill to the bottom of my lungs. Breath is the foundation of the voice, the energy that fuels the sound. Years earlier, in the music room of his house in Auteuil, Professor Valérius had taught me to breathe correctly – 'Expand the ribcage! Engage the diaphragm!' – and drilled me incessantly until the habit formed. Now I did so without thinking. Even if I'd wanted to, at that moment I wouldn't have been able to think of anything except the pressure the Phantom's hands on my waist. I wore no corset — no serious singer did — and the tips of his fingers seared me with tiny flames.

"And exhale. Slowly."

His words stirred the hair on top of my head, heightening my awareness of him. His chest looming over my right shoulder. The weight of his hands on my body. The pressure of his thigh against the back of my leg. The dexterity of those long fingers which could raise stone to build a house, coax music from a keyboard, measure the breath of a singing student.

"Excellent." He dropped his hands from my waist. "You've been taught well."

He stepped toward the piano. "But you must gain firm control of your breath. Sometimes your note wavers." He lit one of the candles in the tall candelabrum standing beside the piano and handed it to me. Then resting one knee on the piano bench, he struck the note "do" on the keyboard. "Sound the note as you exhale slowly. Hold the candle in front of your lips, and make sure the flame doesn't flicker."

A note at a time, he led me up the scale. At "fa" and then at "si" my breath made the candle's flame dance. He struck "si" again, and then spun off the bench, grabbed my free hand and pressed it just below my breastbone. "Support your breath here with the diaphragm."

In the next instant, he slid my hand under his brocade vest and pressed it against the soft linen that covered his hard middle. "I'll show you." As he let out three staccato bursts of air, the muscle under my hand pulsed in time. Then he hit my note and held it. The candle between us burned without wavering, and beneath my fingers the movement of his diaphragm was as gentle as the brush of a butterfly's wing. By the time he released my hand, the heat of his skin had penetrated the fabric of his shirt and warmed my palm.

He took the candle from me, blew it out and carried it back to the candelabrum beside the piano. He seemed unmoved, and outwardly so did I. But inside I reeled. I'd touched other men – my father, Professor Valérius – but not a young man in his prime, and never so intimately. I rubbed my aching hand against the gray serge of my skirt, hoping to soothe the palm scorched by his touch and ease the trembling in my belly.

He bent over a stack of sheet music atop the piano, sifting out a half dozen pages. How could he be so dispassionate? Disappointment pricked me. Did he feel nothing for me? Despite my tumult, or perhaps because of it, when the Phantom resumed the lesson, my notes no longer wavered.

As teacher and student, an unbridgeable gulf yawned between us. In the common parlance, he was my master. And following the custom of the day, he ruled and I obeyed. But when the lesson ended and we parted for a time – he to his work table, me to the shelves of his library – the distance between us dissolved. Later he would return to me as the mysterious angel who had become my dearest friend. At those times he revealed himself to me snippet by snippet, a fragment from his childhood here and a memory from his youth there.

That afternoon I sank into a comfortable leather armchair in his library, too tired to even leaf through the illustrations of *La Vie Moderne* magazine on the table beside me. Instead I rested my eyes on a small painting propped against the books on a nearby shelf. A seascape adorned the unframed canvas, with brooding cliffs rising against a sky thick with dark clouds tinted orange by the setting sun. The picture had none of the clarity of past masters such as Jacques-Louis David or the fine detail of current stars such as Ernest Meissonier. Instead, the painter left his scene indistinct, as if viewed though a thin curtain of mist. Yet one could almost hear the lap of the waves on the sand and taste the salt in the air. I thought the beach with its dark rocks might have been one where I played as a child, and suddenly filled with longing for that place and time, I sighed deeply.

"You don't like the painting?" He came up beside my chair. "Neither did the Academy of Fine Arts. They refused to hang it in the Salon. They prefer grand historical scenes with clear moral lessons. But the world is changing, and painting and opera must change too." He gestured at the small canvas. "This is the vanguard."

"Oh, I like it very much. It reminds me of Brittany. There's a little path up the cliff there." I traced the route in the air in front of the picture. "And just below that rise lies the old church at Perros-Guirec. My father is buried there."

"Ah." He dropped a hand to my shoulder and gave it quick squeeze. "Shall I take you to visit his grave?"

I looked up at him. "Would you?"

"Certainly." He clasped his hands behind his back and leaned down for a closer look at the painting. "I believe I see that trail to the churchyard." He glanced back at me. "When will we go?"

"The anniversary of his death is in January." I blinked to hold back the tears filling my eyes. "Seven years."

He sank to one knee on the floor beside my chair. "And you still miss him."

I nodded, unable to speak because a sob clogged my throat.

"You were crying for your father the first time I saw you, hiding your tears in the cellar. I was on my way upstairs to see the managers, those idiots Poligny and Debienne, and in the corner of my eye caught a flash of gold. Your hair." He brushed a curl that had escaped the black velvet ribbon that bound it. "You were so sad, and that day I was very happy. Playing an angel to comfort a sorrowful child seemed a harmless vanity."

I blotted the last of my tears against my fingers and smiled. "Now look where it's gotten you. A trip to Brittany – in January."

He shrugged. "I like the sea in any season."

"And yet you live here." With a wave of my hand, I encompassed his underground home, the opera house above and the great city outside. "How did that happen?"

He rose to his feet and walked to the sideboard which separated the library from the dining alcove. "When I was fifteen, I lost the ability to sing. All my life, music had been my only solace. I was devastated."

And so I discovered a thread that bound us. In youth we each in our own way lost the music that had been our comfort.

With two deft twists of the corkscrew, he pierced the cork of a bottle of wine. "I was part of a troupe led by an old magician that performed in provincial towns, mostly for farmers and shopkeepers. Lecadre allowed me to stay on, as his apprentice."

Another thread. We had both been traveling performers at one time.

He pulled the cork free. "In the autumn of 1872 Lecadre brought me to Paris. I'd never been before. We arrived at Gare Montparnasse and walked down the hill to the Seine." He poured wine the color of rubies into two crystal goblets. "The magician stopped for a time to inspect the blackened wreck of the Palais d'Orsay before leading me across the river on Pont Royal and stopping again to examine the burned-out shell of the Palais des Tuileries. His

eyes filled with tears at the wreckage and he denounced the 'Communard bastards' who had set
the fires."

"I was more interested in the new boulevards on
the Right Bank. At the marble tables of a hundred
cafes choking the sidewalks. And shop windows
displaying everything from porcelain and perfume
to foie gras and furs. Lecadre led me to the old
opera house on Rue le Peletier." He rolled the stems
of the goblets between his fingers, swirling the
wine, forcing it to breathe. "And the opera! Our box
was in the highest tier. They performed *Rigoletto*.
From my seat I could barely see the wretched
jester's hunched back. But the music!"

Inside the mask, his eyes closed, and he stood
without moving, the goblets of wine gripped tightly
in his hands. "Until then I'd known only two kinds of
songs – sacred hymns or profane ballads. Verdi's
songs had the soaring glory of sacred music and the
pulsing emotion of profane lyrics. Opera embraced
the stuff of life: love, greed, courage, jealousy, loyalty, hatred, desire, sorrow. When the final curtain
came down, music brimmed again on my tongue,
and I thought my heart would burst with joy."

He opened his eyes and smiled. "As applause
erupted around us, I turned to Lecadre and reprised
sotto voce an Act III song that the audience had
cheered: 'The women are unsettled, like feathers on
the wind. Each moment changes their minds.'"

I shivered at the beauty of his voice. No wonder
that captivating sound had worked magic for a
lonely young girl. His voice had confirmed my
father's mystic promise, eased my burden of loneliness, inspired my musician's soul. Now and then in
those years, I had questioned my sanity – only

lunatics heard voices, after all. But deep down I knew I wasn't crazy. And as the opera had returned his voice to him, so the Phantom had returned my voice to me. Yet another binding thread between us.

He handed me one goblet and saluted me with the other. The wine tasted of cherries and lavender and sunshine. He took a moment to savor some before continuing his story. "We descended the staircase into a sea of wealthy patrons, the men in their evening wear a study in black and white, and the women a rainbow of colors with glittering jewels at their necks and graceful feathers in their hair. Their rich fragrances tantalized my senses, and the glamour of it all dazzled me. No farmers or shop-keepers there."

"Outside the theater, the magician took my arm." He mimed the gesture with his free hand. "He steered me along Baron Haussmann's new streets to the place where the Boulevard des Capucines widened into a square. A monumental building glowed white in the gaslight of the street lamps. At the pinnacle, above an ornate dome, Apollo raised a golden lyre. 'That's Napoleon III's imperial opera house,' Lecadre said."

Over his wine glass, the Phantom met my gaze for an moment before his swept on, surveying his underground refuge. "A few weeks later, the magician's troupe moved on, but I stayed in Paris. By day, I was employed as an *ornamaniste* in the opulent foyers of Garnier's opera, working my way through a long list of *ravalements*, carving away slivers of marble on the columns, vaults and walls to free the ornate decorations locked in the stone below. By night, in the deepest cellar, I built this home for myself on the lake beneath the emperor's temple of music. I have been here ever since."

5

*T*HOUGH I WAS only twenty, I already knew that many little lives weave together to create the single lifetime we are each given. Looking back, I could clearly see the boundaries of my little lives: the years with Papa in Sweden; those we spent in the Valérius household before his death in Brittany; and my time at the Paris opera. Time was the only boundary between lives that I recognized then. I hadn't yet learned of other ways to mark the outlines of our little lives – daughter, lover, wife, mother. And when I returned to the opera the next day, I didn't realize at first that in the space of a few hours I'd crossed another invisible but real boundary and begun a new life. The Angel of Music had led a girl from the smallest dressing room in Garnier's opera house, but the Phantom had returned a woman to the world above the ground.

The morning of my return I joined the rest of the cast on stage for a run-through of the upcoming season's opening production, *Les Pêcheurs de Perles*. Georges Bizet set his love triangle among the gem divers of Ceylon, where Zurga and Nadir both renounce their love of beautiful Leila to preserve their friendship. Until that morning, everyone had practiced separately. At first the principal singers and the maestro gathered around a piano while the chorus assembled before the chorus master and a pianist in a cramped atelier behind the stage. When all the singers had memorized their music, they joined a half dozen musicians in a large rehearsal hall where their chairs and music stands could double as scenery – a tree here, a temple wall there. They concentrated on refining their musical inter-pretations – tempo and dynamics – while developing the actions of their characters and working out lines of sight to the conductor to insure a smooth performance. Meanwhile, the dancers gathered with the ballet master and a violinist in their studio beneath the rotunda dome of the royal pavilion. Not until each separate strand of a production had been perfected did the entire cast, singers and dancers, come together on the stage to braid their perfor-mances into a finished opera.

I stood with the rest of the chorus at stage left, ignoring the dance master positioning his girls on their marks and instead balancing on tip-toe in hopes of finally spotting the new tenor, Carolus Fonta, who'd eluded me ever since he'd arrived from Venice a week before. The rest of the chorus girls had settled on a one-word description for our new singer: divine. My search had hardly begun when the chorus master grabbed my elbow. "Miss Daaé. And you four." Pointing a finger, Gabriel ticked off a quartet from the clutch of younger sopranos stand-ing behind me. "Over here, please."

A year before, the chorus would have entered the stage en masse and lined up in curving rows facing the maestro and the audience to sing. But at the end of the last season the Paris opera overthrew tradition. Much to the outrage of some, including the chorus master himself, we now entered in small groups – pairs or trios or quartets – and actually socialized while we sang, reacting with laughter or anger or whatever the action of the story demanded. And the principal singers no longer took their marks and stood still, using only hand gestures to convey the emotions in their song. Now they matched themselves to the music, moving around the stage and interacting with each other, following the cues laid down by the composer as he created the music.

Placing me in the middle, the chorus master arranged his singers in a loose semi-circle behind a trio of dancers that included Meg Giry. Gabriel moved off to assemble another circle of singers just as Francois Devereux, the baritone who played Zurga, arrived to take his mark. Still no sign of Fonta.

"Christine?" I looked down to find that plump little Elizabeth Rousset had fixed her dark eyes on me. "Where were you yesterday afternoon?"

"Yes, Christine." Resentment sharpened Marguerite Loisel's voice. "Perhaps you'll tell us how you managed to get out of a rehearsal that Gabriel said was mandatory, no exceptions?"

Rescue arrived from an unlikely quarter. Mercier, the régisseur and a legendary hothead, who had been crossing the stage in front of the grouped sopranos, suddenly stopped, whirled in our direction and beelined to Marguerite, whose face went pink at his unexpected and unwelcome attention. "Loisel? Is that your name?"

She nodded but didn't speak. The stage director's scowl deepened. "By what right do you, a second-year soprano of doubtful talent, question a singer of Miss Daaé's stature or the authority of the chorus master?"

At his words, the flush of embarrassment on Marguerite's face paled to ghostly white, and her answer came in a squawk. "None, monsieur. I have no right."

"Ah-hah!" Mercier's voice rang with triumph at her abject surrender, and he waved a finger under her long nose. "In future, see that you remember that fact."

The régisseur succeeded in cowing the sopranos around me into silence, but his domineering ways failed to intimidate Meg Giry. Every group of females has its bullies, and Giry was the one feared most by the girls of the opera. Those she favored found life pleasant while those she despised endured the contempt of the entire flock of sycophants which fluttered around her. She didn't carry the weapons brandished by the apaches of Montmartre and the mohicans of Belleville, but her thuggery had similar results. Most denizens of the opera turned a blind eye, including those with the power to put a stop to Giry's browbeating. In part because they didn't want to wind up tangling with her mother, Madame Giry, a harridan who worked as a box-keeper on the grand tier. But mostly because dominance such as Giry's was accepted as the way of the world: In the struggle of life, the strong naturally ruled the over weak.

As soon as Mercier was out of earshot, Giry cast a slow, theatrical glance at me over her shoulder and then leaned her dark head toward Cecile Jammes. "I can guess why Daaé was excused."

Cecile turned her bright blue eyes in my direction and then leaned her auburn head toward Giry. "Tell me."

Over the years Giry had spared me from her harshest efforts, employing the pointed raillery that discomforts rather than the honed cruelty that wounds. And I'd perfected my response: refusing to acknowledge her existence. But that was child's play. Now, for the first time, I squared my shoulders and faced her, fixing my gaze on those bent heads.

"At the request of her protector." Giry threw me another glance, and her eyes widened when she discovered my stare. But she didn't back down. "Her secret protector."

Giry's words rattled me – my heart seemed to leap in my chest – but I managed to hide their impact.

In perfect choreography, Cecile looked toward me again, but whatever she'd been meaning to say disappeared in a nervous gulp when she confronted my stare.

Ever brazen, Giry plunged ahead. "If not her protector, then it must have been the opera ghost."

At the mention of the ghost, Cecile's mouth dropped open and a visible shiver of fear rippled across the bare flesh of her arms. Beside her, Giry smirked with delight at her toady's fright.

"You little fool." I blurted the words without thinking and reached out to give Cecile a quick shake. "Why don't you use the brain the good lord gave you? Don't allow yourself to be ruled by anyone or any silly superstition."

Cecile recoiled from my touch, cringing against Giry, whose smile broadened into pure exultation. At that moment, the orchestra struck up the opening chords of Bizet's overture. The music instantly worked magic, transforming a clutch of bickering young women into poised professionals who took their marks, and the spat ended.

There followed nearly three hours of torture that required every ounce of my performer's discipline to concentrate on the task at hand and to resist the temptation to let my thoughts stray back to Giry's words. My protector?

The opera opens with Zurga on stage with the chorus and dancers, who elect him their leader and then retire to the sides of the stage as his boyhood friend Nadir appears, coming home after a long absence. Even the sight of "divine" Carolus Fonta failed to distract me for long. What was Giry talking about?

Zurga and Nadir's reunion is interrupted by the arrival of a veiled holy woman who turns out to be the pearl fishers' long-lost love, Leila. At the start of Act II, the dancers and the chorus remained in the wings while the principals marked their vocals in hushed voices as they walked through their parts on the empty stage. But I had no chance to question Giry because the dancers had exited stage right while the chorus had exited stage left.

Act II concludes when a mob angry at their sacrilege interrupts Nadir and Leila's reunion at the holy temple, and an enraged Zurga condemns the lovers to death by burning. My mark for the mob scene left me distant from Giry's position, but I decided to follow her off stage at the end of the act. Bizet's opera defeated me when Giry remained on stage for the first scene of Act III in order to receive from the condemned Leila a necklace given to her long before by a man whose life she saved, a necklace Zurga recognizes as the one he gave his savior years earlier. As I watched from the wings, my fingers itched to strangle someone with that preposterous necklace.

Chorus master Gabriel eased my frustration by positioning me within arm's length of Giry for the final scene. To rescue the lovers, a remorseful Zurga sets fire to the huts of the pearl fishers, who rush to save their burning homes. Lovers Nadir and Leila make their escape before the mob returns and throws Zurga on the pyre.

Giry couldn't escape me in the crowd of singers and dancers reeling upstage left around a burning village which as yet existed only in the mind of the set designer. I picked my way through a thicket of swaying performers, clamped a hand around her wrist and practically dragged her off the stage.

She reared back and hissed, "What are you doing?"

"I want to talk to you." I tugged her in the direction of my dressing room. "Alone."

As soon as she guessed our destination, Giry came willingly. She was a prying little thing, forever poking her nose into private places and storing up tittle-tattle to share with her minions. When I opened the door to my dressing room, she struck a pose on the doorstep, looked over the tiny room from top to bottom, and then sniffed. "You haven't done much with it." She flicked a hand toward Papageno's cage – "I heard about the bird" – as she sashayed toward the Phantom's mirror. She paused before it, smoothing her black hair, and finally turned to face me. "The mirror's nice."

I swallowed the laughter tickling my throat and smiled. "Thank you." If she only knew. "I like it, too."

I paused, uncertain how to begin, but Giry knew what I was after and needed no prompting. "You want to hear about your protector, don't you?" She folded her arms across her chest and a note of amazement entered her voice. "You really didn't know!"

I shook my head. "I have no idea what you're talking about."

"Haven't you ever wondered why the men leave you alone?" She studied me from across the room with a look that would have been insolent in a man. "You're pretty enough, I suppose." She sniffed again. "Yet you've never had a suitor, have you? And in the opera house, everyone keeps their distance."

Always alone. Always apart. Of course, I'd wondered. Agonized even. But I wasn't going to let Meg Giry know that. "Tell me."

She shrugged. "You have a protector. Always have. Almost from your first day at the opera. You are left alone by his decree – the managers and the maestro make sure of that."

"He?" I took a step toward her. "Who is it?"

She spread her hands wide and shrugged again. "How should I know? I'm not even supposed to know that you have a protector. Nobody is. It's a secret."

After Giry left, I closed the dressing room door and dragged my only chair over to the mahogany vanity that held Papageno's cage. He tilted his head and looked at me with his bright black eyes as I dropped onto the rush seat. I tilted my head to match the angle of his. "So many secrets, eh, little one?"

I broke a sliver of bread off the *petit pain* on my luncheon tray and poked it between the wires of the cage. After a moment's hesitation, he hopped down from his perch and devoured my offering. So I gave him another. And another.

A secret protector. As soon as Meg Giry described his decree, I knew who it was, of course. Her ghost. My angel. And I even knew why. In law, Madame Valérius had held the title of guardian to the orphan Daaé, but in fact, the Phantom had done the job. That was clear enough. But what I didn't know was how he'd managed it all.

Losing interest in my breadcrumbs, Papageno buried his beak in his golden feathers. I watched him preen his plumage without really seeing. My thoughts led me back to the cellar of the opera house. Last night he'd given me my costume for Siebel. How had he come by it? And the things he'd said. The maestro and the chorus master had been informed. Madame Valérius had received his note. And Poligny and Debienne – "idiot managers" – had met with him in their office suite. Those were his words. But what did they really mean?

6

A FEW HOURS after learning of my secret protector, I made my first true enemy at the opera. La Carlotta's reign as diva began long before the company moved into the Palais Garnier. She rose to stardom in the operas of Meyerbeer, whose love of pageantry and historical themes matched her preference for roles that required a lavish costume and a royal swagger. In those days French opera embraced the barking style, and when shouted singing fell out of favor, Carlotta was among a handful of Parisian sopranos to survive the transition to bel canto, the Italian style of beautiful song. But she endured as prima donna less for her voice than her Spaniard's gift for cunning and intrigue. Until that afternoon, I had been just another ingénue to her, one who might be brought along for soubrette roles where my flirty, fair-haired girl would contrast nicely with her dark, smoldering exoticism. I had no idea as I lurked in the wings, waiting to walk-through my part as Siebel in Gounod's *Faust*, that when the rehearsal ended she would be my implacable and dangerous foe.

On the stage, tenor Carolus Fonta worked with Mercier, the régisseur, to fine-tune his signature gestures as the suicidal Dr. Faust of Act I. Waiting for his turn with the stage director, bass Lucien Canet sat on the boards downstage near the prompter's box, practicing the demonic expressions of his Mephistopheles in a hand-held mirror. My entrance didn't come until Act II, so I waited in the shadow cast by the curtain wall of the crossover. The need to act out his part apparently came as a surprise to Fonta, who protested loudly that singing was the only obligation included in his contract. Though he was quick to anger, Mercier rarely blew up at his principals. He put an arm around the Italian tenor's shoulder and talked to him quietly. In the past year we'd all heard the régisseur's speech about the way our acting would transform the audience's perception of opera. No longer would the singers perform behind a veil of music; from now on the music would mirror actions initiated by the singers. What I found interesting at that moment was the way Mercier's recent insistence on naturalism echoed the Phantom's observation that opera must change along with a changing world.

The curtain wall of the crossover fluttered behind me as two scene shifters emerged, still fragrant with the scent of the tobacco they'd recently enjoyed. They set to work nearby, bending over a batten that had been lowered to the stage and adjusting the clamps for the painted flats that form the first layer of set design. Joseph Buquet, an older man with thinning hair, elbowed his partner. "Look at that fish wife across the way! She's practically breaking her neck trying to get a look at the boxes. She can smell an audience – even a single spectator!"

His partner, Florent, a fresh-faced country boy, gazed across the stage at La Carlotta as she dragged a crate into position to improve her view. "I think she's beautiful."

"From here, perhaps. But up close she's a hornet." Buquet shook his head and returned to his task "You'll feel her sting soon enough."

Buquet's feud with La Carlotta began a few years earlier when the stage director ordered him into a footman's costume as a last-minute replacement for a sedan-chair bearer who fell ill just before the curtain rose for Mozart's *Don Giovanni*. The Spanish soprano played Donna Elvira, a spurned victim of the infamous rake who was supposed to make a grand entrance by stepping from the sedan chair to begin her aria vowing revenge. But Buquet's backstage stumble threw the chair sharply down, somersaulting the diva inside onto her head. When he opened the door, the audience screamed with laughter to see La Carlotta sprawled on the floor with her wig askew. She managed to sing while extricating herself and afterwards gave Buquet such a slap on his face that the thunderclap was heard into the tenth row.

The scene shifter exacted his revenge the following year when his nemesis played Gilda, the hunchback's daughter in *Rigoletto*. Buquet fastened a sprig of catnip inside the burlap bag which concealed the dying Gilda in the final scene and then released a cat that darted across the stage to sink its claws into the bag and into Carlotta. The scream that preceded her final aria that night was not part of Verdi's libretto.

From the safe distance of the width of the stage, I studied the diva, who'd climbed onto her crate and stared intently toward a grand tier box I couldn't see. Even on a day devoted to rehearsal, she dressed the part of prima donna in a flame-colored silk gown that set off fiery highlights in her elaborately-coiffed hair. Despite such comic mishaps, La Carlotta struck terror into most of the opera's singers. She quickly dispatched those she considered rivals by coming down with an endless variety of ailments that prevented her from singing but did not spare the managers from paying the generous salary required by her long-term contract. Subtler means were needed to jettison a few tenacious sopranos. Onstage once with a visiting Italian diva, La Carlotta stared at her rival with feigned dismay and whispered that she'd lost one of her false eyebrows. The Italian soprano dipped her head away from the audience and snatched off the other eyebrow. Not until she returned to her dressing room did the visiting diva discover that she'd been tricked into performing the entire second act with a lopsided face. Too thin-skinned to endure such a public humiliation, the Italian soprano soon scurried back to Milan.

At center stage, Fonta and Canet arrived at their diabolical bargain, a temporary return to youth for Faust and another eternally-enslaved soul for Satan. No matter how many times I heard it, *Faust* moved me with its striking choruses, wonderful arias and unearthly final trio. The stars saved their voices for the real performance by singing so softly that they looked like mimes as the orchestra thundered into the rousing melody that ends the first act of Gounod's opera.

A few feet from me, Florent continued to moon at the distant Carlotta, drawing an exasperated growl from Buquet. "Idiot! She'll take no notice of you." The older man gave his young apprentice a sharp cuff and then jerked a thumb in the direction of the grand tier. "Not while toffs like that one come sniffing around."

Florent squinted toward the darkened auditorium. "Who is it? Do you know?"

Buquet signaled to someone on the catwalk above, and the batten slowly rose toward the fly tower. "One of the *gratin* – de Chagny."

"The Comte?" The boy sent a quick glance to La Carlotta, confusion contorting his face. "But the dancer Sorelli is the Comte de Chagny's paramour."

Buquet wiped his hands on the tail of his blue blouse as he watched the batten rise. "Not the comte. His brother. The Vicomte."

Raoul! A flush of pleasure warmed my face. My friend from Brittany. In Paris. In the opera house. Finally!

"The boy's barely out of the schoolroom and the Spanish screecher old enough to be his mother." Buquet shot a last venomous look across the stage. "But she'll take anything in pants if he's rich enough." Trailed by young Florent, the old scene shifter stalked off and disappeared into the crossover.

A half-dozen men from the chorus took the stage to begin Act II. A few at a time, more singers joined them, drifting in from both sides of the stage to build the crowd of a small-town fair. As the boy Siebel, I would stroll from upstage left to downstage right, observing the merriment without joining in. Walk-throughs don't require costumes but singers sometimes wear them to get accustomed to unusual garb. Thus I wore the hose and doublet given to me by the Phantom the night before. For more than an hour I'd paraded through his house by the lake while he scrutinized my posture, my gait and the swing of my arms from a tall stool beside his work table. "To be a great Siebel, your voice is not enough. You must first walk like a carefree youth." He jumped up to demonstrate a loose-limbed amble. "But when Marguerite appears, shyness must tether you, stiffening your movements." In the next instant, a cloak of inhibition tightened his limbs, transforming him into a knot of embarrassment. Over and over, I'd walked before him, one moment lighthearted and the next bashful, until he pronounced himself satisfied.

Now singers filled the stage before me – students praising their wine and beer, soldiers ready to storm stout fortresses or young women, burghers evading their scolding matrons, and maidens puffed up with the vanity of youth. The orchestra cued my entrance, and I ambled out of the shadows, threaded my way across the stage and took my mark next to baritone Pierre Lantin, who played my friend. From there I would finally have an unobstructed view of the de Chagny box.

Lantin greeted me with the oversize bear hug that the régisseur promised would signal the audience that we were characters, not just members of the chorus. When the embrace ended, as the Phantom had instructed, I propped my fists on my hips and rocked back on my heels to survey the fair. The chorus swirled before me, and I lifted my eyes to the box in the grand tier usually occupied by Comte Philippe Georges Marie de Chagny.

A pair of opera glasses hid his laughing blue eyes. A barber had finally brought order to the wild tangle of his dark gold hair. And his fuller frame now suggested a man instead of a boy. Despite the changes, I recognized Raoul instantly. Perhaps by the eager way he leaned against the rail. Or his frank inspection through those ridiculous binoculars. And the exuberant grin I knew so well.

Raoul's grin had disarmed me the first time we met. I'd been walking with my father among a tumble of pink granite rocks on the seashore at Perros-Guirec. When we reached the beach at Trestraou, we found another pair exploring the golden sand – a tall, bespectacled young man with a bookish air who plodded toward us while an energetic boy danced around him and skipped stones across the waves. The sky had threatened rain when we set out and my father made me bring a scarf to cover my head, wrapping it around my neck until needed. Now the sky had cleared and the walk had warmed me. I tugged the scarf free, planning to shove it into the pocket of Papa's jacket. But a sudden gust of wind tore the scarf from my hand and sent it flying through the air like a red kite. I raced after it and, an instant later, so did the boy.

Up, up the scarf flew as we closed the distance between us. Down, down the scarf drifted as we trailed in its wake, arms upraised in hopes of snatching it from the air. Before we could reach it, another rush of air pushed the scarf out over the water where it finally settled, ever-so-gently, into the sea. My arms fell to my sides, and I groaned in disappointment. The boy flashed me an impish grin, sent up a whoop of delight and plunged into the waves, ignoring the panicked cries of his companion as he waded out waist-deep to retrieve my scarf. I doubled over with laughter at the sight of him carefully wringing the water from the scarf as he splashed back to the beach. He presented it to me with a flourish, and I surprised myself – and him – by planting a giggling kiss on his cheek.

That summer of 1870 we became fast friends. The bookish young man turned out to be Raoul's tutor, and it was his idea that my father should teach the young vicomte to play the violin. Three times a week they came to our cottage from nearby Lannion, where Raoul spent every summer with his aunt. After the lesson, Raoul's tutor took tea with the grownups, leaving us free to roam. Raoul loved Papa's stories as much as I did, which inspired our favorite game. Like beggars, we knocked at cottage doors, but instead of begging for food, we begged for stories. The cottagers complied with Breton legends to match the Norse myths and tales of the Angel of Music that Papa supplied. When summer ended, the Germans had Paris under siege so Raoul stayed on in Brittany, giving our friendship another year to grow. But after the summer of 1871 his annual visits to his aunt came to an end. On our last day together, I overheard Raoul's tutor tell Professor Valérius that our friendship disturbed the older brother who had been his guardian since the death of their parents. From then on Raoul summered with the rest of the *gratin* at Evian on Lake Geneva.

Three years later we met again at the cottage in Perros-Guirec. The world had changed – Papa and the professor both dead, the Empire vanished and Paris burned. I was almost fourteen, a bud about to blossom into womanhood. Raoul was sixteen, a well-made youth on the verge of becoming a hand-some man. For the first time, my heart stirred with a different kind of love. From the feverish look in his eyes, I guessed that he felt the same. The passage of time had swept away the easy companionship of our earlier friendship. I now understood that what had disturbed Comte de Chagny about that friendship was the possibility that an aristocratic boy might form an unsuitable alliance with a bourgeois girl. Raoul knew it, too. We left the words unspoken, but we both realized there was no future for us. And so that final visit was very polite and oh-so-correct. Raoul applauded my decision to enroll in the singing school at Garnier's new opera house, and I applauded his decision to enroll in the Ecole-Navale near Brest. While I conquered the stage, he would conquer the sea, but when he returned to Paris as an officer in the French navy, Raoul vowed to seek me out again. And, at long last, here he was.

On the stage before me, Mephistopheles appeared, and I dragged my eyes and my thoughts back to the opera. All the singers joined bass Lucien Canet for the song – "And Satan leads the dance!" – that precedes his prophesying: Marguerite's brother to die and Siebel's touch to poison flowers. "Are you a wizard, then?" I sang as I backed away from him and his prophecy. When Faust appeared, everyone but that demonic pair withdrew to the wings for the space of their brief duet. I had just enough time to see that Raoul remained in his family's box on the grand tier before becoming Siebel once again.

All in a rush, the men and women of the chorus returned to the stage and began to partner for a dance. At that moment, Gounod made Siebel think only of Marguerite, and I stiffened my body before singing my line: "Marguerite can arrive this way alone." When a maiden asked me to dance, I brushed her off: "It has no charm for me." Then Carlotta appeared on the other side of the stage. I tripped forward: "Marguerite!" Just as Buquet predicted, she played to the sole occupant of the auditorium. I couldn't spare a glance for Raoul because Mephistopheles blocked my effort to approach Marguerite: "Curse that man! Here he is again!"

As the demon wizard, Lucien Canet became Siebel's puppeteer, compelling the love-sick youth to circle the stage in order to leave the way to Marguerite clear for his protégé, Faust. The slow circuit allowed me to look again at Raoul, who still had his opera glasses trained on me. Across the stage, Carlotta startled us all by thundering full-voice her rejection of Faust: "I am no demoiselle, neither am I fair. And I have no need to accept your offered arm." Ignoring the régisseur's frantic beckoning, Carlotta flounced toward me, shooting me a glare that cut like a stiletto as she exited the stage. As the chorus swung back into a waltz, I completed my circuit and followed her.

Before I had a moment to consider the source of the diva's displeasure, the props manager, Claude, took hold of my elbow and waved a bouquet of paper lilies under my chin. "Try these out for us." He pointed to a band of black paper encircling the artificial stems. "As you pick this bunch, crush that band in your fist and every blossom will wither."

In the pit, the orchestra struck up the music for Act III. I took the bouquet from Claude and returned to the stage for Siebel's solo. Opera abounds with tongue-tied swains who need intermediaries to reveal their love, and for Gounod's bashful boy, the role of Cupid is played by a handful of flowers from Marguerite's garden. But first Siebel must overcome the curse that poisons his touch. As Claude predicted, when I clenched my fist, the paper flowers in my hand collapsed against my wrist. The surprise of it made me miss a note, but as I was covering my part sotto voce, no one noticed. Under the pious conventions that governed opera in those days, Siebel needed only to dip his hands in holy water to wash away the curse of Mephistopheles. Rejoicing in my triumph against Satan, I gathered roses and lilies – "I've faith in these flowers alone, for they will plead for me" – and left the bouquet messenger in Marguerite's garden.

"Excellent, Christine." Mercier, nodded his approval as I exited the stage. "There's a bit of the boy in your walk, I'd say."

"And a bit of black magic in those flowers." Claude took the flaccid bouquet from my hand and began to examine it carefully.

With Siebel's part in the opera nearly over, I could relax and let my mind return to Raoul. Would he come to my dressing room after the walk-through? Perhaps such a visit would be improper. Certainly he would know what was correct. Maybe he would seek me out at the home of my guardian, Madame Valérius. No chance of impropriety there – they were already acquainted, good friends even.

At center stage, Carlotta again startled the cast and crew of *Faust* by launching full-volume into the opera's most famous music, Marguerite's jewel song. For a moment, a hush fell over the knots of performers and stage hands standing in the streets of the theater as the prima donna built the song toward its climax.

"There'll be the devil to pay now." The old scene shifter, Joseph Buquet, lifted a hand in the direction of the grand tier. Oblivious to the diva performing solely for his benefit, Raoul had risen from his seat in the Chagny box and turned toward the door. "And I expect Miss Daaé will get the blame. He had eyes only for her."

7

*N*O MATTER how much I pleaded with her, Madame Valérius refused to move into the larger, more comfortable apartment that I now could afford with my soloist's salary. She balked as well when I tried to simply pay a greater share of our monthly bills. In the end, by conspiring with our servant, Victorine, I succeeded in gradually improving Mme. Valérius' standard of living – extra buckets of coal for the fire, better cuts of meat for the table, needed clothing miraculously "found" in the bargain bin at one of the new department stores. I indulged myself as well. Nothing so grand as an entire wardrobe. Although I finally had all the francs I needed to become a woman of fashion, I possessed a strong streak of Swedish frugality. Instead I chose to embellish the clothing I already had: accenting an evening gown with a pair of garnet earrings; freshening a sensible walking dress with a frivolous hat; adding a stylish two-tier cape to wear on promenade.

The morning after Raoul appeared at the opera, I dressed in favorites old and new. To the rich sapphire velvet of a fantail skirt I'd loved for two years, I added an new overskirt and bodice of azure silk faille trimmed with silver buttons at the neck and wrist. I'd risen earlier than usual and taken extra time with my toilette, coiling my long hair into a twist and adding a trace of color to my cheeks and lips. Who was the object of my effort? To this day, I don't really know. Certainly my pulse quickened to andante tempo every time I thought of meeting my childhood friend again. Yet besides a fitting with the costumer in the late afternoon, my only engagement for the day was another lesson with the Phantom. Time and again as I primped and fussed in front of my mirror, my glance dropped to the bright brass key on the crisp linen doily atop my dressing table. He'd pressed it into my hand after showing me the underground passage that led from the house by the lake to a narrow iron gate in the theater's outer wall that opened onto Rue Scribe: "From now on, you come to me." My hand trembled when I picked up the key and slipped it into my reticule.

At 9 a.m. the streets around the opera had barely woken. With the rising sun, the prostitutes had abandoned their doorways in the narrow lanes between Rue de Richelieu and the Palais Garnier. For lack of customers in the cafés on the grand boulevards, the waiters with their bright white aprons occupied themselves re-arranging the marble-topped tables. Businessmen and bureaucrats had already finished their breakfasts, and the *flâneurs* for whom those tables were a second home wouldn't appear for hours. Most of the shops in the neighborhood remained shuttered. Fashionable ladies in need of luggage or carpets or bronzes wouldn't begin shopping until noon. A workman with a bucket of paste paused to post bills advertising new shows – emerald for the Opéra-Comique and wine for the Comédie Francaise – on a Moriss column, and a block away the proprietor of a newsstand arranged a display of the journals published that morning.

I crossed the Place de l'Opéra, skirted the Palais Garnier and turned into Rue Scribe. The Phantom's gate hid inside a shallow alcove in the tiny alley formed by the carriage ramp of the Emperor's Pavilion. The high-walled ramp itself shielded the alley from the street, but until I stepped inside the alcove, I could be seen by passersby on the sidewalk. I paused at the spot where the top of the oval ramp towered over the sidewalk, reaching into my reticule to retrieve the key while surveying the area for onlookers. No one. With the sound of my heart hammering in my ears, I darted down the alley, ducked into the alcove and slid the shining key into the black iron gate. A flick of my wrist, a quiet snick of the lock and the gate silently swung open on well-oiled hinges.

The narrow passage sloped steeply, a blue tunnel in the dim gaslight. When I reached the place where the passage turned sharply before plunging again, I looked back to the small square of daylight barred by iron. Rounding the corner, I discovered a thread of sound rising through the tunnel. An organ, surely, but playing music unlike any I'd ever heard, a fearsome elegy that sobbed with despair. My steps slowed under the burden of the song, which left my heart aching. The music stopped abruptly and a few moments later a brilliant flash of light poured into the tunnel, silhouetting the Phantom standing in his shirtsleeves in the doorway of his house. As I drew near, he stepped forward. "You came."

I unfastened my cape and let him lift it from my shoulders. "Of course."

I untied the ribbons of my bonnet and hung it with my reticule alongside the cape on the hall tree next to the door. "You did say 9:30." I smoothed my hair in the hall-tree mirror before turning to look up at him. "Didn't you?"

"Yes." Behind a simple black satin mask, his dark eyes lit with appreciation as he noticed my new dress. "My nightingale has fine feathers. Very becoming."

He slid his hand around my upper arm and steered me toward the music room. The warmth of his gaze and his words and his touch eased my heartache at the sorrow in his music. The sight of the organ strewn with papers covered with musical notation inspired a conviction that somewhere in those stacks were other compositions – songs of hope and joy and love. He was an angel, after all, and angels existed to rejoice as well as lament. Together we would have reason for jubilation. A rush of exultation left me tingling. I was young and pretty and had a teacher who could help me find my celestial voice.

In the next instant, the Phantom's grip on my arm tightened, and his words rasped harshly in my ear. "Who is he?" He stopped abruptly and I stumbled against him. He reached out his free hand to steady me. "The man for whom you don these fine feathers? The boulevardier who ogles you from the grand tier?"

We faced each other, only inches apart with his hands still loosely ringing my arms just above the elbows. The glow in his eyes had flared into anger. And something else. Hurt? My own fury blunted my curiosity.

"He's no boulevardier." I yanked one arm free of his hand and took a step backward. "He's a friend from Brittany." I jerked the other arm free but held my ground. "And a naval officer."

"A friend?" The rough edge returned to his voice. "Or a lover?"

I laughed up at him, a reaction that left his dark eyes wide with surprise. "How could I have a lover with the guard you keep on me?"

I stared him down, watching a calm wariness replace the surprise in his eyes, willing him to speak, to explain, but he remained silent. When he didn't respond, I counter-attacked. "No denial – so you admit your secret scheming? How did you manage it? How did you make the maestro and the managers do your bidding? Not that their task was so difficult – protecting a fatherless child. Still, Meg Giry says they did as you asked from my first days at the opera. I don't understand why."

"Little Giry." He sighed and looked away from me then, staring at the books in his library though I doubt he actually saw them. He wore no cravat and his shirt hung open at the neck. For the first time I noticed the stubble on his chin. I knew instinctively that for this man such disarray would be unusual. And I wondered what had unsettled him so? Raoul?

"You don't need to understand. Not yet. Not if you trust me." He'd composed himself again, calmed the anger in his eyes and tamed the snarl in his voice. "At this moment in your career, all of your attention, all of your energy, must be devoted to perfecting your voice. And some of my attention and energy must be devoted to guarding you from distractions that might sabotage your success."

I did trust him. More than anyone on earth. Despite my pique at being the last to know of my secret protector, he had kept me safe in a backstage world that abounded with predatory males. His friendship had been a lonely girl's only solace. And his musical instruction had elevated my art to a heavenly realm. Why should I defy him now?

Sensing my surrender, he reached out and gently took my hand. "Tell me about the Vicomte de Chagny."

"We were childhood friends. In Brittany. During the war and the siege and the Commune. He studied violin with my father. And when he enrolled at the Ecole-Navale, he promised to see me in Paris when his studies were complete." I shrugged. "And now he's here."

He pulled my hand through the crook of his elbow, linking our arms, and walked with me to the piano. "When do you meet him again?"

"I haven't met him yet. I just saw him in his brother's box in the grand tier."

"To achieve greatness, you must put aside worldly things. To sustain that greatness, you will need to turn your back on society, whose celebrations of your brilliance will eventually drain the vitality from your art." He dropped my arm, opened a music folio on top of the piano and rifled through the sheet music inside. "One day, perhaps, you'll be able to bestow your heart. But for now your life must be that of a novitiate – disciplined and austere."

The idea of the Palais Garnier as a kind of nunnery made me smile. "And if I renounce society today, what will I gain from that sacrifice in the end?"

He didn't return my smile. "You will have the adoration of the world, and all of Paris at your feet."

I swallowed the little bubble of laughter that rose inside me. His transformation of my voice had indeed been miraculous. Hadn't I described the result as celestial, if only to myself? "You really mean that, don't you?"

"Yes." He found the composition he wanted and lifted the sheets from the folio. "Doubt me if you must. But by the end of this season you'll be prima donna – my prima donna. And then you'll see that what I've said is true."

He tapped the sheet music lightly against the piano cabinet until the corners evened. "Let us begin."

Perhaps the Phantom's prediction of fame and fortune inspired what followed, but I hope not. I confess to my ambition, but I reject the idea that my motives were mercenary. My father dreamed that I would become a diva, and I honored his memory by striving to fulfill his dream. And mine. Under the Phantom's tutelage, my lifelong love of singing had blossomed into a genuine vocation. Even on the most difficult day, I found pleasure in singing. And exaltation on the best. But that day my voice transported me to a new kind of ecstasy. Each note of the warm-up scales had the perfection and clarity of the chime of a bell. After days of trying, I succeeded with the effect known as *filare la voce*, beginning with a quiet skein of sound that spins out to a striking resonance before slowly diminishing again into silence. And I finally let the music invade my soul. As the Phantom promised, I truly did feel it my bones.

When he called for a break, I wasn't tired. I could have kept singing for hours, but I took a seat on the high stool beside the piano and accepted the glass he offered. I sipped the water while studying the sheets of music he'd asked me to look over. "This is the final trio from *Faust*. It's scored for Marguerite."

"I'd like you to learn it – just in case." The Phantom laid a finger against his throat. "Carlotta already has developed a tickle. Imagine what might happen when she actually hears you sing?"

I frowned into my glass. "Joseph Buquet thinks she's already my enemy."

He refilled my glass with the pitcher he'd brought on a tray from the sideboard and gestured for me to drink up. "He of all people would understand her ways."

I set my empty glass back on the tray. "Does anything about this building or its inhabitants escape your notice? I suppose you can even tell me the trick Claude used to wither Siebel's flowers."

"The black tape hides the cement that glues the flowers to the stems." He spread his hands wide. "Crush it in your fist and the flowers instantly droop."

I let my mouth drop open in an exaggerated stage version of surprise, and for the first time heard his laughter, a rich and hearty gust that tickled a laugh from me as well. So much for his earlier lamentation!

He picked up an apple from the tray and peeled it with a silver fruit knife. "I told you about Lecadre, the old magician who made me his apprentice. He was my second great teacher, tutoring me in the arts of the wizard and the skills of the showman."

Inside his mask, a dreaminess invaded his dark eyes. "Like you, I was an apt pupil. I soon mastered the elementary hoaxes common in Europe – spinning an assistant on the sharp tip of a sword or levitating a silk-covered ball above a stone pedestal. My specialty became the more difficult tricks of the East such as the Punjab lasso."

"I fling a hangman's rope overhead with an easy toss." He mimed the gesture with the hand holding the apple, leaving the peel dangling. "The noose hangs in mid-air until recalled to my hand by a snap of my fingers."

He finished peeling the apple, split the fruit into eighths, speared one with the knife and offered it to me. "Lecadre also devoted many hours to teaching me ventriloquism."

I lifted the apple toward my mouth, but in the next instant froze when the Phantom's voice seemed to emanate from the fruit. "The magician wasn't satisfied until, at a moment's notice, I could project my voice from any corner of a room."

I held the apple slice at arm's length and addressed it directly. "Brilliant! Will you teach me the trick?"

"Perhaps." The Phantom's voice now addressed me from the candelabra beside the piano. "In time we became collaborators in devising new illusions such as the phantasmagoria, a magic lantern that projected writhing demons, grinning skeletons and shrieking ghosts on curling pillars of smoke."

I popped the slice of apple into my mouth, savoring the crisp autumn freshness, and held my hand out for more. The Phantom speared another slice and flicked it onto my palm.

"Our greatest collaboration employed the new science of electromagnetism to demonstrate the power of the magician's will." The Phantom's voice now spoke from somewhere behind my stool. "From the audience would come two people, a small boy who easily lifted an empty iron box and a burly man who struggled in vain to raise the same light load because he'd been made 'weak' by Lecadre's will power."

I accepted a third slice of apple. "With all that wizardry to study, it's a wonder you had time to master music as well. That's the real magic."

"Not magic – discipline." The ventriloquist vanished and he pronounced each word firmly. Inside his mask, his eyes steeled. "I knew what I wanted. I knew how to get it. And I allowed nothing to distract me." He covered the hand I'd rested on the piano with his own. "Do you know what you want? Do you understand that if you bestow your heart now, there is nothing more I can do for you?"

My heart fluttered with sudden panic at the thought of losing him. My friend. My protector. My teacher. I was so confused. About my own feelings, which were stronger than friendship for a longtime companion, gratitude for a diligent guardian or admiration for a brilliant teacher. About his feelings as well, especially his fear of Raoul. I never said Raoul was the Vicomte de Chagny, but that's what the Phantom called him. Which meant the Phantom knew Raoul's identity before I even arrived. Why did he pretend ignorance? Just moments after asking for my trust?

Ever so gently, the Phantom tightened his hand around mine. He was here beside me. As he'd always been. "My heart remains my own." Under his hand, I turned mine so that our palms met and our fingers twined. "And my dream remains the one you shared with Papa – to be your prima donna."

8

I RETURNED FROM my appointment with the costumer to find the door to my dressing room ajar and a deep octagonal box beside Papageno's cage on the vanity. My fingertips caressed wood smooth as satin and traced my initials in iridescent shell of palest pink inlaid into the hinged top of the box. I opened the latch of hammered brass and raised the lid. The spicy aroma of cedar tickled my nose as I lifted a Breton *coiffe* of delicate lace from the box. Leaning toward the mirror, I placed the traditional head-dress on my hair and smoothed the wide wings of lace that trailed over my collar bones. The sight of my face framed by the *coiffe* stirred happy memories of summer pilgrimages and feast days with Papa that made me smile.

"It suits you." In the mirror my eyes met Raoul's for a moment before I spun around to face him. Finally! Could he hear the sudden thudding of my heart, which all but deafened me? "I knew it would."

"Raoul! You look wonderful!" In a reprise of our very first meeting, I brushed a kiss across the hard tanned skin of his cheek, but this time I had to rise up on my toes to reach him. "And it's wonderful to see you." I touched the lace head-dress. "Such a lovely *coiffe*. You shouldn't have."

"On the contrary. That *coiffe* and everything else in the box saved my sanity. I was so discouraged at first at the Ecole-Navale. An old sailor told me the only way to forget the hardship and my loneliness was to remember a sweetheart and to carefully choose the treasures I'd bring back to her with my sailor's valentine." He fingered the lace that grazed my left ear. "I chose this first – in Brest."

I dipped my head to hide the color staining my face. "I found it hard here, too. And lonely."

Raoul lightly touched my cheek. "My poor Christine. All alone in the temple of music." His tone brightened. "Where you now reign as queen, with a box of treasure freshly delivered to your throne."

As ever, Raoul didn't allow himself or his companions to remain glum for long, and his gaiety proved infectious. At his urging, I reached into the octagonal box and pulled forth a large rectangle of red wool elaborately embroidered with threads of gold. "Oh, beautiful!" I draped it over my hand, as weightless as down. "So soft."

"I bartered very hard for that at the souk in Algiers. The *della'l* said it was fine enough to be a bridal gift for a Berber princess." Raoul lifted the lace *coiffe* from my head, replaced it with red wool shawled like a veil and turned me until I faced myself again in the looking glass. "You're just as I imagined – the beautiful Fenena, daughter of the Babylonian king in *Nabucco*."

Our eyes met again in the mirror. "But you told me you knew nothing about opera."

"I didn't, but I've learned since then – on four different continents!" He didn't look away, and neither did I. Somehow the mirror made our confessions easier. "I went to the opera whenever I could because it made me feel closer to you."

With one hand, I lifted the veil across my face, hiding my smile and leaving only my eyes in view. Even before the Phantom extracted my vow to spurn society, I hadn't allowed myself to imagine this reunion with Raoul. We had parted six years before as friends. But his words – sweetheart! – and his treasures suggested greater regard.

He reached into the box and, with a flourish, presented me with a single dainty feather of silvery-gray. "Plumage from the neck of a sooty albatross." I held out my hand and he placed the feather in my palm, the barbs like tiny strands of silver. "I traveled farthest for that. There's nothing to be found on the Kerguelen Islands but wind and ice and birds."

I looked up from the feather in my hand. "I don't know where that is."

He laughed. "You're not alone. It's a little spray of islands in the great southern sea at the bottom of the world." For the first time, he turned his attention to Papageno, pointing to his cage. "Your little canary would have added a spot of color among the penguins, petrels and terns who watched us as we mapped the shoreline. One day we came upon a fine beach that reminded me of Trestraou at Perros-Guirec. I found your feather there."

"What sights you've seen!" I let the veil drop from my face and gently stroked the small albatross feather. "How far you've traveled!"

76

He thrust out his chest and squared his shoulders into a stiff military posture but softened the effect with a smile. "I've circumnavigated the Earth. And I've just been made a member of an expedition that will explore Antarctica next year. That's more than you can say for Christopher Columbus or Jacques Cartier. Perhaps one day I'll be in the history books as well."

Distress at the danger Raoul would face smothered my temptation to laugh at his boasting. The man certainly hadn't lost the high spirits that had endeared the boy to me. His eyes still shone with adventure and mischief, and he still possessed a special vibrancy that somehow made me feel more alive. "You will be careful, won't you?"

"Never fear, Christine." He snapped a crisp salute, and his smile widened into a grin. "I'll always come back to you."

How those words jolted me. I sank onto the rush seat of a chair. Year in and year out I'd stood alone and apart, a tribe of one in a world designed for pairs. But no longer. Two men now claimed me. The Phantom laid the world at the feet of his prima donna. Raoul promised to be constant to his sweetheart evermore. All my life I'd longed for the home I'd never had, the chance of a real family that I'd lost when my mother died, the loving circle of a brood of children overseen by two devoted parents. And I'd also longed for operatic success, the dream now becoming a reality, of a talent nurtured into a celestial voice that would allow me to create my own destiny.

My thoughts tumbled in confusion as Raoul presented the rest of his treasures – a bolt of crimson silk from Indochina, a string of black pearls from Tahiti, a madras Creole cap from Guadeloupe. I managed to keep my composure as he filled my lap with gifts, but my mind still clamored when he laid the last on top – a smaller octagonal box containing an intricate seashell heart under glass.

"That's a true sailor's valentine. From Martinique."

"It's beautiful." My voice barely rose above a whisper. "It's all beautiful."

Papageno flew across around his cage in alarm when Raoul lunged for the other chair on the far side of my dressing table. He dragged it so close our knees touched when he sat down. "I didn't mean to overwhelm you, Christine. It's just that I've thought of you and nothing else since we finally set sail for home."

For a moment, he chewed on his lower lip. "I asked my brother, Philippe, if you were free." He took my hand in both of his. "He knew of no attachment."

Still clasping my hand, he leaned forward, resting his elbows on his knees, until only inches separated our faces. "I've been at sea so long. And I have such plans for us – the races at Longchamp, boating parties on the Seine, promenades on the grand boulevards, dinners at Lapérouse, champagne at Café Riche." He squeezed my hand gently. "Plans for our amusement, Christine. No more than that. Not yet."

He released my hand and sat up straight, his show of patience belied by expectancy that tensed his shoulders. How those entertainments tempted me! I allowed a sigh to escape as I gathered up his gifts, placing them atop my dressing table before I turned back to him. "Raoul, do you remember the Angel of Music?"

His blue eyes widened in surprise. "Of course. 'Little Lotte loved most of all, when she went to sleep, to hear the Angel of Music.' Your father's wonderful stories."

I knotted my fingers in my lap. "Just before he died, Papa said, 'When I reach heaven, Christine, I will send the Angel of Music to you.' And he did." Before he could reply, I rushed on. "I have a new teacher. He's strange and wonderful – a genius. In six months he's transformed my voice."

Raoul stiffened. "Are you saying this man is your—"

"Oh, no!" I threw up my hands to stop his words. "He's my teacher. Nothing more. But he is very strict. And I've promised him that, for now, I'll put aside the pleasure of society and devote myself to music."

He frowned and leaned toward me. "For how long?"

"For this season at least. Perhaps only until May."

"May!" Raoul jumped to his feet, and I shrank against the back of my chair. "But soon after I'll be going away again." He punched the fist of one hand into the palm of the other. "And I'll be gone for a year at least."

He stomped across my dressing room, his face scowling with indignation, then turned on his heel and stomped back until he stood towering over me. "This is an outrage, Christine. You can't be serious. To make me wait again – after I've already waited six long years?" He injected a tone of command into his voice. "I insist that you dine with me tonight. We'll discuss this then. Shall I call for you here?"

I gazed up at him mutely, as stupefied as one of his sailors who'd just had his first taste of the lash.

"Eight o'clock? Here?" Raoul flashed me a brittle smile. "Very well. I'll see you then."

He stalked out of the dressing room and was gone before I had a chance to respond.

No sooner had the door swung shut behind him than the Phantom's mirror gaped from the wall. "So that's your sailor boy. A brash pup."

He strolled to my dressing table, pulled three grapes from the pocket of his waistcoat and dropped them between the tiny bars of Papageno's cage. The canary immediately fluttered down to investigate. "And here is your teacher. Nothing more."

The Phantom's snarling echo of my words raised the hair on the back of my neck. He wore again the pale mask that fit like a second skin, presenting a countenance as bland as a china doll. "I meant no—"

He swiveled toward me so suddenly that I flinched. "Spare me, Christine. I've had a lifetime of 'nothing more.'"

He reached out, gently took hold of my chin and turned my face so that the light from the gas lamp behind me fell across my features. "Perhaps you should ask about those plans the Vicomte has for you. Surely you don't believe they include a home at Hôtel de Chagny in the Faubourg St. Germain?"

He dropped his hand. "More likely he intends you to serve as his courtesan, as La Sorelli serves his older brother." His voice sharpened. "I doubt he thinks you're just a *putain ordinaire*."

I didn't react to his insults. And I refused to look away. My father had been content with his life, and I'd been spared the lessons of anger that many children learn. But I'd seen how dogs that cower invite further beatings. So I remained as silent and still as a stone sculpture, my face as expressionless as the blank mask the Phantom showed to the world.

"These boulevardiers are all the same, showing the kind of devotion to their cafés that patriots reserve for their countries. They arrive each afternoon at one and play cards or dominos until seven. Off to dinner and the theater then back to the café to talk and talk, the more malicious the better." Under his second-skin mask, the Phantom's lip curled with scorn. "And perhaps a promenade? But only on the Boulevard des Italiens, and only on the north side, the left side. Above all else, a boulevardier defers to the fashion of the day."

He stared down at me, his dark eyes unreadable. I knew so little of men. Yet I understood that the two who now claimed me viewed each other as rivals. The Phantom wanted his prima donna. But what did Raoul want? The entertainments he'd outlined for us were those of a man of fashion, an elegant *flâneur*. What the Phantom said was true enough. The France Raoul had returned to was the one he'd left. Nothing had changed. Aristocrats still found their sweethearts among the *gratin*. And they still looked to the bourgeoisie for other kinds of companionship.

In his cage, Papageno fussed over his grapes. On the wall, the gaslight flared suddenly from an impurity in the line. And still the Phantom and I remained frozen in silent confrontation, faces impassive but hearts raging.

A dream of light and laughter drew me to Raoul, whose sunniness and simplicity offered a welcome escape from the intrigues of the Palais Garnier and the barrenness of my life outside the theater. A darker, more complex desire lured me toward the Phantom – our shared passion for music, certainly, but much more than that. Even now, in the face of his anger, I remembered the hard heat of his chest against my palm. And somehow I couldn't summon the indignation I should have felt at discovering his hidden observation of my tête-à-tête with Raoul. Or stop myself from wondering how long it would be before the Phantom trusted me enough to reveal the mystery he hid behind his masks.

And so, as the moments passed, I renounced one by one the temptations Raoul had dangled before me. After all, I'd never cared for the races. Our maid, Victorine, could accompany me on promenade. Eventually my time would come for elegant dinners and expensive champagne. And when I wished for an outing on the Seine, I had only to approach the large painting that dominated the Phantom's dining alcove to join the revelers feasting *en plein air* at Chatou.

"His plans don't matter." At my words, the Phantom's mouth softened, his lips no longer a grim line. "Yours do."

He took my hand as I rose to my feet. "If I insist, will you dine with me tonight?"

I tried to withdraw my hand, but he held tight. "Absolutely not."

He raised my hand to his lips and brushed a light kiss across it. "If I ask, will you dine with me tonight?"

I gave him my most brilliant smile. "Of course."

He waited silently while I locked my dressing room door, covered Papageno's cage and turned down the gas. When I was finished, the Phantom pulled my arm through his and led me once again into the darkness behind the mirror.

9

MY CHOICE, once made, changed things between us. During my lessons, the Phantom remained a strict master, guiding the development of my voice with a firm hand, while I undertook my studies with a fierce new resolve, a fresh passion that animated each note I sang. But when the lesson was over, the Phantom was more at ease with me and I with him. Our silences grew companionable and so did our conversation, restoring the rapport that had been upset when the voice that was my friend suddenly materialized as a man.

Madame Valérius applauded my choice. "They would have approved!" Blinking back tears, she grasped the medallion hanging around her neck and smiled at the framed photographs of my father and the professor on the marble mantelpiece of our drawing room. "This is what they both wanted for you!"

She didn't question the strange and sudden appearance of the teacher she called my angel. As her health slowly deteriorated and her life narrowed to the confines of our small flat, Madame Valérius became more and more eccentric. She grew to believe that her husband and my father remained with us in a form mortal eyes couldn't perceive. She embraced the spiritualism of mediums such as Madame Blavatsky, collected pamphlets about the apparitions of the Virgin Mary at Pontmain, Lourdes and La Sallete, and wore the miraculous medal struck by the Sisters of Charity on Rue du Bac. Always an obedient child, I'd hurried home from the Palais Garnier the first time I heard the Angel of Music and told her about the strange voice in the cellar of the opera. "He's come at last. Your father's final gift!" She'd cupped her hands around both of mine. "Let him be a comfort to you, as the Professor is to me. We talk every morning after I've finished my coffee."

Our maid, Victorine, had seen nothing alarming in the conversations between Madame Valérius and her dead husband. "She's a sick, old woman, Miss Christine, with nothing to dream about but her past and your future. So she chats with the Professor. So what? Where's the harm in that?"

From then on I'd carefully edited the version of my life that I shared with my benefactress, telling her nothing that might disturb her delusion of benevolent spirits hovering around us to cheer each step I took on my road to operatic glory. Now, with the Phantom, I could finally be myself. As the October days shortened in the streets outside the opera, the hours lengthened that I spent in the Phantom's house by the lake.

I was not at home when Raoul called at Rue Notre Dame des Victoires. Madame Valérius received him warmly, and Victorine remembered his fondness for little madeleines when she served their tea. Only six of the sweet shells remained on the plate she offered me later that evening. "He gobbled those cookies like the boy he was, but he's grown a handsome man, Miss Christine. Still no airs about him, for all his fine looks and fat purse. Never was."

I waved the plate away but softened my refusal with a smile. "How did you find him, Madame?"

"As spirited as ever." Madame Valérius' eyes sparkled at the memory. "And quite forthright about his unhappiness with your angel. 'If she is free, why does she take orders from this man?' he asked. I said, 'No singer like Christine is ever really free. They are bound by their art, and the strongest tie is to their master.'" She touched her fingertips to her lips. "Master! He didn't like that!"

Much as I tried to avoid it, our confrontation was inevitable. A full week passed before Raoul finally found me in my dressing room. In that time the room had been transformed by Jean Bataille, a scene artist at the opera who specialized in clouds. He'd covered the walls with a springtime dawn of blue and rose and gold that spangled across a ceiling of clouds, and he'd dragooned the wood-working shop into providing gilded furniture to match. Papageno's cage now stood on its own pedestal opposite the Phantom's mirror, and in place of the scratched dressing table and doorless wardrobe, my dressing room now featured a three-seat sofa upholstered in rose damask, a Louis XVI armoire with lyres carved on the doors and a vanity topped with white marble. Jean also wanted to gild the Phantom's mirror, but I wouldn't let him. "Oh no! Don't touch it," I cried when I walked into my dressing room to find the painter examining the mirror to see how the carved frame attached to the wall. Jean gave me a peculiar look as he took a step back, and I modulated my voice to remove the thread of panic. "It's perfect just as the way it is. Really."

At that moment Raoul appeared in the doorway with a large bouquet of yellow roses filling his arms. Jean bobbed his head at me and then at Raoul, showing us both a crown of paint-splattered brown hair, before slipping out the door. Raoul brushed his lips against the hand I offered. As I carried the flowers to my dressing table, he surveyed the freshly-painted room. "At least this master of yours treats you well."

Lacking a vase, I arranged the roses in the porcelain pitcher of my wash basin and considered Raoul's comment. Was my new dressing room a gift from the Phantom? I didn't really know. Until that moment I hadn't given the matter any thought. I'd been so engrossed in my work that I just accepted the refurbishment without question. After all, none of the other private dressing rooms contained battered walls and ramshackle furniture.

I turned to face my visitor. "Such sweet flowers and such sour words."

"Surely you don't expect sweet words for the man who persuaded you to stand me up the other night?" For the first time, I noticed the hurt in Raoul's blue eyes. "Not a word, Christine. Not a note. Nothing but a locked door."

"I'm so sorry." I gestured toward the sofa. "Please, do sit down, and let me try to explain."

What a fix! A librettist who wrote a story based on such an unlikely coincidence would be dismissed with one word: preposterous! In all the world I had just two friends – one from my childhood in Brittany and one from my youth at the opera house. For so many years I had stood alone and apart. Now those two friends each sought to claim me and both named the same price: my friendship with the other. The age-old triangle with a new twist, except that this was not a story in an opera but my own life.

Raoul's posture remained stiff as I sank onto the sofa beside him. He stared across the room at the roses standing on my dressing table, presenting me with his profile. "That last day in Perros we were awkward youths unable to recapture our childhood familiarity. We parted as friends but with no promise for the future."

I edged my hand across the cool damask toward his, which rested on the cushion beside his leg. "Six long years and both of us lonely. You eased your loneliness by dreaming of a sweetheart." His skin warmed the tips of my fingers. "A sweetheart who had no idea of your affection."

At those words, he recoiled, but I grasped his hand. "I am deeply honored by your affection, Raoul. In those years I thought of you often. With great fondness. But I am today what I was then: an orphan who must make her own way in the world. While you were at sea, I have been here working to fulfill my dreams."

I let go of Raoul's hand and spread mine wide to encompass the entire Palais Garnier. "This is why Papa allowed Professor Valérius to bring us from Sweden to Paris. Finally I am standing on the threshold." I swooped both hands back to his, gathering it between them. "I do not believe the selfless boy has grown into a selfish man. I do not believe you would have me put aside my father's dreams – and my own – because you want a play-mate."

For a moment, he showed no reaction beyond a flush that stained his neck before creeping up to rouge his cheeks. "*Merde!* What an ass I've been!" He turned toward me then, his eyes pleading and without guile. "Christine, can you forgive me?"

"Of course."

Before I could say more, he rushed on. "But not to see you at all – except from our box? You always on the stage and I always in the grand tier? Surely we can meet now and then?"

"Of course." I nodded, still cheered by his reasonableness in seeing things my way. "Perhaps on a Sunday afternoon."

"This Sunday!" His eyes danced with pleasure. "We'll go to Argenteuil in my carriage. We'll watch the sailboats on the river. And dine in a brasserie that comes highly—"

"Raoul!" I threw up both hands to fend off the torrent of words. "You must give me an invitation, not a command. If I am free – and if your invitation is convenient – I will accept. But, first, you must ask."

A knock at the open door prevented his reply. "Miss Daaé?" A young stylist from the wig shop danced from foot to foot in the doorway, her fingers knotting the crisp linen of the apron which covered her dress. "Your pardon, mademoiselle, but the wig mistress begs to see you soon about your Despina hair."

I lifted the silver pendant watch pinned just below the lace collar of my blouse and discovered that I was fifteen minutes late for my appointment. I dropped the watch and sprang to my feet. "I'll come this instant." Raoul automatically rose when I stood. I flashed him an apologetic smile. "Forgive me again, but I must fly."

I offered my hand as I moved toward the door, and he took it at once. "I'll send you a note about Argenteuil, Raoul, when I know for sure."

In the corridor outside my dressing room, I gave his hand one quick squeeze before turning after the young wigmaker and plunging again into the backstage world that now absorbed all my time and attention. Before I'd taken a half dozen steps, the problem of Raoul and his plans for Argenteuil faded from my mind. My rededication to the Paris opera eclipsed even the impetuous young man who was my oldest friend.

The golden light of a fine October bathed the white marble of the Palais Garnier during the next few weeks, but I seldom felt its warmth against my face. I had two new parts to learn for comic operas that would open in December and in January. As the scheming maid Despina in Mozart's *Così fan tutte*, I would help persuade the two sisters who employed me into dalliances to betray the fiancés who'd taken bets on the honor of their future wives. As the busybody peasant Giannetta in Donizetti's *L'Elisir D'Amore*, I would spill the secret about the hero's inheritance, leading him to mistakenly attribute to a love potion his new success with greedy girls. Even secondary roles such as Despina and Giannetta required demanding preparation. I hadn't yet begun to sing the parts because the Phantom insisted that I first memorize the music and perfect the pronunciation of each libretto. Only then would he allow me to focus on my songs to develop my performance – emotions to color my notes, places for me to breathe, passages to sing louder or softer.

Late one afternoon I remained at the Phantom's piano long after my lesson ended, plinking out the notes of a descant by Giannetta which soars above the peasant chorus that opens Donizetti's opera. At the opposite end of the house, the Phantom leaned over his large work table. He retreated to that spot after most lessons. Although he'd never expressly asked me not to follow, I'd never entered his work-shop. But from the library, dining alcove and music room of the house by the lake I'd studied the tubes of paint and sticks of pastel scattered on the shelves above his work table, counted the jumble of brushes stuffed into an empty jar and the stack of drawing pads anchoring one corner of the table, and wondered why he seemed to spend so much time cutting cardboard into small pieces and piling up little blocks of wood.

I took a break from mastering *L'Elisir D'Amore* when I discovered that his pursuit this afternoon was something entirely new. On one side of his work table lay a mound of fabric squares in a rainbow of colors and on the other a pile of papers. The Phantom dug into the heap of fabric, sorting through the squares until he found the one he wanted. He pinned his selection to the top paper in the pile, tossed the pairing to a basket on the floor beside him and resumed his search through the mountain of fabric.

As I wondered about the purpose of the Phantom's task, he suddenly turned in my direction and caught me watching him. I froze on the piano bench, one hand still arched over the keys of my descant, until he smiled and summoned me to his side.

As I approached the work table, he waved me onto the high stool he sometimes used. "Please be seated."

He stood before me, blocking my view of the table while he held a square of fabric beside my left ear. "Don't turn. Be still." I followed his command, but from the corner of my eye made out a rich blue moiré silk patterned with burnished gold. He lifted another swatch into position beside my right ear, a rich golden brocade sprinkled with blue. After a moment, he dropped the brocade and raised a final sample, a piece of indigo velvet edged with plain gold braid.

Behind his satin mask, his dark eyes traveled from one scrap of blue to the other and back again. He held the velvet atop my head like a little cap. "The gold braid picks up the color of your hair." He folded the silk over his fingers and held it across the bridge of my nose. "But this is the true color of your eyes."

Our eyes met across that bar of blue. "What are you doing?"

"Selecting a fabric for your Juliette." He grabbed a paper off the pile on the table behind him, pinned to it both swatches and handed it to me. "At the costume shop they'll have to look some more."

The paper held a sketch of a dress in the baroque style with a low and square neckline, a stomacher bodice and paned sleeves that puffed out over ribbon ties. "My Juliette?"

He retrieved the sketch from my hand, scribbled a few lines beside the picture and set it to one side. "I've decided on Juliette for your debut in a leading role." He indicated an array of wooden blocks faced with shapes of cardboard that, I discovered on closer examination, depicted the timbered walls and nail-studded doors of medieval buildings. "A revolutionary production with a Paris setting. It will be our season finale."

He'd decided. A simple enough statement, and one I no longer questioned but accepted as fact. If it concerned the Paris opera, the Phantom decided. Why that had come to be and how he managed it all, I didn't know. But that he did, of that I had no doubt.

10

A FEW WEEKS after I first entered the Phantom's house by the lake, he finally allowed me to enter his life. He revealed himself to me slowly and in parts. I learned about his daily existence, the commonplace details of ordinary days. I learned about his musical vocation, the great mystery resolved into a series of stunning professional facts. And I learned about his fortress heart, the stronghold of indifference that protected his wounded soul from a tormenting world.

A ringing bell prompted his first revelation. We'd been working on Despina, Mozart's saucy maid. Comedy didn't come easily to me. My repertoire had never included humorous tunes. My father and Professor Valérius believed audiences preferred sentimental songs from children, and both men were too strait-laced to approve of clownish behavior in a little girl. The Phantom showed me that oftentimes humor arose not from what I did but when. Timing was all.

"I've made a change in the start of the finale in Act II." He dug through the sheets on the music stand of the piano. "The bass tempo won't suit

Canet so I've had to rearrange your notes as well. *Sacre bleu* – where is it?"

Rearranging Mozart's notes – can you imagine such audacity? Wonder rooted me in place until a bell sounded and broke the spell. I spun on my heel, searching for the source of the sound. "What's that?"

"Martine. My housekeeper." He rifled a few more pages, then sighed and rose from the piano bench. "Once she was frightened of me. Now she shies from my guests. In this house the servant rings the bell to summon the master."

He started toward the dining alcove but stopped abruptly. "My bedroom." He half-turned back, looking at me over his shoulder. "Fetch it for me, will you, Christine? Look on the cabinet across from the bed. Or the chair next to the tall chest of drawers."

The bedroom of a dead man. That's the sinister picture of the Phantom's chamber drawn by M. Leroux's novel. Black-hung walls trimmed with a musical staff endlessly repeating the *Dies Irae*. A music book inscribed with notes the color of blood. And a canopy and bed curtains in red brocade that surrounded an open coffin. The props of a villain in a melodrama. I'm quite certain the novelist borrowed the coffin from the actress Sarah Bernhardt. She toured with hers on both sides of the Atlantic, using it to great effect to rouse the public's interest and increase her ticket sales. As for the notes of the Latin hymn from the Requiem mass? Surely just a lucky guess. I didn't learn until much later of the significance to the Phantom of that hymn describing the Day of Judgment. Still, I believe M. Leroux merely wanted his melodramatic villain to have a suitably ghoulish song, and therefore settled on the most famous – and most frightening – in Christendom.

In reality, the Phantom's chamber appeared at first glance to be in keeping with the mode of the day for a gentleman's furnishings: a large walnut bedstead whose coverlet picked up the gold of the Wilton carpet covering the floor, and other pieces – armchair and footstool, wardrobe and chest of drawers, cabinet and side tables – in wood and fabric to match. In the dim light of the low-turned gas lamps on three walls, I spotted a sheaf of papers on the cabinet he'd mentioned and headed toward it. But as I arrived at the dresser a small painting hanging above distracted me from my errand.

A copper shimmer from the rising sun laid a shining path across the sea. The suggestion but no more of a forest of masts obscured by the morning mist. In silhouette, distinct and yet insubstantial, a dory – or two? or three? – approaching the shore. The painter's every brushstroke visible on the surface, bold dabs of vivid color – all the blues, all the greens, all the oranges in the world's palette – that blended into joy within my heart.

I turned up the gas lamps, one after the other, and in the brighter light discovered other paintings hanging on the stone walls of the Phantom's bedroom. In his man-made cavern far below the city streets, the paintings offered windows into other worlds. Under arching tree limbs, in shade which cooled my face, a youth hummed tunelessly as he filled his pockets with chestnuts. The piping lilt of childish chatter reached me from a little girl carrying a bouquet of poppies as she trailed behind her mother through a fragrant field of wildflowers on a sun-struck afternoon. The breeze which filled the sails of the boats on the river, sending them scudding over white-capped water, also tugged tendrils of loose hair around my face. Who needed panes of glass or the light of the sun when one had windows like these?

I'd returned to the painting of the seaside dawn when the Phantom came looking for me. "I see you've found Monsieur Monet's *Impression*." He walked up beside me and rested his fingers against the ornate gold frame. "Would you like to hear what the critic at *Le Charivari* said about it? 'Wallpaper in its embryonic state is more finished than that seascape.' Even today the painter would count himself lucky to receive 100 francs for his finest canvas."

"But it's beautiful." I rested a fist against my breast. "It fills my heart."

The Phantom sifted through the music on the dresser until he found the sheets he wanted and then took my arm, steering me out of his bedroom. "Critics are creatures of little talent whose only reason for existence is to carp at their betters. We will vanquish them by the genius of my vision and your voice."

At the sight of a white cloth spread across the dining table, he postponed further elaboration about the stupidity of critics and the power of our genius. "Martine has brought in a meal for us."

A feast, in fact. Farm chicken with dainty roast potatoes from a rotisserie. Two bottles of Beaujolais from a wine shop. Paté de compagne and marinated leeks from a charcuterie. A crusty loaf of bread and a tarte tatin from a bakery. Chèvre and Roquefort from a fromagerie.

"And salade mixte from Martine's own hands." Across the table, he covered a small plate with greens and pushed it toward me. "On that I insist because her vinaigrette is the best in Paris."

I ran the tines of my fork over a piece of escarole and tasted Martine's tart yet sweet dressing. "Mmmm. Wonderful! But you mean she doesn't cook?"

"Never. Not even for her husband." He refilled my goblet and then his own. "Gaston is also my driver. When she sends him out to pick up my meal, he picks up theirs as well."

In truth, Martine's cookery by shopping wasn't all that unusual. By tradition, most Parisians relied on the rotisserie for their poultry, whether buying their chickens, ducks, geese and turkeys already cooked or selecting a live bird in a stall at the poultry pavilion at Les Halles and dropping the plucked carcass at the neighborhood spit to be roasted. In the old sections of the city, kitchen ovens were too small for a bird or a joint of meat, and served mostly to warm the food brought in from nearby shops. At midmorning in most quarters of the city a line formed outside the bakery, with each housewife or serving girl carrying a dish to be cooked for the midday meal.

In those days many Parisians lived their lives in public places, withdrawing only to sleep their six or eight hours each night. They washed at a public bath, ate in a café or restaurant, and scanned newspapers and magazines in a public library or reading room. For Parisians who wanted to pray, churches remained open. For Parisians who wanted instruction, many lecture rooms charged nothing. For Parisians who wanted to promenade, public gardens and Haussmann boulevards awaited. And for the price of only a few sous Parisians could gain admission to a theater for entertainment, an art gallery for inspiration or a ballroom for romance. In a city that lived to see and be seen, the Phantom's servant sounded woefully out of place.

I savored a morsel of roast chicken, as moist and sweet as any I ever tasted from the farms of Brittany. "She certainly sounds odd for a servant. Why do you keep her?"

The Phantom shrugged as he picked up his goblet of wine. "My rooms are neat. My clothes are clean and mended. In here, she stays out of my way." He lifted his wine toward the ceiling. "Out there, she keeps my secrets."

Some of those secrets he revealed to me one night soon after as I followed him through a maze of narrow passages hidden inside the ornate walls of Garnier's opera house. No doubt somewhere in that vast building a night watchman struggled to stay awake as the clock crept past midnight, but we moved about freely and never encountered him. The Phantom lit our way with the lantern he carried in one hand as he led me out of the cellar.

We spiraled into the auditorium on an iron staircase hidden inside the huge carved column that separated his spot on the grand tier – Box 5 – from the one beside the stage that had been designed for France's last emperor. The Phantom reached up into the darkness and a moment later a crack appeared in the round wall that surrounded us. Slowly and silently the fracture widened as the column slid in upon itself until a narrow opening gaped before us. I stepped through and found myself standing behind two rows of paired chairs, armchairs for the gentlemen and open chairs for the ladies. The ghost light glowed on the stage below.

I turned to the Phantom as he came up beside me. "To have constructed this hidden labyrinth, you truly are a genius."

His laughter rang out across the darkened auditorium. "I can't claim credit for that. No doubt Garnier heard the order from Napoleon III himself. The Emperor wanted a carriage entrance to protect him from assassins. I suspect he wanted hidden passageways to escape murderous mobs. The Bonapartes knew how much the people of Paris love revolution."

He sidled through the chairs and leaned his hands on the gilt edge of the box as he surveyed the theater. In his posture I detected none of the awe that always flooded me when I viewed the stage from this angle. But in the tilt of his head, the ease of his stance and, especially, the possession casually declared by his hands, I thought I saw the deep satisfaction of a ruler appraising his realm. His next words confirmed that notion. "However, I did add certain improvements to Garnier's creation that have made this opera house my own."

As the moon drifted across the dark skies over Paris, the Phantom showed me his improvements. Sliding panels here, two-way mirrors there, and traps everywhere in between – his hidden maze offered unseen passageways and undiscoverable doorways that had allowed the Phantom to foment a revolution of his own. Yet the seeds of his rebellion had been planted long before the Phantom arrived in Paris by Lecadre, the old magician who taught him the art of magic.

Far more subtle were Lecadre's lessons in showmanship, magic of a very different sort that focused on people rather than props. Before one performance of Lecadre's circus troupe, the magician led the Phantom to a stool positioned in the darkness behind the orchestra and instructed him to study the audience – en masse and individuals – to find out what moved them and why. Hovering nearby during rehearsals, the Phantom watched Lecadre fine-tune the show – perfecting the timing of an entrance, adjusting the sequence of stunts, calling for more volume from the orchestra's brass. Seated by his master's side during auditions, he learned to dissect the current lineup of acts, considering which, if any, could be excised to make room for a new spectacle. Of those that remained in his circus, Lecadre pushed gently but firmly for innovations to freshen their appeal, new marvels to amaze audiences who thirsted for novelty. No detail was too small to escape the showman's interest: a row of glass beads to add a shimmer to the acrobat's flame-colored costumes, an upswept twist to highlight the beauty of the equestrienne's ivory neck, a daily manicure to call attention to the menace of the dancing bear's claws. In time, Lecadre solicited the Phantom's own ideas to improve the circus and incorporated many. More than once, he laid a gnarled hand on his apprentice's shoulder and pronounced his benediction: "You have the makings of an impresario, my boy."

With the help of the old magician, the Phantom discovered his vocation, and when he stood beside Lecadre in the shadow of the Palais Garnier, he found his life's work – shaping the Paris opera company into the greatest in the world. To that end, he first made the necessary improvements to the hidden passageways. Then from his secret vantages throughout the opera house, the Phantom worked tirelessly by day to master the intricacy of vocal coaching, the complexity of orchestral arranging, the challenge of set design and the subtlety of shrewd casting. By night he stepped through the hidden doorways, entering any room he pleased.

Later on he would take me into the opulent office shared by the opera's managers and the private music room that was the maestro's retreat. That night we left the auditorium and made our way first to the atelier of set designer Achille Meril, a sky-lit room filled with work tables like the Phantom's and similarly scattered with the paraphernalia of the artist. He carried his lantern from desk to desk, studying the sketches and set models on the work tables. At one he picked up a charcoal pencil and made corrections. At two others he crumpled sketches in one hand and shoved the balled paper into the side pocket of his coat. When he got to the largest work table, which belonged to Meril himself, he set down his lantern and crouched beside one corner so he could study at eye level the model of a set. After a few minutes, he flicked a finger against the miniature set, flattening it, and then withdrew from a chest pocket inside his jacket a tight roll of papers tied with a thin red ribbon and tossed it onto the rejected model.

"Does he mind?" I fingered the ribbon and then looked down at the Phantom. "That he gets the credit for your work?"

"Perhaps at first." He rose to his feet, making no effort to keep the scorn out of his voice. "But in the end they were all eager to claim the works of my genius as their own."

In Eugenie Savatier's costume shop the Phantom took no notice of the rank of sewing machines along one wall or the unfinished costumes hanging from a rod on the other. He didn't pause to inspect any of the half-dressed mannequins – one for each principal singer and dancer in the company – that formed a headless crowd in the middle of the shop. He ignored everything except the single sketch that lay in a small cleared patch in the center of the fabric- and paper-strewn work table of the costumer. My Juliette costume. The one he'd sent back with two swatches of fabric and a scribbled notation to look further. A new square of sapphire fabric adorned this fresh sketch, pinned alongside three gold cords in various weaves.

"Let's have a closer look." He lifted the sketch and set the lantern in its place. Then he held the sapphire square of blue next to my eyes. "Perfect." And trailed the braids of gold across the hair on top of my head. "This one." He unpinned the rejected cords from the paper and placed the sketch of my costume, with his selections, back on the work table. "Eugenie, at least, follows my instructions."

And, of course, so did I as my voice lessons continued. Much of the Phantom's instruction now focused on my acting. As a member of the chorus, my performances required little acting because the singers play crowds rather than parts. But principal soloists do play parts and thus, especially with the opera's new emphasis on acting out our roles, I had much to learn. To speed my improvement, the

Phantom often joined me in duets. The ones I liked best were the love duets that required us to hold hands, lock eyes and embrace. I played the woman warrior Odabella to his rebel Foresto in Verdi's *Attila* for the Act I duet that begins with his suspicion of betrayal and ends with an ecstatic embrace under a fast and brilliant *cabaletta*. I played the druid priestess Adalgisa to his Roman proconsul Pollione in Bellini's *Norma* with our alternating arias that end with an arioso duet. And I played unhappily married Laura to his exiled Enzo, lovers who grab a fleeting moment of happiness under the Venetian moon in Ponchielli's *La Gioconda*. Day after day my lessons required me to become a woman in love. Is it any wonder that my heart began to turn toward the man who played my lover? He sang so passionately and held me so tenderly. As I stood within the circle of the Phantom's arms, his mask hardly registered in my mind and my last fear of him drained away.

But the Phantom kept his own heart closely guarded. He'd banished his wounded soul from the world of love just as surely as he'd banished himself from the society of men. Yet I began to hope that someday far in the future, when we'd reached the pinnacle of art he strove for and shared the joy of that achievement, he might open his heart to me. And sometimes the gentleness of his touch and the light in his eyes promised as much.

The hours I spent in the opera house began to seem like an artificial interlude that intruded on my real life, the one I lived underground. Preparations for the season continued through an endless round of practices with the orchestra, adjustments of costumes and wigs, decisions about makeup, hours spent posing for publicity pictures, and rehearsals in part or in whole. Raoul persisted in his attentions, stopping by my dressing to renew his invitation to Argenteuil in person if I happened to be there or in a scrawl on the back of the calling cards he left when he found me out. Late one afternoon I returned to my dressing room to find a florist's box and wrapped fruit basket on the low table in front of the sofa. I searched in vain for a card and decided my anonymous admirer must be the Vicomte de Chagny. But opening my gifts put the lie to that idea. Inside the box, the flowers lay limp and dead, and underneath the wrapping, the apples teemed with worms. Even so, I wasted little time speculating about the identity of the enemy who'd sent those cruel gifts. As always, my thoughts quickly returned to the Phantom and our life in his house by the lake.

11

"*C*ESAR IS MISSING. Did you hear?" Meg Giry fluffed the lace ruffle on the bodice of her *Faust* costume, pointedly ignoring me and addressing her words to the seamstress standing at my side. "You know the one I mean, Delphine. The horse that ate Carlotta's flowers during dress rehearsal yesterday?"

"Such a scolding she gave those stable boys!" The seamstress shook her head and grabbed another handful of the back of my doublet, pinning it in place. "Perhaps they fear for the poor beast and have taken him out of harm's way."

I took a breath to test her new seam but could barely sip the air. "Not so tight! I won't be able to sing."

Delphine ducked her head in apology. "I'm sorry, mademoiselle." Then she plucked another handful of burgundy satin. "But I must follow Madame Savatier's instructions: 'Make sure she shows a woman's curves inside those boys' clothes.'" Her blue eyes danced with amusement. "You're not here to sing, after all. Only for the photographs."

Little Giry paid no attention to our exchange and continued with the mystery of the missing opera horse. "I talked to the head groom myself. Lachenel says none of the stable boys saw or heard a thing. Even after a taste of the strap, they all insisted they had no idea what has happened to poor Cesar."

The golden sunlight of late October streamed through the soaring windows of Nadar's studio, painting us with the mellow tint of autumn. This was my first visit to the garish red building at 35 Boulevard des Capucines that housed the atelier of France's most famous photographer. We all had been instructed to visit Nadar – even Carlotta, despite her screeches of protest. Everyone assumed the idea for the picture postcards of the opera's principal singers and dancers came from the managers, but I knew better. The instructions certainly came from Poligny and Debienne, and undoubtedly that pair would also pocket the profits if the new souvenirs became popular. But as with everything else at the opera, the postcards were the Phantom's idea, and they made me uneasy. I wasn't sure I liked the emphasis on my woman's curves or the thought of a complete stranger owning a photograph of me.

Delphine rocked back on her heels and inspected her handiwork. "And what does your mother say? Does Madame Giry see the diva's hand in this disappearance?"

Meg shrugged. "Perhaps. In any case, she thinks Cesar wound up at a *boucheries chevalines* in the Marais. She says many people developed a taste for horse meat during the siege."

The horror of her words soured my stomach. An old and docile horse well-known for eating scenery, Cesar earned the diva's ire by munching all the roses in Marguerite's garden during Carlotta's performance of the jewel song. His meal delighted the small audience for our dress rehearsal of Gounod's *Faust* and their laughter infuriated the Spanish diva. Vindictive to a fault, Carlotta answered every slight – real or imagined – with her own brand of cruelty as I'd learned so recently by her gift of dead flowers and wormy apples. Was it possible she'd extracted deadly revenge against Cesar?

Delphine gave my doublet a final tweak. "Poor beast. I hope she's wrong."

"There is another possibility, I suppose." Meg Giry tossed a glance at me, her dark eyes glittering with malice. "If Carlotta's not to blame for Cesar's disappearance, then he must have been taken by the opera ghost!"

I forced out a sigh of disgust and turned my back on them both, refusing to allow Little Giry to bait me. The next instant Nadar's assistant, a diminutive redhead with the bearing and voice of one of Napoleon's field marshals, opened the dressing room door and poked her head inside. "Come. Now. He's waiting."

Later that evening I learned to my astonishment that Meg Giry was right. Cesar had been taken by the opera ghost. A few weeks earlier the Phantom had begun supplementing my voice lessons with outings to theaters like the Comédie Francaise, the grand *café-concerts* near the Champs-Élysées and the simple cafés of Pigalle. The women we watched would soon be my rivals, he explained, and studying their performances would help me perfect my own. On those evenings he came for me at Rue Notre Dame des Victoires in his carriage, sending his driver, Gaston, up the stairs to ring the bell while he waited in the shadows beside the stoop.

That night I'd intended to mention my uneasiness about the picture postcards. All afternoon I'd planned my argument, and I rehearsed it again as I crossed the vestibule. Publicity was a necessary evil in a metropolis like Paris where dozens of newspapers and magazines clamored for readers and dozens of stages competed for an audience. But until recently photographs had been expensive, personal mementos reserved for families, sweethearts and friends. These new picture postcards were tawdry souvenirs with a risqué reputation.

As I stepped through the door, a cone of light from the street lamp fell upon the Phantom's horse. I recognized Cesar immediately, and my uneasiness dissolved under a tide of joy.

"It was you!" I darted down the stairs and greeted the old horse with a stroke of his velvet neck. Despite my veil, Cesar seemed to recognize me and snorted a greeting. "Everyone thinks Carlotta's taken him for revenge."

The Phantom opened the carriage door and offered me his hand. "She might have if Cesar hadn't retired from the opera."

I gave his gloved hand a quick squeeze before sinking back against the leather seat. "Retired by you! Nothing escapes you – not even the horses."

"Especially the horses." He rapped on the front window to signal Gaston that we were ready. "Once they were my only friends."

Lifting the veil that covered my face, I draped the lace back over my hair and turned toward him. "Tell me."

The carriage rolled forward, raking his face with patches of light and shadow as we passed through the city streets – here bedazzled by the brilliance of a gaslit promenade, there smothered by the sinister gloom of a squalid alley. Through it all his face remained impassive under the second skin of his mask. "By the time I joined the circus, people didn't interest me." He shrugged. "From their cruelty I'd learned to feel nothing but contempt for mankind. Instead I befriended the circus animals."

He stared straight ahead. "Animals seemed to me more clever than men. They decided to give or withhold affection based on conduct alone. I liked the horses best – their power, their spirit, their dignity."

"In the late afternoon, most of the troupe watched the crowd gather, but I always took a curry comb and joined the horses." A wistful note entered the Phantom's voice. "I liked the weight of their foreheads against my chest as I secured the feathered crests between their ears. The sweet tang of their sweat perfuming the air as I braided ribbons into their manes. Their warm breath tickling my neck as they teased for treats."

My heart ached for the lonely boy he had been and the solitary man he had become. I longed to comfort him with a tender word and a gentle touch, but the rigid line of his lips warned me off. He'd lived apart for so long that he didn't easily surrender his solitude, and moments of revelation often ended with a harsh retreat.

He turned toward me and in the glow of a street-lamp gave me a tight smile. "I knew by then that when you love no one, you are free."

I struggled to keep my face impassive even as my mind rang with denials. I knew he'd loved those circus horses. I believed he'd loved the old magician, Lecadre. I suspected he'd loved the weeping orphan who once hid in the opera cellar. And I'd imagined the day that he would love the woman I'd become as well. Our evenings out – and his obsession with protecting my reputation – fueled that fantasy. The Phantom insisted that at all times I wear a veil to obscure my identity. Even so, he feared that was not enough to insure my anonymity and took other steps to protect me. At the theater, he made sure to arrive at our box just moments before the performance began, to withdraw behind the privacy curtain during intermission and to depart before the applause died away. At *café-concerts*, he chose the inexpensive tables behind the orchestra seats. And in the smoky cafés in Montmartre his preferred the darkest corner. The Phantom insisted that the world would worship the celestial voice of his prima donna all the more if they could also venerate her angelic purity. In our strange garb, we made an unusual pair and drew many stares. But this was bohemian Paris, and however much people stared, they kept their distance and their tongues. Despite the Phantom's mask and my veil, on those evenings I could almost believe we were an ordinary couple, and I avoided anything that might break the spell. So I swallowed my denials and put off mentioning the picture postcards for another day.

How I loved our evenings together! In those days the high and low of Paris mixed each night as the aristocrats of the *gratin*, the riffraff of the *canaille* and everyone in between thronged into the streets to pursue their pleasures. I should have been too tired to enjoy myself. The Phantom had refused to let me begin work on my Juliette: "Not yet. For Juliette you will just be yourself." But in addition to my five other roles for that season, he'd decreed I would also learn Carlotta's tragic parts – *Faust's* Marguerite and *La Juive's* Rachel. "To thwart her conniving," he said. "And, of course, because tragedy is the pinnacle. Heartbreak. Despair. Terror. You must learn to embody those emotions as well." By the end of each day exhaustion weighed upon me like a lead shawl, and I staggered home to be doted upon by Madame Valérius and Victorine. Yet I had no trouble reviving for my evenings with the Phantom. I loved sitting close beside him in the privacy of his darkened carriage or in the comfort of a theater box. No matter where we went, the Phantom's precept remained the same: emotion, emotion, emotion.

"All performance is emotion. All music is emotion. All opera is emotion," he told me on our first evening together. "Bad luck to have Sarah Bernhardt touring America. She plays the audience like a virtuoso, inspiring the emotion she seeks at the moment she chooses. Still, enough talent remains in Paris to teach you the when and why and how of audiences and emotion."

One evening the Phantom took me to Nouvelle Anthènes on Place Pigalle, a café popular with the artists he admired. As he escorted me to a table, he exchanged nods with a man who sat near the tiny stage with a sketch pad open on his knee. The Phantom ordered glasses of house wine and then positioned his chair close to mine, leaning toward me until our heads almost touched. "The artist is Edgar Degas. You've seen him at the opera?"

"No. But I've heard the name. All the dancers talk about him."

"All of Paris will be talking about him soon." He paused while the waiter poured our Bordeaux. "He's done a sculpture of Little Giry that will set tongues wagging."

"Is it—" I looked at him over the rim of my glass. "Is it indecent?"

"No, but the Salon will reject it anyway. It's true – a real opera dancer, not a mythological goddess." He touched his glass to mine. "Just as my operas will be true."

That night the subject of my study was a singer fresh from the provinces, a short girl with brown hair in a single plait, chubby pink cheeks and a good though untrained voice. She began with a silly song called *The Turbot and the Shrimp*, and for the first few lines the audience ignored her as she stood in the center of the stage, moving only her lips as she sang. Price lured people to Nouvelle Anthènes, not the entertainment, and the work-weary men and women who filled the tables – laundresses and laborers, fish mongers and railway porters – concentrated on their drinks and their cigarettes until the singer suddenly began to move. In an instant, she was reborn as the coquette of the song, prancing across the boards to engage an invisible partner. Her liveliness gradually captured the crowd's attention, conversation dropping off table by table until only stray whispers competed with her song.

Even the waiters stood with their trays hanging at their sides, ensnared by the vivacious chanteuse.

"When she was a statute, people ignored her because statues belong in cathedrals and palaces." The Phantom's murmur stirred the hair above my ear. "The pageantry of bishops and kings is done. Today the people rule and they prefer emotion, performers who move and stories taken from real life."

Another evening the Phantom took me to Eldorado, a *café-concert* on Boulevard de Strasbourg that featured singers, dancers, jugglers, clowns, acrobats and lion tamers. The respectable bourgeoisie occupied the loges, leaving the cheaper orchestra benches to the bank clerks and shop assistants, gamblers and prostitutes, artists and students who could scrape together two francs for admission and another 50 centimes for a drink. The Phantom selected a table tucked away in the back near one of the bars and ordered a bottle of Veuve Cliquot. Once Rosa Demay took the stage, I left my champagne untouched.

A single diamond sparkled against the black velvet ribbon that circled her slim neck and a red silk butterfly adorned the tower of black hair atop her head. She wore a stunning gown of red silk trimmed with black lace, but the illusion of elegance vanished as soon as she opened her mouth. Demay's popularity stemmed from her gutter humor and the bawdy songs she performed with vulgar gestures and endless gusto. I'd never seen anything like it – neither Papa nor Madame Valérius would have allowed it! Time and again she breached the fourth wall of the stage – leaning into the orchestra to tweak a musician's ear, shaking

114

her fan at an outraged matron in a balcony seat, winking suggestively at a fresh-faced youth on a bench in the pit. At the height of the uproar, the Phantom touched my hand, momentarily drawing my attention from the stage. "They laugh now. But soon she'll have them in tears."

A few minutes later, his prophecy came true. The orchestra struck a single thunderous chord. Demay half-turned from the audience and stood with her clasped hands raised to her breast as the *tricolore* dropped from the wings. A hush fell over the hall.

"In the old French city lives an iron race with hearts like a furnace and flesh bronzed by fire. All its sons are born on the straw. For a palace they have only a slum. This is the rabble." She swung around to face the audience, arms spreading wide. "And so am I."

The crowd sang along as each new chorus named another member of the iron race. "It is the honest man whose hand with pen or hammer wins his piece of bread." In a single smooth motion, she whipped open her fan and swept it before her, including everyone in the pit. "It is the man with spirited laughter who scoffs at your contempt." With a flick of disdain, she closed her fan to underscore the scorn she pointed at the conservative burghers in the balcony. "It is the child in his twentieth year who enters our battalions, cannon fodder for the battle, and succumbs without a cry." By now most of the audience swayed on their feet before her, tears streaming as they roared the refrain and joined the final chorus. "But today when old France calls them under its flag, they will say to the enemy: 'This is the rabble. And so am I.'"

As with all the singers and actresses we saw, the Phantom chose Rosa Demay to show me a secret of performance. "Hers is the most potent of all," he said as we waited on the sidewalk for Gaston to arrive with the carriage. "She inspires a frenzy by touching feelings that are already there."

Yet the hostile pride of the *canaille* was not a feeling I shared. I was no longer the Swedish peasant I'd been born, and I didn't belong at places like Eldorado and Nouvelle Anthènes with their raw ensembles and raucous crowds . Even hidden under my veil and with the Phantom close beside me, I felt exposed and out of place. Only in a handful of grand theaters was I truly content.

But my contentment came to end the first night Cesar pulled the Phantom's carriage. He brought us to the Odéon, a theater for classical drama near the Palais du Luxembourg where students from the nearby university filled the stalls and aristocrats from the nearby mansions of St. Germain filled the first and second tiers. Three boxes away from our spot in the grand tier, Raoul de Chagny sat among the cream of the *haut monde*, including an exquisite girl who wore a low-cut gown of vanilla satin embroidered with tiny beads that sparkled each time she leaned her dark head against the Vicomte de Chagny's shoulder and whispered in his ear. I did my best to keep my attention on the stage, where a rising young actress played the title role in George Sand's *Claudie*. Inside I burned with resentment at the social conventions and rank hypocrisies that required my veil and the Phantom's mask.

Half-way through the first act, the Phantom murmured in my ear. "Your sailor boy has a pretty friend. Do you know her?"

I shook my head, not trusting myself to speak. I pretended absorption in the travails of poor seduced Claudie, but I couldn't help seeing the movement sweeping across the balconies as playgoers turned their opera glasses away from the stage to look at the beautiful girl at Raoul's side. Of course Raoul's attention had wandered. How could I expect to keep his friendship when I wasn't allowed to see him? Yet he hadn't completely given up on me. Just the day before he left his card repeating his invitation to spend Sunday afternoon in Argenteuil. By the end of the act, I'd gathered my courage to ask the Phantom if I could accept Raoul's invitation.

"A ride in his carriage, a promenade along the Seine and luncheon in a brasserie?" He closed one of the heavy privacy curtains, sealing out the intermission hubbub in the auditorium. "Will your maid be free to accompany you?"

"Of course. Victorine adores Raoul." I threw back my veil and looked up at him. "And Madame Valérius spends Sundays in church."

He stared down at me, studying my face from behind his impassive second-skin mask. "You've been working very hard." He reached out a hand and gently cupped my chin. "A bit of fresh air and sunshine will do you good."

12

*S*UNDAY CAME at last with the kind of glori-
ous blue-sky autumn weather meant to
backdrop a perfect day. Yet with the exception of the time Raoul and I spent walking along the
bank of the Seine, the hours of the day unwound in
a series of small disasters. At the breakfast table,
Victorine leaned over to slice the brioche and
knocked Madame's prized porcelain chocolate pot
to the floor, shattering the Limoges into a thousand
pieces scattered through a sticky puddle. Dressing
for church, Madame Valérius shut the door of her
armoire on the hem of her favorite dress and ripped
a jagged tear when she stepped away from the
wardrobe. Waiting by the window as Raoul arrived
in an open landau with his brother and Comte
Philippe's paramour, La Sorelli, in the opposite
seat, I briefly considered whether leaving Victorine
behind would harm my reputation with the world or
the Phantom and quickly decided the pleasure to be
gained far outweighed the risk of disgrace.

Blame my naiveté. What did I really know of the
demi-monde or the fate of the *déclassé*? Only what
could be found in stories like *Claudie* because I'd

been sheltered from the sordid side of life by the generosity of Madame Valérius and the protection of the Phantom. By chance or design, some people fell away from legitimate society. As always, women paid the heaviest price, especially those from honorable stock. Some fell victim to family scandal – a bankrupt father, a libertine brother, a ruined sister. Others let their hearts overrule their heads – abandoned first by their husbands and eventually by their lovers. A lucky few became pampered demi-mondaines kept in high style by rich men eager to flaunt their wealth, inhabitants of a luxurious world that lacked only respectability. Well-known entertainers like Sorelli were the most highly prized courtesans. But nearly all fallen women ended up being passed from man to man until the authorities forced them to register as a *fille soumise* and submit to periodic medical examinations at the Préfecture de Police. Both fates seemed to me equally unimaginable on that sunstruck morning. After all, I was only twenty years old and knew for certain that I would not – and could not – fall.

Almost immediately I regretted my rash decision. The Comte greeted me cordially but without warmth. La Sorelli welcomed me with a sly smile. And Raoul forced me to sit closer than propriety allowed by taking possession of my hand as soon as we set off. Over the next hour I noticed neither the city streets nor the country lanes we passed through because the Comte and Sorelli demanded my complete attention as they chattered away. I knew none of the people they talked about and had visited few of the places they mentioned. As long as I smiled or nodded at the appropriate time they didn't seem to mind my silence. Raoul appeared happy enough just holding my hand, so I let their gossip wash over me and tried not to show my distress.

By the time the carriage approached the wide silver swath of the Seine at Petit Gennevilliers, I'd studied the other pair long enough to conclude that the Comte's feelings ran deeper than Sorelli's. He hung on her words, really listening to everything she had to say, and his gaze lingered on her as if she were a rare treasure. Despite the armor of aristocratic reserve he showed to the world, Philippe Georges Marie de Chagny was besotted with his prima ballerina. On the surface, La Sorelli more readily showed her feelings – touching his arm and smiling up at him. But the dancer's smiles never reached her eyes and her touches seemed perfunctory. Her detachment was as evident to me as his passion, and I found it strange that such a powerful man had been ensnared in a lopsided affair. Perhaps he didn't care; more likely he simply didn't know. For all my naiveté I was sure that a proud man like Comte de Chagny would find La Sorelli's insincerity unendurable – if he knew.

Liaisons with wealthy men were expected of opera dancers, whose brief careers failed to provide income to last the rest of their lives. They came to the ballet school as children of seven or eight, enduring long days at the barre without pay. Those accepted into the corps de ballet earned only 300 francs a year, and even girls lucky enough to dance in a small ensemble as a *coryphée* received only 1,500 francs for their labors. A prima ballerina like Sorelli could expect an annual stipend of 20,000 francs but only for a few years. A rich protector was an essential accessory for an opera dancer and, as every ballet student knew, a handful of the clever-est girls set themselves up for life by picking the right admirer. The children Virginie Oreille bore to the Duc du Berry had insured his lifelong support, and Marie Taglioni had gained an eternally useful title from her brief marriage to Comte Gilbert des Voisins. Time would tell if Sorelli was clever enough to lure her infatuated comte to the altar.

"Jacques! Stop!" Raoul sat forward, tossing a smile of thanks to the startled driver who hiked around in his seat to see what was amiss. He aimed his next words at his older brother. "Would you mind if Christine and I stopped here for a time, to walk on the promenade? We'll catch up with you at the brasserie in, let's say, ninety minutes?"

For a moment, the Comte surveyed the river where a handful of sailboats raced across the water. "A pretty girl and some pretty boats – which entices you more, I wonder?" He grinned at Raoul. "Off you go, then. And see that you don't make us wait!"

Golden leaves showered around us as Raoul steered me along the path atop the grassy riverbank. "That blue boat's the exact color of your eyes. We'll call her the *Christine*. She's sure to win."

I laughed. "Because she's the exact color of my eyes?"

"Because the best sailor's at her helm." He stopped and dragged the toe of his boot through the dirt to make a diagram. "They're running before the breeze now. But just before they reach the island, they'll have to come about and finish the race sailing into the wind. That fellow has the *Christine* right where she must be to sail close to the wind on the return course. He'll have her close-hauled and halfway to the highway bridge before the others have finished their turns."

So the Comte guessed correctly. The sailboats had lured Raoul out of the landau. I didn't mind. I was free of the confines of the carriage and the city and the opera. As always, the Phantom was right – the sunshine and fresh air did do me good. And the companionship of Raoul even more. He stood beside me transfixed by the small fleet scudding across the water under their triangles of white. I hadn't understood a word he said about the wind. And I couldn't make out any pattern in the movements of the boats. Instead I studied the man beside me as he leaned toward the river with fisted hands and narrowed eyes as the boats neared the island of Ile Marante. All at once one boat broke free of the flotilla – the blue boat – to streak in the opposite direction.

"Hah!" Raoul's eyes danced as he punched the fist of one hand against the palm of the other. "Just as I said! The Christine outsailed them all!"

I slipped my arm through one of his. "You really love it, don't you? Boats and sailing?"

"And ships and the sea." He set off again down the path along the Seine, the sailboat race forgotten now that his prediction had come true. "Just as you love the opera. Perhaps you'll come to love the sea as I do. My liking for the opera has certainly grown."

"So you said." I scuffed through a small pile of leaves, enjoying the crunch under my heels. "Tell me more about this new affection."

"It began with a performance in Brest by a visiting company. All the cadets were ordered to attend. I'm ashamed to admit I can't exactly recall what we saw, but I'll never forget that moment. A passionate scene." A smile tugged at his lips as he gave me a sideways glance. "The lovers didn't notice the dog that wandered onstage during their duet. The mutt had eyes only for the conductor's baton, expecting the stick to be thrown. He followed that baton with his head, back and forth, back and forth, as the duet approached its crescendo." Raoul let his tongue hang out and waggled his head. "Just before the peak, as the tenor clasped the soprano and began to lower her to the floor of their hidden bower, the dog ran out of patience and began to bark. The shocked tenor lost his grip. The soprano hit the stage." He flashed a wicked grin. "And bounced!"

An eruption of laughter stopped me in my tracks, the kind of great belly guffaw that I hadn't felt in years. The weight of it doubled me over and I hung there helplessly, while Raoul gently patted my back. When I recovered I was relieved to find that we were alone on the path, without witnesses who might have been shocked by my lack of decorum.

With a gentle tug, Raoul set us in motion again. "Of course, I also quite liked a performance of *Rigoletto* in Indochina. That was an amateur troupe made up of *colons*. Just as a group of aristocratic hangers-on started mocking the hunchback jester, his deformity began to slide. By the time the scene was over, Rigoletto had been transformed into a normal man with an enormous bottom."

Although my shoulders shook, this time I managed to restrain myself from completely abandoning good manners. But the gleam in Raoul's eye warned that he wasn't done with me yet.

"I suppose my favorite operatic experience was the performance of *Norma* that I saw in Martinique. The stage, of course, was set with an enormous gong that must be struck with a hefty mallet to make a sound." Again he acted out the part with an enormous swing. "The druid priestess hauled back her arm, caught the tenor in the nose and laid him on the stage unconscious."

I gasped and then bit my lips to keep from exploding again and shuddered with silent laughter until tears ran down my cheeks. Raoul rocked back on his heels and beamed at me. After a moment, he pulled out a linen handkerchief and gently wiped the tears from my face. "That put a bit of color in your cheeks. You're altogether too pale and too serious these days, Christine."

For a moment I leaned against his hand. "You always did make me laugh."

He bent forward and brushed a light kiss against my lips. "You need to laugh, darling Christine."

Raoul stuffed his handkerchief in his pocket and, taking my arm, turned back toward the road to Argenteuil. We kicked leaves like children as we walked along the river path. And on the sidewalks of the town we checked the contents of every shop window and inspected the front garden of every private home just like all the other Parisian couples out for a Sunday in the country.

Until Raoul accused me of being too serious, I hadn't realized how oppressed I'd been by the Phantom's expectations and my own. Now I compared my sailor and my teacher. I couldn't imagine spending a lighthearted day with the Phantom. In every way that Raoul was sunny and simple, he was dark and complex. One man I knew only through his professional obsession and the other only through his holiday merrymaking. Perhaps a similar intensity came over Raoul on the bridge of a ship. His love of the sea provided an obsession of his own. But on land he was a typical sailor on liberty, devoted to pursuing what he missed most aboard ship – pretty women, fine food and endless laughter.

"He we are." Raoul held open the brasserie door, and I stepped into a bit of old France – stained glass windows, quaint wainscoting and a low, timbered ceiling. The autumn sun streaming through the front window left jewels of light on the table where the Comte and Sorelli shared a platter of oysters and a carafe of white wine.

"You're not late, but we started without you." Philippe lifted an oyster shell and poured the flesh into his mouth as Raoul seated me and then himself. "And we may stay right here as long as the oysters and the Tokay hold out."

The Comte winked at Sorelli as a bald and rotund waiter refilled her green-stemmed Alsatian wineglass before pouring glasses for Raoul and me. "Eh, my love?"

Raoul conferred with the waiter and then ordered oysters, cassoulet and salad for our *dejeuner*. I sipped the wine and found the combination of spice and smoke wonderful refreshment for an autumn afternoon.

The Comte sat back in his chair. "So, Miss Daaé, have you all of your parts for the season?"

I set my glass back on the table and prepared to give Raoul's brother my full attention. Again. "Yes, I—"

"Impossible!" Sorelli's exclamation cut off my words. Her eyes blazed with scorn. "How could you know? We haven't even been told the title of the final production, let alone given parts. And still the managers dither. Nitwits! Do they think if they wait long enough someone else will decide?"

Panic set my heart thumping. She couldn't know about the Phantom. Still, I blurted a resounding dissent. "There is no one else!"

Sorelli turned toward me with a raised eyebrow and an appraising stare.

Cheeks burning, I dropped my gaze and kneaded the tablecloth between my fingers. "You're right, of course. I misspoke. We're all waiting for our final parts."

The exchange disturbed neither man, but the last glow of happiness from my time alone with Raoul faded. All I wanted was for that unfortunate outing to come to an end so my indiscretions could disappear with the dawning of a new day.

A new day, a fresh page, a chance to begin again. Once upon a time that familiar formula yielded redemption. Perhaps it still does for ordinary people. But not for titled members of the *haut monde* like the de Chagny brothers or principal players of the Paris opera like La Sorelli and Christine Daaé. Their deeds are chronicled – and misdeeds endlessly rehashed – by a slavering pack of journalists who like nothing better than a scandal as juicy as their *andouillettes*.

I had no inkling of that fact of life when I headed down the sloping tunnel leading to the Phantom's door for my voice lesson the next morning. The day was clear and the air was fresh so I'd dawdled a bit before stepping into the darkness. Soon winter would be upon us and everyone in Paris would remain indoors hugging their hearths.

Pausing by the door to hang up my coat and hat, I called a greeting to him. He didn't reply but stood looking at me from the library at the other end of his house, his face impassive as always behind his second-skin mask. One of his hands rested on the newspapers stacked on the library table beside him.

I pasted a contrite frown on my face and prepared to apologize for being late. Before I found my voice the Phantom lifted one of the newspapers from the table and began to read. "'Sighting: Regatta of two on the promenade at Argenteuil for the Vicomte de Chagny and opera beauty Christine Daaé.'"

He let the newspaper drop to the floor and picked up another. "'Among the window shoppers in Argenteuil on Sunday...naval officer Raoul de Chagny – yes, those de Chagnys – and the Palais Garnier's newest songbird, Christine Daaé.'"

He dropped the second newspaper and picked up a third. "'Foursome: The brothers de Chagny, Philippe and Raoul, dined Sunday at Brasserie B— in Argenteuil with Sorelli, the opera's prima ballerina, and soprano Christine Daaé, who debuts next week in Gounod's *Faust*.'"

I watched the final newspaper drift to the floor and then raised my eyes to meet his across a room that suddenly seemed as vast and cold as Notre Dame. "Rags like these can destroy you, Christine. Acclaim turns to infamy overnight because tearing down is so much more fun than building up. With an opening like this, your enemies will have no difficulty peddling scandal to their friends in the press. Already Carlotta is whispering in the corners."

"But it's so unfair." I spread my hands wide. "I've done nothing wrong." His eyes sparked, and I tripped forward. "But I did disregard your wishes, and for that I'm truly sorry."

He kicked the newspapers on the floor. "Now do you understand? Now will you obey?"

"Yes." I strode toward him. "Absolutely."

"Then you will not mind that you're forbidden to see de Chagny without my express permission." He watched me approach, his dark eyes now as expressionless as his mask. "Or that you will never be allowed to see him outside of this opera house."

Outwardly I remained calm but inside I ached. "May I have your permission to explain this to Raoul?"

"No need." He took my elbow and guided me toward the piano. "I sent Gaston to Hôtel de Chagny with a note an hour ago."

13

OR THE NEXT WEEK the publication sched-
ules of the daily newspapers dictated the
rhythm of life at the Paris opera. Not because
of gossip items about me. There were none. But
with the opening of the Palais Garnier's new season, the audience received the first hint of the
revolutionary changes the Phantom planned for
their beloved theater, leaving the city's opera aficionados – and their newspapers – abuzz with curiosity and consternation. The principals moved around
the stage and acted out the story as they sang?
Imagine! The chorus no longer trooped from of the
wings en masse but wandered out in twos or threes
or fours? Unheard of! Many devotees viewed the
slightest change as an attack on the French tradition of grand opera.

And it was grand. Picture the scene on that
opening night in 1880. Backstage, the cast and
crew jammed the streets of the theater: dressers
rushing about with costumes; scene shifters rolling
sets into position and lifting flats through the maze
of ropes and pulleys in the fly tower; members of
the chorus and corps de ballet milling about the

common dressing rooms while they waited for their calls; the principal singers in their private dressing rooms humming to ready their voices and pacing to steady their nerves. In the auditorium corridor, box keepers stacked footstools on the Venetian mosaic floor and ushers hoisted armfuls of programs while in the grand foyer barmen iced champagne and polished glasses. In the outer vestibules below the grand staircase, boot cleaners, cloakroom attendants and ticket takers moved to their posts.

On the sidewalks outside, queues formed in the side galleries leading to the ticket counters, made up for the most part of gentlemen because workingmen couldn't afford even the cheapest four-franc tickets and ladies weren't allowed in the orchestra seats. Around the corner at No. 29 Boulevard des Italiens, professional applauders gathered by the *chef de claque's* table at the Café du Helder, hoping to be hired for the evening and given the assignment of encouraging this or that player from a free seat directly under the crown-of-pearls chandelier. And across the river in the Faubourg St. Germain, elegant women wrapped their necks with diamonds and donned new gowns from the shops of Worth or Laferrière while drivers pulled their carriages through stately porte-cocheres to await their passengers for the drive down Rue du Bac to the Right Bank.

For much of the audience, the performance merely provided a pretext because the real purpose of a night at the Paris opera was to be seen. Many arrived long before the curtain rose and wandered through the Palais Garnier until the gasmen lit the footlights. For many years the house lights remained up during an opera so hawkers could move through the crowd selling food and drinks. Theaters finally went dark only at the insistence of Richard Wagner, a composer whose obstinacy equaled his genius.

In my dressing room, Papageno fussed with a section of orange the Phantom had left in his cage while Victorine draped the end of my lilac silk sari over my left shoulder and pinned it to my cropped blouse. "There. How does it feel?"

I raised and lowered my left shoulder and then thrust it forward and back. "Perfect. No pinching."

"And no stretching." The maid smoothed the smooth silk. "A strange garment, but it keeps its shape. The Vicomte won't be able to take his eyes from you."

I laughed lightly. "He'll need very good eyesight to find me among the throng that crowds the stage tonight. I'm just another girl in the pearl fisher's village."

As a member of the chorus on opening night, I had no reason for nerves, but I paced on the Phantom's behalf. Subscribers of the Palais Garnier expected colossal scenes and epic stories based on the feats, passions or sufferings of historical figures, not a humble village of fisher folk, however exotic their locale or their catch. Performances at the Paris opera were required by law to feature at least one ballet, and by tradition the dancers appeared soon after 10 p.m., the hour that members of the Jockey Club arrived in their boxes after dining out. That night the 10 p.m. dance would be so short that the briefest delay at the restaurant would mean the clubmen arrived too late to see their opera girls perform. If that happened, the Jockey Club might ruin the show just as they had twenty years earlier when Wagner decided the ballet belonged in the first act of his *Tannhauser* and drew the wrath of clubmen who disrupted the first three performances. The claque in all its variety also counted as an honored institution: laughers who whooped at every joke, weepers who dabbed handkerchiefs at invisible tears, encorers who shouted "Again! Again!" Impresarios who failed to pay for the claque's acclaim inevitably earned their catcalls. All of this the Phantom knew, but none of it he respected. And so I paced as the hands of the clock moved toward 7:30 p.m.

Ten minutes before curtain time, a call-boy knocked on my door. "Footlights are lit, Mademoiselle Daaé, and they're taking their seats."

As the orchestra struck up the overture, I waited in the wings with the rest of the chorus, each of us solemn and alone inside cones of silence that wouldn't dissolve until our individual performances began. As that moment approached, I picked up the straw basket at my feet. When it arrived, I linked arms with Elizabeth Rousset, pasted a wide smile on my face and strolled out of the wings.

My memory of opening night 1880 ends here. In my mind, when I step onto the stage, I am alone and playing Siebel in my debut as a principal singer. The days between those two moments in time have vanished. Raoul insisted he came to my dressing room after the curtain fell on opening night to apologize for compromising my reputation and Victorine refused to let him in. I do not recall. Madame Valérius always said I raced her to the newspapers the next morning. My mind is blank. On the day of my debut, did I hum through three octaves to tune up my instrument or sing through my role in half-voice in a final practice? I can't be certain. One thing I do know: sometime between the season's opening night and my debut four days later, the Phantom told me how to deal with a hissing claque. "Remember the fourth wall of the stage, and come alive inside those walls. Be real." His words echoed through my mind when Carlotta's minions greeted my debut with boos.

The howls of the claque surprised everyone on stage. This was Siebel's first entrance but not his moment. That would come with a solo aria in Act III. Here in Act II, I sang only a few lines. Still, the unexpected bawling shredded the fourth wall for me. I fought a wobble as I sauntered across the stage toward Siebel's friend. When I drew near, baritone Pierre Lantin raised a false eyebrow and then gave me a wink. After we greeted each other with a hug, I retreated into my character, the loyal and brave Siebel, rocking back on my heels as the Phantom had directed.

A flash of light in the grand tier caught my eye. The yowling of the claque suddenly diminished by half. A rectangle of light streamed from the Phantom's box, filled with a phantasmagoria of shifting shadows. The open door between Box 5 and the grand foyer briefly silhouetted a scuffling knot as ushers dragged the interlopers from their seats. A final shape appeared – I recognized the warship bosom of Madame Giry, the boxkeeper – and shut the door.

As Act II spun out, I rebuilt the fourth wall, each tiny success raising another stone to protect me from Carlotta's paid mob – my ringing profession of loyalty to Valentin; my tremolo of confusion inspired by Mephistopheles' curse; my wistful longing when Marguerite appeared. When the moment came for my debut, I had become Siebel, seeing nothing but Marguerite's garden, hearing nothing but the orchestra and feeling nothing but adoration for my beloved.

After it was over, Victorine met me in the wings with an enormous bouquet of red roses. "Your teacher insisted you receive these the moment you stepped off the stage."

I gathered the fragrant bundle into my arms, inhaling the heavenly scent. "Thank you."

"Flowers!" La Carlotta sneered from the side curtain, where she waited for her entrance cue. "If a man tries to give me only flowers, I laugh in his face."

I spun around to face her. "Really? I would have guessed you'd spit in his face."

The prima donna lunged toward me, her fingers stretched out like claws. I held my ground. She stopped short and snorted. "Another time I'll teach you to mind your tongue."

"Better be quick, you and your jackals." For a moment, I buried my nose in roses and then handed the bouquet back to Victorine. "I fear your day will soon be done."

Just before the final curtain, Victorine slipped out of my dressing room and into the grand foyer to assist Mme. Valérius, who'd accepted Raoul's offer of a seat in the de Chagny box for my debut. I was still in costume when the Phantom pushed the mirror from the wall. I stood at the marble-topped vanity with my back to him as I arranged his roses in a crystal vase, but a wisp of stale cellar air alerted me and I turned to face him.

For an endless moment he simply stood there looking at me, one hand still grasping the mirror's carved frame. Then a smile slowly crept across his lips. "You are the one."

"What do you mean?" I tilted my head in confusion. "I am the one – what?"

His smile widened into a grin as he sprang toward me, caught me under my arms, lifted me into the air above his head, and spun us both around in a dizzying circle. "The one I've waited for. The one I've needed. The one I've finally found. Right here in the opera house. All the time you were right here."

I rested my hands on the pristine black shoulders of his frock coat, giddy with his praise and the thrilling warmth of his touch. "So you are pleased with my debut?"

"Beyond pleased." He gently lowered me to the floor. "I would have paid that claque myself if I'd known how well you'd face them down. Your performance surpassed my greatest expectations. You were superb."

He took my hands and drew me toward the rose damask sofa. "At the end of my first season, I revealed myself to Poligny and Debienne and told the managers what I required. Protection for the orphan Daaé. Twenty-thousand francs a month. Absolute artistic control. My own prima donna." He tugged Siebel's cap and wig from my head, freeing my hair which cascaded around my shoulders. "You fulfill my last requirement."

I combed fingers through my hair, gathering it into a single plait. "Carlotta has a huge following. Why do you need another prima donna? Why do you need me?"

"A transcendent voice – your voice – will allow me to lift my artistry to a new plane." He circled his hands in the air before me, like an oracle conjuring a dream. "Think back to your arrival, and the operas performed here then. The stage always a castle or a cathedral, the costumes a warrior's armor or a king's robe, grotesque pageants of rulers for the republican citizens of France."

He brushed the knuckles of one hand along the line of my jaw until they came to rest under my chin. "My Juliette will come from the *canaille*, a beggar's princess from the *cour des miracles* who I'll dress in rags and house in a tumbledown shack. Art must be true to life. Your extraordinary voice will silence the outraged shrieks as I wrench this company away from outmoded spectacle and into the forefront of *verisimo*."

Such extravagant praise for my voice! Such unshakable confidence in his vision! Such infinite ambition for us both! Is it any wonder that I was in thrall to the Phantom? I would have followed him anywhere and done anything he asked. I dipped my chin and gently rubbed my cheek against his knuckles. If only he would ask!

I'd hoped the Phantom would lead me down to his house by the lake to celebrate our first success. Instead he sent me home in his carriage, leaving me to ride silent and alone through Paris streets thronged with the wild gaiety of a Friday evening. In my bedroom under the eaves in Rue Notre Dame des Victoires, I lay awake for hours savoring memories of him – every admiring word, every gentle touch, every happy smile. When I could not be with him in the flesh, I contented myself with daydreams.

Madame Valérius woke me early the next morning, shuffling into my bedroom with a cane in one hand and a clutch of newspapers in the other. She perched on the edge of my bed as weightless as a bird to share the reviews, and I propped my pillows against the headboard and settled against them.

"First, *Le Temps*, because their words carry the greatest weight." She lifted the newspaper into the stream of light coming through the narrow window. "'As welcome as the return to grand opera with Gounod's *Faust*, however unorthodox the staging, was the exemplary performance of Mlle. Christine Daaé whose Siebel captured the youthful vigor and radiant song of that unhappy man.'" Madame Valérius smiled. "That will please the Professor. He sets such store by their opinions."

She offered me *Le Temps* and she raised another paper. "*Le Figaro* has the keenest critics. 'The unique brilliance of Christine Daaé's voice, which reminded this listener of the glimmering northern lights of her native Sweden, inspired one aristocratic admirer to challenge the bleating claque. We salute them both.'"

I leaned forward, craning to see the words on the page. "What are they talking about?"

Madame Valérius arched an eyebrow at me. "Raoul, of course. You didn't hear him? He was wonderful!"

As my heart took a little somersault, I shook my head. Raoul was so good, so loyal! "I heard only the orchestra. I couldn't let myself hear anything else."

Victorine caught the end of our exchange as she bustled in with cups of hot chocolate for us both. "'Shame,' he shouted whenever the louts threatened to start again. 'Shame!'"

Madame Valérius accepted a cup. "Others joined in, and soon the claque was cowed into silence."

"And on the other side of the curtain La Carlotta was in a frenzy of rage." Victorine stood in the doorway, arms folded across her chest and eyes glittering with malice. "But she's gone too far this time. Sneaking *claquers* into the opera ghost's box! Madame Giry had to call the municipal guard to have them removed before he arrived. The managers won't like to hear that."

I carefully set my cup back in the saucer. "The ghost's box? How can you believe that old woman's fancies? Has anyone actually seen this ghost?"

"She hasn't seen him, but she hears him. She talks to him!" Victorine stuck out her chin and gave an emphatic nod. "I believe her because I've seen proof of the ghost with my own eyes. On opening night the opera ghost's lady left her fan in Box 5, and Madame Giry showed it to me."

"His lady!" My cup rattled in the saucer. A woman? The Phantom had a woman? "What lady?"

Victorine shrugged. "Sometimes he brings a lady. When she comes, he always asks Madame Giry for a footstool. And after they're gone her rose scent lingers in the air." Victorine spread her hands wide. "On opening night I saw her fan – carved sticks of the finest ivory and lace as sheer as a gossamer wing – and I smelled her rose perfume."

Victorine's story captivated Madame Valérius, whose wide eyes belied the sensibleness of her question. "But that could have been anyone's fan. And anyone's scent."

"I thought the same myself. But before last night's show, Madame Giry showed me the little shelf in Box 5 where the ghost leaves francs for her.

That's where she left his lady's fan." Again Victorine spread her hands wide. "Later as I crossed the grand foyer to the de Chagny box, Madame Giry waved me over to Box 5. 'He's gone,' she said. 'Arrived at the start of Act III and went off in the middle. But see what he's left me.' And so I went straight back to that shelf. The fan was gone, and in its place he'd left ten francs and a box of English sweets!"

Madame Valérius and Victorine exchanged the sly smiles of eager conspirators. For my benefactress, the opera ghost was another welcome piece of evidence that the spirit world intruded on our own. For our maid, the opera ghost was another fleeting spectacle to distract her from the drudgery of life. In the days to come they'd parse through all the unanswered questions about the mystery of Box 5 and eventually wonder why the opera ghost came only for the first half of *Faust's* third act? I already had that answer – by then I'd finished my debut singing Siebel's aria. Which left me with only one unanswered question: Had the Phantom sent me home alone in his coach the night before because another woman waited for him in his house by the lake?

14

*T*HE TWO MONTHS following my debut were the happiest since my father's death. On the four days each week the opera was dark, voice lessons with the Phantom nourished my musician's soul. On performance days – Monday, Wednesday and Friday – Raoul's visits to the Palais Garnier touched my heart. As autumn segued into winter, brisk Sunday walks with Victorine gave way to lazy afternoons roasting chestnuts on the hearth, reading aloud the stories in *Les Soirées de Médan* and writing letters for Madame Valérius. Only two things marred my deep contentment: Carlotta's stealthy campaign to undermine my position at the opera and the disquiet that came from knowing the Phantom had another woman. But I refused to let either disturb me. I was truly happy and very busy, and I had no difficulty brushing aside trifling imperfections. When thoughts of the diva's plotting rose in my mind, I remembered that in secretly understudying her roles my voice had surpassed hers. And when worries about the Phantom's other woman nagged me, I remembered the wonder in his eyes when he'd exclaimed, "You are the one!"

The start of the season didn't slow our pace. Repertory companies like the Paris opera cycled through a number of works – performing some, preparing others and maintaining productions on hiatus. *Les Pêcheurs de Perles* retired first so that *L'Elisir D'Amore* could open. I lost my easy performance as a member of the chorus and now sang three secondary roles each week – Siebel, Despina and Giannetta. In addition, I had to learn my songs as Princess Eudoxie in *La Juive*, Carlotta's songs as Rachel in *La Juive* and the part of Juliette in the finale production that the Phantom promised would put our company in the vanguard of *verisimo*.

"Can opera ever really be true to life?" I stood beside the Phantom's work table, lightly fingering tiny models of stage sets. In place of *La Juive's* gothic 13th century German city, he planned to fill the stage with a contemporary Black Forest village. In place of the 15th century Italian palazzos of the Montagues and Capulets, he imagined the decrepit slums of Louis XIV's Paris. "Doesn't the audience come to escape from real life?"

"Fairy tales are for children. Art should grip people here." He laid a fist against his chest. "Your Juliette will break their hearts."

My concerns about *verisimo* didn't extend to playing Juliette. She came to me easily because to play her I had only to be myself. We were close in age, after all, and equally inexperienced. The Phantom began my preparation with Juliette's short Act I aria rejecting her the idea of marriage – "The heart falls in love and happiness is gone forever" – and embracing the freedom of youth – "Let my soul have its springtime!" The words of the song might have been written for me so well did I understand Juliette's emotion. But Gounod's notes presented the greatest challenge of my brief career, opening the song with measure after measure of demanding coloratura. Rapid high notes of elaborate ornamentation came again and again in Juliette's waltz, which built to a final crescendo that required me to be pitch-perfect and strong at the top of my range. Week in and week out we worked on that *valse arriette,* the Phantom unwaveringly confident in the face of my doubts and endlessly patient with my quick frustration.

"For now just get the aria," he said. "Once you have the song, you'll find those notes. You have a nest of nightingales in your belly."

And then late one Saturday afternoon, I sang it perfectly for the first time. Pausing only long enough to refill my lungs, I sang Juliette's waltz a second time.

Before I could launch into another reprise, the Phantom rose from the piano bench. "*Brava.*" He smiled down at me. "Who sent you to me? God?"

I laughed, buoyed by this proof that he was right: I was the one he'd waited for. "I sound like an angel to you? You didn't always think so. For years you looked for your prima donna and never noticed me."

"I'd never heard you sing. All I knew of you was what I'd been told – orphan of a brilliant but eccentric violinist and ward of the impoverished widow of an esteemed music professor. A charity case." He shrugged. "Then Gabriel invited you to join his master class, and I finally heard your voice."

As I followed the Phantom to the dining alcove, I allowed memories of that day to flood my mind. Publicly, Gabriel's invitation had signaled my candidacy for principal singer. Privately, the chorus master's notice had confirmed my secret belief that the magic had returned to my voice. After taking a seat with a half-dozen other sopranos in a semi-circle of chairs in Gabriel's studio, I'd idly studied the large, ornate mirror behind his piano and wondered if the chorus master would offer – *when* he would offer – private voice lessons. That first day I'd credited my good fortune to the healing effects of time, which had eased my grief at Papa's death and allowed me to become comfortable with life at the Palais Garnier. Now I recognized that I owed it all to the Angel of Music and the happiness I'd found in his friendship. And he'd been right there behind Gabriel's mirror all the time!

At the sideboard I picked up a silver knife and cut two wedges from the prune and raisin clafouti left by Martine during our lesson. I handed the plates to the Phantom, who continued his explanation while carrying them to the table. "What a revelation to detect the ferocity I'd been searching for in the voice of a girl I already knew so well."

I poured out two cups of tea, adding lemon to his and sugar to mine before turning toward the table with a cup and saucer in each of my hands. His smile warmed me. "Over the years she'd revealed so much to me – how her head was always filled with songs, how music alone could touch her soul – that I knew I could awaken that wildness and tame it. And I realized that our collaboration was meant to be."

Snared by the portent in his words, I set our tea beside our plates of fruit flan and then focused all of my attention the Phantom, on the dark eyes glowing behind his mask.

"Why else did I reach out to another for the first time in my life? Why else did you find your way into my underground world? If there is a God above, this is his design." He leaned toward me, and for a moment I thought – hoped! – that he would kiss me. Instead, his voice dropped to a husky whisper and his eyes burned with a new intensity. "If heaven is empty and stars rule our destiny, then the universe aligned to bring us together. I was meant to be your teacher and you my prima donna."

Raoul made the same claim. Destiny drew two children together on the golden sand at Trestraou ten years before and had reunited them now. "Why else did I think only of you as I sailed around the world?" he asked. "How else can you explain why the most beautiful girl in Paris remained unclaimed when I returned?"

I'd expected Raoul to be angry after receiving the Phantom's letter outlining the new restrictions on our meetings. Instead, he was contrite, begging forgiveness for compromising my reputation. "After six years at sea I've forgotten the proprieties that must be observed on land." I found no trace of guile in his blue eyes. "I promise to be the soul of decorum if you'll give me another chance."

Solemnity never suited Raoul for long, and soon he was making light of the new rules. He found especially irksome the decree that my dressing room door must be open at all times when he visited. He liked to tease me by standing in the doorway and soliciting the opinions of passersby. "Now I ask you, my good man," he said one afternoon to a passing carpenter named Charles Gautier. "Tell me the truth. If I move the door here" – Raoul positioned the door at a 45 degree angle – "do you consider it open?" Gautier nodded so vigorously that a lock of dark hair fell across his eyes. He swept it aside as Raoul moved the door until it was only a foot from the jamb. "And here?" This time the carpenter ruled just as quickly, firmly shaking his head as he mumbled something under his breath. "Ajar, you say? Not open but ajar." Another aristocrat might have raised hackles with such pranks, but Raoul's friendly nature won over even the lowliest of the opera's workers, who all pronounced him a good fellow.

As winter came on I fell into the habit of drinking tea in the late afternoon and Raoul often arrived at my dressing room in time to join me. Victorine would arrange a plate of *sablés* and then, careful to leave the door wide open, set off in search of another round of gossip and speculation about the opera ghost with Madame Giry. Between bites of Victorine's delicious butter cookies, Raoul spoke of the future – his and ours. "We'll have a half dozen small boats – I'll be in command of one – to explore the shoreline foot by foot, to chart the depths of the water and measure the great sheets of ice. And when we find a suitable place, we'll build a permanent station."

"Permanent for what?" I refilled his cup. "I don't understand the point of your exploration. What is there in Antarctica besides penguins and ice?"

"Darkness! In Paris it's easy to forget the stars. In the Southern Ocean – never." He leaned toward me, his eyes gleaming eagerly. "Antarctica is the darkest place on Earth, and from there astronomers can look deep into the sky. And clean! No smoke from the factory or dust from the farm – Antarctica is as unchanged by man as Eden when

God first made it. We need somewhere pure in order to measure how the rest of the world has been befouled by man."

"I see." I held out the plate of cookies. "But is it safe?"

"Safe enough." He snatched two *sablés* and grinned at me. "And I'll only be gone a year!"

A year sounded like forever to me. Now that he'd become part of my life again, I wondered how I'd bear the quiet and solemn days without Raoul's lively banter and hearty laughter. My dread of his leaving must have shadowed my face because he set aside his tea cup and took my hand between both of his. "I'm not leaving yet. And when I come home, we'll be together. Forever."

Victorine wanted to shoo Raoul out when it was time for me to dress, but he cajoled her until she granted permission for him to remain while I did my makeup. As I searched among the pots and jars, sponges and brushes, on my dressing table, Raoul sat on the sofa and read aloud the day's installment of *L'Evénement's* serial novel, which ran across the bottom of the front page. Early on he'd surprised me by his devotion to proclaiming aloud the frequent letters to the editor on political topics from Emile Zola and Victor Hugo. "Forget about my title – I'm no royalist." He snorted with disgust. "How you wound me, Christine. I'm a sailor honored to serve the Republic." For the sake of my makeup, he was under strict instructions to hold off sharing what he called the funny bits until after the glue had set on my false eyelashes. And as soon as I finished my maquillage, Victorine retrieved his coat and hat from the stand by the door and sent him on his way.

On the afternoon of the grand Christmas gala, Raoul and I were laughing over some nonsense in the newspaper when a firm knock sounded at the wide-open door of my dressing room. I looked up to find the conductor – the maestro! – standing on my doorstep.

His given name was Georges-Jacques Chénier, but no one called him that. To one and all in the Palais Garnier he was the maestro, and his word was law. Tall and thin with a riot of curling black hair that bounced in time with his wand, the maestro ruled the musicians and singers by demanding perfection and helping them to achieve it. In a company of close to 300 performers, only Carlotta dared to talk back to him. But no matter what she said – or how she screamed – the maestro remained unmoved.

An apologetic smile flitted across his lips as he nodded to Raoul before addressing me. "Mademoiselle Christine, I wonder if I might have a word?"

When the door closed behind Raoul, the maestro waved away my offer of a seat on the sofa and came to stand beside my dressing table. "I've just been informed that Carlotta is not available tonight. By all reports she was pale and trembling when she left the theatre a half hour ago, so she may actually be ill. I'd like you to take her place on tonight's program."

"Me?" I clutched my throat, simultaneously thrilled and horrified at a command performance in a starring role. Would the Phantom approve? "What will I sing?"

"Your teacher tells me your Marguerite is superb, so you'll simply replace Carlotta in the prison scene and final trio from *Faust*, which ends our program." He gave me a warm and reassuring smile. "He also says you've made a wonderful start on Juliette, so you can begin with her waltz."

In the next hours I learned for the first time what it meant to be prima donna. I was still at my dressing table, still in shock at the maestro's command, when Eugenie Savatier – the costumer herself – swept into my dressing room followed by two assistants, one clutching a brace of evening gowns and the other toting a casket of jewels. Mme. Savatier quickly sorted through the dresses, holding the fabric of each against my cheek for a moment before pronouncing judgment. "Too pink. Too dull. Too green. Too bright. Perfect."

She chose a simple gown of ivory satin and gauze piped with shimmering gold cord and finished with a standing collar and short puffed sleeves of lace. As she pinned the bodice, fitting it snug enough for looks but loose enough for singing, I pulled at the short train. "How will it look when I move?"

"Movement – bah! Modern nonsense." The top of her gray chignon barely reached my chin, but Mme. Savatier's authority in costuming was unquestioned. She looked up at me and rolled her dark eyes."It is a ball gown. It is meant for dancing."

After fitting the gown, she turned to the jewels, sifting through the glitter to extract a simple pearl choker with a clasp of brilliant diamonds. She smiled as she fastened it around my neck. "Don't worry. It's paste."

Following the costumer came the hairdressers, who wove ropes of pearls and diamonds through my hair as they curled and coiled the strands into an elegant coiffure. The makeup master came to assess my earlier effort and add a few touches of his own before pronouncing my face perfect. Other accessories arrived in the hands of breathless assistants – stockings of the sheerest silk, satin slippers embroidered with shiny beads, long kid gloves with pearl buttons at the wrist.

Through it all my thoughts returned again and again to the Phantom. Would he approve? Did he know? Would he come to Box 5 tonight? Finally, I beckoned Victorine, who'd hovered on the edge of the crowd after being pushed aside by the deluge of experts. "Run up to the grand foyer," I whispered behind an upturned hand. "Ask Mme. Giry if the ghost attends the Christmas gala."

Victorine returned ten minutes later. "Sometimes he comes, sometimes he doesn't." She shrugged. "But Mme. Giry says Charles Gounod will be in the house tonight. The composer of all your songs!"

When the orchestra struck up *Roméo et Juliette* and the curtain parted to reveal me standing in the mouth of the wolf, I spared no thought for the composer in his seat somewhere on the grand tier. I glanced only once at the box where Mme. Valérius had joined Raoul. All of the attention I could spare from my song I gave to Box 5 and the man who might not even be there to hear my performance. As the notes of Juliette's coloratura poured out, each one a brilliant perfection, I sang only for him. As my feet carried me into a dreamy waltz, I danced only for him.

Applause thundered down as tenor Carolus Fonta joined me on the stage for the final love duet from *Faust*. He faced my side and joined the clapping. "No *claquers* tonight. It seems the world has discovered another Swedish nightingale."

With the confidence of an experienced player, Fonta guided me through the aria's choreography as Faust slipped into Marguerite's prison cell and the doomed lovers remembered the early days of their love in the village streets and her fragrant garden. He squeezed my hand in appreciation at the emotion coloring my notes as Marguerite resisted Faust's effort to lead her to freedom. And he warned me with a stabbing glance to stage left of the arrival of bass Lucien Canet as our nemesis, Mephistopheles, for the soaring final trio. Still, I had eyes only for Box 5.

"Pure and radiant angels, carry my soul up to heaven!" Marguerite's plea rang out in an epic melody of martyrdom that I aimed only at him. "God of justice, I give myself up to you! God of mercy, I am yours, forgive!"

As Marguerite repeated her plea, Mephistopheles sang out his warning that Faust must flee or be abandoned by his satanic protector. And Faust added a third strand of song begging Marguerite to follow him to freedom.

"Pure and radiant angels, carry my soul up to heaven!" Marguerite's prayer rose in steps toward a thrilling climax that was meant all for him. "God of justice, I give myself up to you! God of mercy, I am yours, forgive!"

Matching me step for step, Fonta and Canet marched the songs of Faust and Mephistopheles toward the same pinnacle, spinning their melodic lines around the peak I built with Marguerite's entreaty. As the trio reached its zenith, a pale hand snaked out of the darkness of Box 5 and gripped the gilt balustrade of the grand tier. His hand.

The audience erupted like a maddened mob, cheering, clapping, sobbing as they rose to their feet. Flowers rained around us, flung down from the boxes and tossed up from the seats beyond the orchestra pit. I staggered under the onslaught, undone by exhaustion and emotion. Carolus Fonta wrapped an arm around my shoulder to prop me up while Lucien Canet scurried across the boards to gather an enormous bouquet of tributes that he gently placed in my trembling arms. Again and again we bowed and still the audience clapped and cheered.

"There'll be hell to pay tomorrow from the subscribers." The tenor gave my shoulders a quick squeeze. "That I guarantee."

"How dare you keep such a treasure hidden!" The bass barely managed a squeaky falsetto. "With a voice of such splendor in the company, why should we listen to La Carlotta?"

At last the audience released us, and I made my way through a throng of well-wishers to my dressing room. The Phantom waited inside, standing by Papageno's cage and stroking the tamed bird with a gentle finger. He looked up as I came through the door and reached out with his free hand. "Your angel wept tonight."

Before I shut the door completely, a commotion erupted in the hall outside, squeaks of alarm and the heavy tramp of feet. I peeked back out. A sextet of workmen came toward me, struggling under the burden of a stretcher covered with a tarp. "What is it?"

"It's Joseph Buquet." I hadn't seen Meg Giry among the knot of squeaking dancers crowding the hallway. "He was found in the second cellar, hanging from the set of *Le Roi de Lahore.*"

For a moment, horror robbed me of speech and breath and sense. I could only stare as the workmen passed with the shrouded remains of a man I'd seen every day for years. I remembered how he mussed his thinning hair with impatience at the set designer's endless debates over the exact placement of a painted backdrop, how the pipe he smoked left a fragrant tang in its wake, and how he earned the secret admiration of many by daring to say out loud that Carlotta sang and behaved like a fish wife.

In the next instant, Little Giry gasped and covered her mouth with both hands. I followed her gaze over my shoulder and found that I'd let the door to my dressing room swing open, framing the reflection of the Phantom in the mirror over my dressing table. The glow of the gas lamp playing over his face clearly showed the edge of his mask, spotlighting it like a honed blade.

Raoul arrived at that moment, dodging around the stretcher and slipping through the wave of *coryphées*, led by Little Giry, which followed Joseph Bouquet's procession. He, too, saw the Phantom and frowned. "Christine?"

I stepped into the hallway and closed the door behind me. "He is my teacher."

Raoul stared at the closed door. "He wears a mask." He faced me then. "Why?"

"I can't tell you. I wish I could." I dipped my head, unable to meet his eyes. "You must go. And I must return to my teacher."

15

*T*HAT NIGHT I slept for the first time in the bedroom the Phantom had prepared for me in his house by the lake. Without another word, Raoul had turned on his heel and followed the ballet dancers flocking behind the procession of workmen carrying the body of Joseph Buquet. As I reentered my dressing room, I staggered from exhaustion and emotion.

The Phantom rushed to my side, offering the support of his arm. "Are you very tired?"

"Tonight I sang only for you." For an instant, I let my head rest against his shoulder. "And I am dead."

"Then once you've had a cup of Martine's hot chocolate, you'll go straight to bed."

He waved away my half-hearted objections and covered Papageno's cage, locked the door and turned down the gas before leading me into the dim tunnel behind the mirror. As soon as I was in bed, he'd send out the necessary notes: an explanation to Mme. Valérius with a request for a week's worth of clothing; instructions to the Maestro to substitute understudies as Despina and Giannetta in upcoming performances; and advice to the managers, Poligny and Debienne, about exploiting the interest that was sure to follow my triumph at the gala and absence from the Palais Garnier. "What Propertius said of lovers is also true of divas: Absence makes the heart much fonder."

He'd outfitted my small bedroom with gilt wood furniture in the Louis XVI style, matching the pale blue silk upholstery on the chair to the coverlet on the bed. Martine had draped a night dress of embroidered lawn and a wool wrapper across the pillows and left a pair of crocheted slippers on the thick blue carpet that covered the stone floor. A single gas torchiere hissed above the bed, throwing light on a quartet of paintings – more magic windows by his favorite vanguard artists – that the Phantom had obviously chosen just for me.

On the wall closest to my pillow hung the small seascape with brooding cliffs that had reminded me of Perros-Guirec, now elegantly framed in gold-painted wood. A large pastel dominated the wall beside the door, drawn by the familiar hand of M. Degas and featuring a well-known chanteuse singing full-throated on the stage of a *café-concert*. The wall behind the chair featured the rooftops and chimney pots of Paris as twilight descended on a snowy day while summer reigned above the bureau with a bouquet of flowers spilling out of a Chinese vase.

Despite my exhaustion and the soothing effect of Martine's hot chocolate, I couldn't sleep when I finally nestled into the pillows. "Your angel wept tonight." My mind echoed with the Phantom's words. I turned the gas low, leaving only enough light to trace the outline of the cliffs in the Perros painting. Next month he would take me there so I could visit Papa's grave on the anniversary of his death. His many kindnesses – that trip and this painting – suggested more than a teacher's affection for a favorite student. And yet the Phantom never went beyond what was courteous or correct. Unlike Raoul, he never snatched a kiss or took possession of my hand or let his linger on mine longer than was strictly proper. What would he do if I tied that woolen wrapper around my waist and sought him out now? At his desk if he was writing those promised notes or in his bedroom if he'd finished that chore and retired for the night? I shivered, at once tempted by my desire for more of him and wary of his need for concealment. Somehow I would find a way to draw him out of his solitude.

That week I worked harder than ever before. Together the Phantom and I marked up Juliette's score, deciding where I would breathe and noting when I would sing louder or softer. Then I began to spend all my free time memorizing the part – fifteen scenes over five acts – while the Phantom focused his lessons on my technique. One exercise smoothed the portamento of my voice as it glided from one pitch to another. The next concentrated on perfecting passage notes, the links between my head, throat and chest registers, to produce a seamless voice throughout my range. He sent Gaston to fetch a fainting couch and had him position it in the music room near the piano so I could learn to sing while reclining, preparing for Juliette's wedding night duet with Roméo. But my hardest task proved to be mastering the Act V emotions of Rachel in *La Juive*.

"You must infuse your voice first with terror and then with determination." The Phantom didn't look up from the keyboard as he once again stated the instructions he'd first given me that afternoon and now repeated again long after dinner. "She is terrified of the cauldron of boiling oil but chooses to die as a Jew rather than accept Christian baptism."

"Why can't I do this?" I knotted my hands and reared back in mock fright. "Did it come easily to Carlotta?"

At my question he looked up, noted my melodramatic stance and frowned. "Stop that at once, and forget Carlotta. Her voice has no warmth, no humanity. At best hers glitters, but even at its worst your voice glows." He rose from the piano, crossed to his work table and rummaged through a pile of wardrobe notions for a few moments before returning with a red ribbon in his hand. He pulled mine behind my back and loosely secured my wrists with the ribbon. "Let the music lead you, and convey Rachel's emotions with your voice."

Over and over he played through Act V – sometimes the orchestra's score, sometimes my notes alone – until I saw that there was a reason for everything in the music. Every note and everything about the notes – each cadenza, each crescendo, each vibrato – was set down by the composer on purpose to capture what his characters felt at every moment of the opera. Eugène Scribe had written Rachel's words in his libretto, but Fromental Halévy had distilled her emotions into music. That evening the Phantom taught me the depth of music, and by the time his lesson ended, the essence of Rachel's terror and determination infused my voice.

He swung around on the piano bench, pulled me between his legs and untied the ribbon that bound my hands. "You have her. Your voice is absolutely true." Gently, he rubbed my unmarked wrists. "You worked very hard today, and you've earned a reward."

A bright moon over the Bois de Boulogne clearly lit the road behind the grandstand at Longchamp where Gaston drew the brougham to a stop. At half past ten on a cold winter night, we had the vast park to ourselves. Even the hardiest mohicans and prostitutes had left for warmer climes. Before helping me out of the carriage, the Phantom wrapped a soft woolen scarf around my neck and offered me a thick fur muff for my hands. "Never let it be said that this music teacher neglected the proper care of his prize pupil." He drew on leather gloves and looped an arm through one of mine as we set off along the road with Gaston and the carriage trailing close behind.

The stars overhead sparkled like diamonds tossed across black velvet. I sent a silent wish toward the brightest one before launching my salvo at the Phantom. "What about your music teachers? You've never mentioned them."

I forced myself to act naturally, to walk and breathe evenly as the seconds passed and his silence drew out. Clearly I'd gained a measure of his trust, but would it be enough? Just as the first dark tendril of despair unfurled in my heart, he finally replied. "There was only one."

I hugged his arm, hoping to appear spontaneous, and smiled up at his profile. "Then, dear music teacher of mine, tell me about that one."

As the seconds drew out, I studied his pale face, which appeared stiff under the mask, almost frozen. The smile I'd pasted on my lips bespoke the genuine interest of a loving friend. Would he look down? Yes! Would he trust me?

For an instant when his eyes met mine, his features softened. Then he looked away and his face hardened again. "When I was small, the village children shunned me. The girls shrieked as they ran away, and the boys threw rocks before they followed. When the schoolmaster found me listening under his window, he shooed me away. I learned to avoid the village and roamed the countryside instead."

An owl hooted from a distant tree and, behind us, César whickered at his partner in harness, but the Phantom didn't seem to hear the night sounds around us. He walked steadily forward, looking straight ahead. "One day I came across a crumbling ancient wall and discovered a magical place behind it. The wall hid an old orchard with every kind of fruit tree imaginable – figs, peaches, apples, pears, cherries – and beside the orchard stood a chapel that rang with wonderful music Sometimes just an organ, sometimes just a choir, sometimes both. I climbed the wall and hid high in the trees, gorging on fruit and music."

Bare branches formed an arch in the icy night air overhead, but in my mind's eye a warm sun shone and fruit hung heavy on leafy branches hiding a lonely little boy.

"Over time I learned the songs, though I didn't understand the Latin words. I never saw anyone else in the orchard, but someone must have heard me singing because one day the voice of a woman called up to me, asking me to come down. I stopped singing immediately and remained in the tree." A smile ghosted across his lips. "After few minutes, she said, 'All right then. If you won't come down, I'll come up.'"

He marched on, his eyes fixed on the darkness ahead, while I clung to his arm and gazed up at him. "I knew what to expect – one look, a scream and she would vanish. But that didn't happen. She was old, a nun, but she was spry and soon was perched beside me. At the sight of my face, she just blinked. 'You have the voice of an angel, my child,' she said. 'And the devil's face,' I replied. She reached out a hand, lifted my chin and looked me in the eye. 'You're wrong. Here on Earth, in God's creation, the Devil was a beautiful angel. He became a demon because he fell.'"

He stopped then and swung around to face me. Behind us Gaston spoke softly to the horses and pulled them to a stop. "Soeur Adeline undertook my education. She taught me to read and write. She taught me to play the wheezing organ in the chapel. And she taught me to discipline my voice by mastering ancient hymns. After she died, I left my village and joined a traveling circus, earning my way by exhibiting my face and my voice."

So now I knew. What the Phantom hid behind his mask had been with him all his life. From childhood. Perhaps from birth. The children who should have offered friendship stoned him. The men who should have offered protection shooed him away. The women who should have offered comfort screamed. Everyone had shunned him except an old nun who'd looked him in the eye and told him he was an angel. Would he ever give me the same chance?

Our nightly visits to the Bois de Boulogne did not go unnoticed. Neither did my absence from the Palais Garnier. As Carolus Fonta and Lucien Canet predicted, the subscribers and the critics demanded to know why the nightingale Daaé had been given pants roles and cast as a soubrette when her gala performance showed she had the voice of a prima donna? The explanation offered by the Maestro and the managers – that the radiance of my voice was developed only recently by a new teacher – simply made things worse because they would not, indeed could not, name my tutor. When no one at the opera explained my absence, the newspapers quickly recast it as a disappearance. My "disappearance" inflamed the opera and the popular press with rumors about the mysterious teacher who had transformed my voice and speculation about what the future might hold for Carlotta now that a new diva had emerged to challenge her supremacy. Then an item appeared one morning in a gossip column in *Gil Blas*: "Opera aficionados clamoring to hear the Palais Garnier's missing Swedish nightingale are advised to look for her between 10 and 11 p.m. on the drive behind the Longchamp racetrack where she promenades each evening on the arm of a well-dressed man. Her teacher, perhaps? Or..." And so for the paltry reward of two sous a newspaper spy brought our evening outings in the Bois to an end.

The smutty suggestion of that grubby journalist also threatened to destroy my oldest friendship. Raoul read the column, of course. And he rejected the scandal implied by those three simple dots. Yet despite his faith in me, a poisonous seed had been planted. I had explained as best I could the promise I'd made to my teacher and the reasons for it, both his and mine. But I couldn't provide ordinary details about the man – his name, his address. Raoul had seen with his own eyes the most extraordinary detail about my teacher – his mask – and heard my refusal to account for it. Perhaps with that momentary glimpse of my masked teacher he'd also sensed my attraction to his rival. And thus a speck of doubt found its way into Raoul's heart.

Soon a more dangerous scandal eclipsed my concern about newspaper gossip. My absence from the opera spared me from witnessing the way Joseph Buquet's death had thrown the company into disarray. To his many friends at the opera, the chief scene shifter had been a rock – serious, sober, steady – and news of his death naturally came as a shock. The manner of his death proved even more devastating. And the inquest's verdict of suicide most stunning of all. Buquet's mourners at the opera reeled with disbelief. Why would he kill himself? He'd been happy enough. What could have made him do it? His life had been free of disappointment and hardship. A question without an answer provides fertile ground for a scandalmonger, and Carlotta had two. What had happened to Joseph Buquet, and where was Christine Daaé? By the time I returned to the Palais Garnier, the prima donna's whispering campaign had persuaded half the company that my "disappearance" was connected with the chief scene shifter's death.

16

MADAME VALÉRIUS and I spent a quiet holiday at home, observing traditions from both Sweden and France. On Christmas Eve, we placed our shoes beside the fireplace in hopes that Père Noel would fill them while we slept, but we made sure to leave a bowl of porridge out for Tomte, the gift-bearing gnome who lives in Scandinavian attics. On Christmas morning, I joined Madame for mass at the little church of Notre Dame des Victoires and lit candles at the feet of the Virgin in thanksgiving for the kindness of Soeur Adeline and the magician Lecadre. Their generosity to an outcast boy had twice opened his heart and inspired hope that I could do the same. As I knelt beside Mme. Valérius on the cold stone floor, I studied the hundreds of inscribed marble devotional plaques left by the faithful: "A miracle was necessary and you gave it to us;" "Recognition to Mary and St. Joseph for your protection at the time of the Italian war;" "Fidelity, love, hope." Then I bent my head and asked for the fidelity, protection and miracle that I needed as well.

I'd given Madame her gifts at breakfast – a box of linen handkerchiefs, a magnifying glass on a pretty chain she could wear around her neck and a rosary from St. Peter's in Rome that had been blessed by Pope Leo XIII. For Victorine I had a bottle of her favorite perfume, a large box of chocolates from Marquis and a chic bonnet from Mlle. Esther on Rue de Richelieu. For all of us I'd ordered dinner from a nearby restaurant and laughed with pleasure at their amazed delight when a trio of liveried waiters arrived just after 1 p.m. and carried in a banquet from Escoffier.

We started our feast with caviar blinis, foie gras mousse and fresh oysters. We merely sampled the cold consommé albion and hot almond cream soup before lingering over the grilled paupiettes of sole with crab, roast young venison with cherries and capon stuffed with Périgord truffles. Madame and I waved off the Bénédictins blanc-mange but Victorine indulged. Then our maid had to loosen her stays when I served the Bûche de Noël on plates dusted with powdered sugar snow and decorated with sprigs of spruce, fresh raspberries and meringue mushrooms. Afterwards we gathered around the fireplace, where a stout Yule log burned, sipping champagne while we admired the crèche on the mantelpiece, sang Christmas carols and thanked each other again and again for the gifts we'd received.

Two other gifts remained unopened in my bedroom. A few weeks earlier, I'd run into the artist Degas in a corridor at the Palais Garnier and on impulse called after him. "Monsieur?" He stopped and turned back to me, a raised eyebrow his only reply. "We've never met, but you know a friend of mine. I was with him recently when he exchanged greetings with you at Nouvelle Anthènes." After a moment's hesitation the artist nodded, inviting me to continue. "He so admires your work, I hoped perhaps you might consent to draw my portrait in pastels. As a gift. For Christmas?" His dark eyes narrowed as he cocked his head and examined me, searching my frame from top to bottom as a farmer studies a prize pig. Finally, Degas smiled and lifted his hat. "Perhaps." When I returned to my dressing room following my stay at the house by the lake, I found the portrait propped against my mirror and by the shape of my singing mouth instantly recognized the moment he'd sketched. Degas's portrait captured Marguerite's epic plea for rescue from the final song of my gala performance. I couldn't wait to present it to my teacher.

The other gift might never be opened. After my sojourn underground, I'd gone back to the studio of Nadar to sit for a photographic portrait. I left Victorine behind at the Palais Garnier, where she could settle in for another gossip with Mme. Giry. I saw no harm in going alone since the distance from the opera to the atelier on Boulevard des Capucines was hardly more than a block. No one bothered me as I walked to my appointment, but on my way back a wild-eyed *flâneur* grabbed my arm and forced me to stop. "Mon Dieu, it is you!" He swayed before me, his breath smelling of absinthe. "You're an angel, did you know that? And your voice is divine." He clawed at his chest, jamming his hand beneath his coat, and drew out a small rectangle of cardboard. "I bought your picture. See?" He shoved the postcard in my face – all my women's curves displayed in my doublet and tights as the youth

Siebel – and the request which followed added a second outrage. "Will you sign it?" With a sharp swing of my elbow, I managed to free myself from his grasp and safely scurried away before the tipsy man recovered his balance. My first brush with fame left a sour taste and, for me, tarnished the gift I'd so carefully chosen for a beloved friend, a gift further blemished by the fact that I hadn't seen or heard from Raoul since the night of the gala.

A few days after Christmas, the maestro informed me that the opera's managers had accepted an invitation for me to sing with Carolus Fonta on New Year's Eve at the salon of the Duchess de Zurich. This time I didn't have to wonder if the Phantom knew about the command performance. I now understood that orders from the maestro or the managers originated with him. He never explained to me the methods he used to impose his rule on that trio of ambitious men. Yet if the answer to the question of how remained elusive, the answer to why was readily apparent. Since the Phantom had taken the helm, the revenue and reputation of the Palais Garnier opera had soared, and the current season looked to surpass all others. Even before the announcement of our final production, almost half the tickets had been sold and only a few seats remained available for the other five shows.

With his good looks and wonderful tenor, Carolus Fonta played a large part in our current success, and I knew he'd offer sound advice on preparing for our private performance. Late one afternoon I knocked on his dressing room door, eager to hear his thoughts on my choice of songs. I'd almost given up hope of getting an answer when the door finally opened. La Sorelli tossed me a cool smile as she slipped past my shoulder while Carolus called out a merry greeting from his leather couch across the room. "Ciao, nightingale. Again we sing together."

"So I'm told." He waved me in, and I sank into the matching armchair opposite the couch, where he'd stretched out in a silk robe and balanced a glass of red wine on his stomach. "Will you help me pick my songs and tell me what to expect? I've never been to a salon."

He suggested I start with a folk tune from Sweden, and after I'd sung several for him, we both liked *Herr Mannerlig* best. No need for Carolus or anyone else to know that the ballad told the story of a mountain troll spurned by the handsome knight who captured her heart. To follow he recommended a well-known song with lots of vocal fireworks and pretended to swoon when I sang the Queen of the Night's passionate second aria from Mozart's *Die Zauberflöte*.

"Two songs for each of us and then a final duet." He swirled the wine in his glass. "Something from the season to tease them back to the theater. But not a showstopper, or else why buy a ticket?" He closed his eyes and hummed snatches of a half dozen songs before breaking into a grin. "'*Il m'aime, il ne m'aime pas.* He loves me, he loves me not.' It's perfect!"

I nodded agreement. "So how will it go? As I said, I've never been to a salon."

He sat up and tossed off the rest of his wine. "We arrive at the appointed time – about an hour before the buffet. We perform, circle the room once to receive compliments and then depart. The next day a servant will bring us our pay."

I smiled. "And what is the fee for three songs?"

"High, my little nightingale, very high." He raked a hand through his black hair. "Demand payment every time you perform. Never give it away. And don't fool yourself that you've been invited to this salon as a guest. You're the entertainment. Without that voice, the noblesse wouldn't let you in the door."

I certainly could have passed for a duchess on the night of the salon. Again the costumer dressed me, this time in silk the color of lemons. "The women of the *haut monde* aren't stupid. You won't see gas in their drawing rooms. And yellow is the only color for candlelight," Eugenie Savatier explained as she placed a half dozen jeweled hair pins on my dressing table. After a brief discussion with the hairdresser, she nodded at the gloves and stockings an assistant held out for her approval and inspected the black velvet evening coat trimmed with sable before calling out one last bit of advice as she swept out my dressing room. "Mind the jewels tonight. Those are not paste."

As our carriage rolled across Paris on a cold New Year's Eve, snow softened the burned-out hulk of the Palais des Tuileries and swirled over the dark water of the Seine when we crossed Pont Royal onto the Left Bank and headed up Rue de Bac into the grand and stately heart of Faubourg St. Germain. This was an aristocratic world of immense wealth that I knew only from stories I'd read in books and magazines and newspapers – Raoul's world – and one that had no place for me. When we arrived opposite the Hôtel de Zurich, where an army of uniformed servants loitered around the magnificent porte-cochere and torches brought daylight to the cobbled courtyard beyond, our carriage didn't stop. I turned to Carolus, who shrugged. "That's for guests. We go in through the back."

A liveried servant in knee breeches and powdered wig met us in the servant's vestibule, a plain hall with unadorned walls, and escorted us to the ballroom, where the guests had gathered. We followed him through the green baize door and down a long gallery of paintings framed in gold leaf and lit by a string of crystal chandeliers. He led us up one branch of a grand double staircase with ornate wrought-iron banisters and pink marble steps, and through four large reception rooms that opened one into the other, each more lavish than the last, with frescoed ceilings, soaring windows and thick carpets that swallowed the sound of our steps. The ballroom's three double doors stood open, and Carolus and I paused on the threshold of the middle pair, standing side by side until we were announced by another footman in even more elaborate livery.

The clever use of mirrors magnified the Duchesse de Zurich's huge ballroom with endless reflections of glittering chandeliers and gilded chairs beyond counting, making the space appear as large as the auditorium at the Palais Garnier. At the far end rose a low stage with a gleaming piano and a pair of upholstered benches. Behind the stage lay a conservatory with towering palm trees and a marble fountain with spouting swans. For a moment, the servant's words silenced the assembled guests, who turned in their seats to see us. In the next instant heads bent toward one another, mouths opened behind lacy fans and a speculative buzz rose that set the ballroom humming like an enormous bee hive. I took the arm Carolus offered and did my best to smother the fluttering in my belly with a wide smile.

"A brilliant strategy." Carolus set a slow pace as we walked down the wide aisle between the chairs. "First hide the latest novelty for a week and then bring her back only long enough to tease them all over again." He grinned. "Our maestro is a genius!"

Was this evening also part of his plan? That the Phantom was a genius I had no doubt. Hadn't I used that very word in explaining the transformation of my voice? And I'd learned that his genius extended beyond music – to casting, to set design, to wardrobe. And publicity? Was that the purpose of Nadar's vulgar postcards? And my "disappearance?" And the revelation by *Gil Blas* of my late night walks in the Bois de Boulogne? Had the Phantom contrived it all to serve his grand scheme to transform the Palais Garnier company into opera's vanguard?

Thank God for the brilliant advice of Carolus Fonta. I arrived beside the piano with thoughts of the Phantom spinning my mind and anxiety about the avaricious audience tightening my nerves. But the familiar melody of *Herr Mannerlig* instantly relaxed me. I'd sung the song since girlhood and performed it hundreds, perhaps thousands, of times. Warm memories of Papa flooded through me and into my voice, spilling out in a sparkling performance that drew rousing applause. The glow of their approval hadn't worn off before it was time for me to sing again. Chin held high, I looked over their heads, fixed my eyes on the luminous halos of light on the far chandelier and delivered the Queen of the Night's dazzle of rapid high notes. This time my reward included shouts of '*Brava!*' When we finished our duet from *Faust*, the audience followed the lead of their hostess in the first row and stood as one to applaud until the Duchess de Zurich released them by stepping forward to thank us. Thus began our polite procession around the ballroom. The single circuit for compliments that etiquette demanded passed in a blur of faces and a slur of titles until we reached a familiar pair. "I believe you know the Comte de Chagny?" She smiled as Philippe lifted her hand to his lips. "And his brother, the Vicomte Raoul?"

"Your grace." Raoul bowed to the duchess and took my hand. "With your permission, I'd like a private word with Mademoiselle Daaé."

Without waiting for a reply, he tugged me to his side and steered me toward the conservatory. Surprise robbed me of all conversation beyond inane platitudes. "It's a lovely room. And a lovely party! Are you enjoying yourself, Raoul?"

He sent a distracted glance around the room before returning his attention to me. "I only came because Philippe said you'd be here. I've longed to see you."

"I've missed our teas as well." I tried to retrieve my hand and failed. "Have you been out of town?"

He leaned toward me, his blue eyes narrowing. "You sent me away! After the Christmas gala."

A hot flush spread through me. "Not for good. Just for that night. I've explained my promise to my teacher again and again."

The fragrance of damp earth scented the conservatory air and strange gold fish with bulging eyes swam inside the wide marble basin. Raoul took a seat next to a spouting swan and pulled me down beside him. "You haven't explained your disappearance. Or his mask." I couldn't look away from the anger flashing in his eyes. Nor could I offer the explanation he wanted. "At least I've seen for myself that he's just a man."

His grip on my hand loosened, and I gently tugged it free. "What do you mean by that?"

He folded his arms across his chest, his eyes suddenly steely. "You haven't heard the latest news about La Daaé? Philippe told me just before you arrived. It seems that the corps de ballet has decided your mysterious music teacher is none other than the opera ghost."

By the rush of heat across my cheeks, I knew that my blush had deepened. Trust Little Giry to jump in where Carlotta left off. "That's ridiculous." I gave Raoul's upper arm a gentle stroke. "If you're not afraid of ghosts, you'd be welcome to come to tea. Very welcome."

His façade of reserve melted instantly to reveal the eager young man I loved, who countered my invitation with one his own. "If tonight you'll be my partner for the buffet and reserve the midnight waltz for me?"

"I can't stay, Raoul. I'm not a guest." I looked back to the ballroom where Philippe stood alone now and openly watched us. Was that a smile of affection for his brother or a smirk of derision for me? "I'm here as an entertainer. And now that my performance is over, I must go."

I started to rise but Raoul caught my elbow so I sank back onto wide lip of the marble fountain. "But you're the most beautiful woman at the party. Of course you must stay."

Poor Raoul. First he stood accused of impropriety for taking me on an outing with his brother's courtesan. Now he stood accused of impropriety for treating me like a member of the *gratin*. No wonder he was confused. Perhaps it was selfish of me to allow our friendship to continue. We came from such different worlds. Could they ever be reconciled? That problem didn't arise with the Phantom. Hearing about his childhood had filled me with memories of my own. We were so alike, he and I. Both born of peasant stock. Both one-time traveling performers.

"I'm sorry, Raoul." Despite the restraint of his hand, I rose to my feet and took a step away from the fountain.

I waved to Carolus Fonta, who stood just inside the ballroom door, signaling that I'd join him in another minute. My gesture arrested the footsteps of Philippe and the Duchess of Zurich, who each had started toward the conservatory from their separate corners of the ballroom. Both no doubt intending to rescue the poor Vicomte from the clutches of a woman of inferior birth. Even when we were children, Raoul's family had disliked our unsuitable friendship so much that they'd stopped sending him to the sea shore. The sight of those two aristocrats bearing down on me reopened a wound I'd thought was fully healed and raised anew a doubt I'd thought was laid to rest. Surely Raoul wasn't blind to the nature of the relationship that his brother had with La Sorelli? Did he only feign ignorance of propriety? Did he hope that flattering my vanity would lead to a liaison with an opera girl of his own?

I turned back to Raoul and, in my best imitation of the Duchess de Zurich, offered him my hand. "Goodbye, Raoul. It's been so nice to see you again."

He brushed his lips across my knuckles. "Until next year, then. Thank God it arrives in two hours!"

"My apologies, Raoul. I've just remembered." To underscore my feigned ignorance, I momentarily rested my fingers against my lips. "I'm going to Perros with my teacher. For the anniversary of my father's death. I don't know how long I'll be gone." I gave him my chilliest smile. "Perhaps sometime we'll meet again."

17

MY TRIP TO Perros-Guirec turned out far differently than either I or novelist Gaston Leroux imagined. The Phantom came for me in his carriage, and we drove to Gare Montparnasse to catch the Brittany express. But citing urgent and unexpected business, he left me at Lannion, promising to join me in Perros the next afternoon. As I boarded the stagecoach that would carry me the last seven miles to the coast, I forced myself once again to banish thoughts of his other woman. With or without the Phantom, the purpose of the trip remained unchanged – to honor my father's memory. I was the only passenger in the diligence and the only guest at the inn called the Setting Sun. The moon-faced landlord lit a fire in my room while his stout wife bustled in with a pitcher of warm water and the promise of tea. Pleading exhaustion, I asked them to send my supper to my room. After washing the travel grime from my face and hands, I carried my cup to the dormer window. Frost rimed the heath under a slate sky as a pale winter sun sank into the darkening sea, a bleak scene that matched my mood.

My heart remained heavy the next morning as I walked through rare winter sunshine to the ancient chapel for my father's memorial mass. In the burial ground beside the church, I knelt at his grave, resting my forehead against the tombstone carved of rock quarried from the pink granite headlands Papa had loved so much. He'd been gone for seven years. In Paris I felt his loss as a dull ache, but here in Brittany my bereavement felt fresh. Had it been distance and not time that eased my pain?

I expected an empty chapel because midmorning mass was uncommon on weekdays in Perros. But by the time the priest entered from the sacristy, a half dozen worshippers had scattered through the pews behind me. In the jeweled light cast by the Virgin's window knelt Ginette Cerdan, who'd come with us to Perros as an apple-cheeked maid and, when she decided to marry a local man, arranged for her cousin Victorine to take her place. On the aisle halfway back sat Marcel Boulanger, the wizened village cobbler whose atelier had often hosted my father's impromptu performances. And just inside the door stood Edouard Truffot, gray head bent over the pocket watch that timed the opening and closing of the small shop where he sold the odd assemblage of canned food, hardware and dry goods that stocked a village store. The others I didn't recognize until they introduced themselves after the mass. When I'd said goodbye to the last of my father's mourners, Père Etienne rattled off the names of a dozen others who'd sent their regards along with apologies for being unable to free themselves in the middle of a weekday morning. The kindness of all who came or sent greetings generated a radiance that dispelled my melancholy. What joy to know my father still lived in their hearts as well as my own.

Beyond the graveyard the heath rose gently toward a crest overlooking the sea. Under a blue sky, I climbed the slope and sat down in golden sunshine on a familiar rock at the top. As children Raoul and I had come here frequently, by night to look for *korrigans* dancing at the rising of the moon and by day to follow the path twisting down the cliff to the beach. From that vantage I was more convinced than ever that this was the headland in the seascape hanging in my bedroom at the house by the lake. No need today to imagine myself into the painting in hopes of recapturing the soothing sound of the sea. Down below the waves rolled against the shore with the ceaseless pulse of a beating heart, washing up the sand and ebbing back in time with my own breathing in and breathing out. After seven long years in the bustling din of Paris, the hushed rhythm of the Perros sea entranced me, holding me spellbound on my childhood seat as the morning spun out. The sun had almost reached the noon zenith when a footfall broke my reverie. "Do you think the *korrigans* will come this evening?"

I felt no surprise at Raoul's appearance. He belonged in Perros as much as I did. But the distress darkening his blue eyes and the lifeless pallor of his cheeks belied the teasing question. I withdrew a hand from my fur muff and touched the sleeve of his woolen top coat. "Raoul, you're unwell. You shouldn't have come."

"I had to come, Christine. I took the evening local and sat up all night thinking of nothing else." He dropped to his knees beside me, his eyes now level with my own. "I have to tell you what I wanted to say on New Year's Eve. That I love you. And I can't live without you."

I touched his pale cheek. "Oh, my dear." The anguish in his eyes dispelled all of my doubts. Raoul wasn't like his brother and never had been. He was my oldest friend, and he deserved the truth. I resolved to give him as much of it as I could. "Sit here." I patted the vacant rock beside me. "I've decided to tell you something serious. Very serious."

Without a word, he slid onto the rock, and I began my story. "You remember that first day you came to my dressing room? I told you that on his deathbed my father promised to send the Angel of Music to me."

His steady gaze never wavered. "I remember."

"When I came to the opera, I was sad. Very sad and very lonely. I found a little hideaway where I went whenever I needed to cry." I looked away from his sympathetic eyes, turning to face the sea. "One day when I was hiding a voice spoke to me, a wonderful voice with comforting words. And I knew my father had fulfilled his promise. The Angel of Music had come."

I glanced back to Raoul, who still stared at me, before turning again to the sea. "He told me I didn't need a teacher. I had the chorus master and the maestro for that. Instead the Angel of Music became my friend. My only friend. And for a long time that was enough. For him and for me."

"As the months and years passed, my singing hardly improved. My voice lost something when my father died." As I spoke, the misery of those years bloomed again inside me, clenching my belly and fisting my hands inside the fur muff. "And no matter how hard I tried, no matter how hard the chorus master tried, we couldn't get it back. The dream that first brought us to France was slipping away – shriveling, dissolving – and nothing I or anyone else tried could stop it. I would still have a singing career in the chorus. But I would never become prima donna."

I paused, blinking back sudden tears, uncertain whether they rose from sorrow at my lost voice or joy at the Phantom's miracle. "Then last spring the angel told me the time had come for him to be my teacher. In six months he transformed my voice. And one Sunday morning he appeared in my dressing room himself." I faced Raoul again. "The man, not just the voice."

His mouth curled in distaste as he spat out a question. "The man in the mask?"

I nodded. "My teacher."

Now came my turn to watch as Raoul sat silently staring out at the grey winter sea. For the first time in hours I felt the day's cold and realized the sun had passed behind a towering mass of clouds. Inside my heavy manteau, I shivered, and the movement immediately drew Raoul's attention. He reached out with both gloved hands, turned up the collar of my overcoat and let his hands linger on my shoulders. "Christine, do you expect me to believe that this man is a mystical messenger sent by your father from beyond the grave?"

The question was so unexpected that I had no immediate answer. Was that what I believed? In all honesty, I didn't know. For years and years I hadn't questioned, just accepted.

Raoul's fingers tightened on my shoulders and his eyes narrowed. "Well, I don't believe it. I'm not

178

so gullible as you. I think this man, whoever he is, is using the memory of your father – his promise, his ambition for you, even his grave – to manipulate you for his own nefarious ends."

Gullible! A horrible thing to say. But I bit back the irate words now dancing on my tongue, refusing to give in to anger. Above all things, my reply must be rational and intelligent. "What nefarious ends? That I sing the best I ever have? That I achieve my goal in life? That I visit my father's grave?"

His eyes flashed and hostility infused his voice. "To have power over a beautiful young woman. To control when and where and how often she sees her friends. To whisk her away without explanation at his whim to some secret spot where God only knows what he does with her."

I shrugged his hands off my shoulders and made no attempt to suppress an icy tone. "Your insinuation is insulting. My teacher is an honorable man and treats me always with the utmost respect. He has never snatched a kiss from me. He has never held my hand longer than was proper."

Raoul's face colored at my allusion to his own improprieties, but he didn't back down. "His secrecy, his mask – you must see how strange his behavior appears to others. I understand that you're grateful for his tutoring, but you must admit that the circumstances are more than a little bizarre."

I didn't answer right away, avoiding an admission that would escalate our snarling match and instead aiming for a warm and reassuring tone to defuse the argument. "If you understand my gratitude then you should also understand why I gave him the power to control my life for this opera season. There is no nefarious plot. And in May the promise I made to him expires."

At this point in his novel, Gaston Leroux preferred argument, depicting me running away from Raoul in fierce anger. Hours later, I reappeared, the novelist wrote, and Raoul followed me to my father's grave where I fell on my knees at the stroke of midnight when an unseen violinist started to play. After I left the graveyard, Leroux wrote that an unseen hand rolled human skulls at Raoul, who followed a shadow into the church, encountered a terrible death's head – "face to face with Satan" – and fell unconscious before the altar.

In fact, Raoul and I parted amicably. He apologized for intruding on such a solemn occasion. I assured him he needed no special invitation to visit me in Perros or in Paris. And we resolved to resume our afternoon teas when I returned to the opera the next day.

However, the novelist was right about some things. Later that day I did return to my father's grave, and the Phantom accompanied me. The sun hung low over the sea when he came for me in a hired carriage. On the short drive to the graveyard, he took a violin from the case resting on the seat beside him.

I smiled across at him. "Did Soeur Adeline also teach you the violin?"

He shook his head. "I learned by trailing after the gypsy fiddlers who joined the circus for a month or a season. None of them welcomed my attention. As I passed from one to the next, their cruel nickname came with me. Despite their disdain, they taught Don Juan well."

He carried the violin in one hand and a large bunch of red roses in the other as we made our way to Papa's grave. I knelt on one side, but the Phantom remained standing on the other. After I finished my prayer and opened my eyes, he leaned down to prop the roses against the pink granite tombstone and remained bent over the grave for a moment, his lips moving with silent words. Then he straightened and addressed me. "I wanted to come here with you to thank a man I never met for giving me the greatest gift I will ever receive."

My cheeks burned as I rose to my feet.

He stood across from me with his hands hanging at his sides, violin in one and bow in the other. "I wondered what would be the proper mark of respect to express my gratitude to the man who gave me my prima donna? And then I remembered something you told me long, long ago."

The Phantom tucked the violin under his chin, raised the bow in his hand and began my father's signature song, *The Resurrection of Lazarus*. The music evokes the awesome emotions described in the Bible story – the sisters' grief at the death of Lazarus, their wonder at the miracle that brings him back to life, their joy at having their brother living among them again. And about the Phantom's rendition Leroux was right as well. He played the most perfect music. Never before had the song been executed with such divine art. If the Angel of Music exists, that heavenly being could not have played better than the Phantom did at my father's grave as twilight fell across the wild Breton sea.

With his violin, the Phantom resurrected my father as well. Tears rolled down my cheeks as I listened to his music in that empty graveyard. By bringing me to Perros, the Phantom had returned my father to me. No longer was he a fading memory beloved by me alone. I now knew that others cherished him as well. Even one who'd never known my father in life had embraced him after his death. And I understood at last that as long as Papa remained alive in our hearts he was not truly gone.

With that realization came a rush of love for the Phantom. What caring he'd shown by bringing me to Brittany! I didn't need a passionate word or a caressing touch to prove that he loved me.

When the last note of the Phantom's violin faded to silence, he lowered the fiddle and the bow to his sides. I walked around my father's grave, slid my arms around the Phantom's waist and leaned against him. After a moment's hesitation, he wrapped his arms around me and returned the embrace. I'd been in his arms before – as Juliette and Rachel and the tragic heroines of other operas. But that was the first time we'd embraced as ourselves – a man and a woman. From deep down came the urge to lift my lips toward his, but I resisted the desire. His arms must be enough. For now.

18

I UNLOCKED THE DOOR of my dressing room early the next morning and instantly forgot my invitation to Raoul to join me for tea. The Phantom and I had taken the overnight train from Brittany, and he loomed behind me as the door swung open, stirring up clouds of fine, soft feathers that spilled from slits in the upholstered couch to cover the floor. Smears of black greasepaint defiled the beautiful dawn painted on my walls with foul words of anger and hate. A jagged scratch bisected one of the lyres carved on the doors of the armoire. An oozing pile of makeup and perfume stained the white marble top of the vanity. And on its pedestal, Papageno's cage stood uncovered and empty, the bent door hanging from a single hinge.

"Oh, no!" I started forward.

The Phantom gripped my shoulders from behind, and I stopped. "Let me."

For a moment I leaned against him. Then I nodded and turned back into the hallway as he stepped into my dressing room and quietly closed the door. He emerged a few minutes later with the still body of Papageno in his hand, the golden feathers hidden inside a linen handkerchief.

I touched my pet's burial shroud and raised tear-blurred eyes to the Phantom. "Who would do such a thing?"

"You can guess as well as I." Behind the mask, his dark eyes flashed. "This seals it. Now she must go." His voice softened. "Until your dressing room is repaired, you'll stay with me. We'll soon finish Juliette."

I spent the next two weeks at the house by the lake. The Phantom wanted me to perfect his Juliette before I began rehearsals with the other principal singers. Any day the managers would announce the opera that would close out the Palais Garnier's season. Speculation ran rampant in the press, with columnists trading insults over their pet theories. Some predicted a debut for the nightingale Daaé. Others prophesied a new opera of gritty realism in the style of Zola. A handful championed a Carlotta revival while one lonely Luddite derided speculation and suggested simply waiting for the announcement.

On this visit, the Phantom resumed our nightly outings to the Bois de Boulogne. With my performance at the Duchess de Zurich's party, the newspaper's interest in my "disappearance" had faded and a new sensation had caught the journalists' attention – a very pretty aerialist from Poland who performed with a troupe of famous fliers each night at the Folies-Bergères. Safe now from prying eyes, we continued as before, walking each night along the dark street behind the Longchamp grandstand while Gaston followed with the carriage. Sometimes I longed to feel the warmth of the sun upon my face, but I contented myself with the brilliance of the stars and the moon. Our visit to Perros was an exception. During daylight hours the Phantom preferred to be underground.

With work on the current season winding down, the Phantom turned his attention to selecting next year's productions. A table beside the piano bore a stack of opera scores and one in the library a matching stack of librettos. He spent less time at his work table, which had been cleared of all miniature sets except for *Roméo et Juliette*, but late one afternoon he lingered there with a pile of fabric swatches, all blood red. I put aside the book I'd been reading in the library and wandered over, taking a seat on a stool and leaning on his table to study the sketch he was working on. A man's costume with a doublet over knee breeches, a short cape and cuffed boots, all in brilliant red, plus a full-face mask of brightest white. The outfit might have worked for the masquerade scene in *Roméo et Juliette* except for that mask – a grinning skull.

"Who is it?" I pulled the drawing closer to me. "And what's it for?"

"My costume for the Mardi Gras ball. We must decide yours soon." The Phantom tossed me three swatches of fabric. "I'll go as Red Death, a role I played for years."

Just like that he opened another door into his past and allowed me through it. I'd detected the change in him before I could name the cause. A new ease in his manner. A new lightness in his step. Not until the long train ride back from Brittany did I understand the reason. He was happy. When it began I didn't know. The night of the gala, when he declared, "You are the one?" The day after

Christmas, when he unwrapped my gift? Yet when it began didn't really matter. What mattered was that happiness seemed to provide a shield against the pain in his past, and that shield enabled me to learn more about him.

As we sat at his work table that afternoon, the Phantom described his time as Red Death so vividly that I had no trouble seeing the troop of clowns romping in and out of a single spotlight as a curtain of black gauze dropped behind them. In the darkness beyond the curtain, stagehands wheeled into place a platform draped in gaudy red silk and topped with a golden throne. Dressed in matching silk, he took his seat. When the throne was new, his small boots dangled above the cloven-hoofed feet, his little fingers couldn't stretch to the ends of the clawed arms and his mop of dark hair fell far below the crowning horns. But by the time of his last performance his frame fit Lucifer's throne so well that the fallen angel's horns appeared to sprout from his own head.

"Ladies and gentlemen." A somber voice stilled the clowns frolicking before the dark curtain. "Mesdames et messieurs." The clowns departed, and for a few seconds, the spotlight remained empty. "Damen und herren." Into the spotlight stepped a gypsy who tucked a violin under his chin. "We have a most unwelcome visitor." A light came on behind the curtain to reveal the back of the golden throne. "Face of a devil, voice of an angel." As the curtain rose and the violinist struck up Mozart's *Requiem*, the throne spun slowly to face the audience. "I give you Red Death."

Revulsion swept across the crowd like a wave, a crescendo of gasps and moans and wails as his face came into view. A thousand nights on that throne he'd endured their loathing, but their reaction didn't wound him. The secret to his serenity was his music, the power of his voice to replace their disgust with wonder. "Day of wrath and terror looming, heaven and earth to ash consuming." And then, as the meaning of *Dies Irae* penetrated their awe, their wonder turned to terror. "What horror must invade the mind, when the approaching judge shall find and sift the deeds of all mankind."

The Phantom fell silent, his gaze drifting to the fabric swatches spread on the table before him. I pushed the trio he'd shown me back to him and let my hand brush against his. "But you stopped playing Red Death. And you stopped singing."

He raised his head, his dark eyes distant and locked on something I couldn't see. "When I was fifteen, I lost the ability to sing. The notes rose from my throat and danced on my tongue, eager for release, but I couldn't free them. They remained locked behind my teeth."

Only when he was alone could he unleash his music at will. Cruelty had kept him silent so long that in front of an audience he required some sign to free his song. Soeur Adeline had told him he was an angel. At the circus he'd always found a sign somewhere in the eyes of his audience – a grandmother's grief for any wounded child, a young girl's sympathy for any sorrowful friend, a wise man's benevolence for any suffering he saw. Even for a devil child, the light of compassion had always shone in someone's eyes.

But that night the circus performed in a Prussian garrison town and the tent filled with the

Kaiser's soldiers. And he was grown, almost a man. That night he found no sign of mercy.

For the third time, the violinist repeated his cue to sing and then let the fiddle fall silent. He remained stone still on the throne, offering no hint of the turmoil within, the agony of unsung notes stinging his lungs like a swarm of angry bees. A whisper threaded the hushed tent. Then a murmur. And another. In the front row, a soldier tossed a quip to a comrade who replied with a loud guffaw. In a moment, they'd begin throwing things at the throne.

Slowly, he rose to his feet. If he could no longer sing, he would speak instead. "When the wicked are confounded, doomed to flames of woe unbounded." He stepped down from the throne and walked to the edge of the ring, stopping in front of the unlucky soldier, who stank of beer. "When the Judge shall sit, whatever is hidden shall be seen, nothing shall remain unpunished."

The soldier's smirk vanished. Offering his red-gloved hand, Red Death pressed his advantage. Wide-eyed, the warrior cringed away from his touch. Following Red Death's lead, the violinist drew the bow across the strings, underscoring the soldier's fear with a raucous howl.

Finally, Red Death let his hand drop to his side and stepped backward until he reached the throne, his gaze still fixed on the soldier. "We'll meet again." With a poof of air from above, the gauze curtain drifted down. He smiled at the drunken soldier. "Soon."

The sneer twisting the Phantom's face faded into a smile. "After that night, Lecadre retired Lucifer's throne and Red Death's act." Behind his mask, the storm had left his dark eyes, leaving them calm, almost serene. "But I remained with the troupe as the magician's apprentice. And I took up the violin."

Afterwards I brooded about the Phantom's revelations. Red Death troubled me. He enjoyed frightening his audience. He enjoyed taunting that soldier. He enjoyed exercising power over other people. I told myself that Red Death was just a character, one that the Phantom had abandoned many years ago. Still, the disclosure of that part of his past left me uneasy because I'd given him power over me.

A few days later I received a note from Madame Valérius that turned my fretting in a new direction. She'd had a visit from Raoul, who told her that his anger at being stood up for tea had turned into worry about my well-being. When he arrived at my dressing room at the appointed time, Raoul said he found the door locked, but days later his brother overheard the opera dancers whispering about an attack on Christine Daaé. Raoul rushed to the managers' office, where Poligny and Debienne assured him that I hadn't been attacked even as they explained my absence as a sick leave. So he'd come to our flat without invitation to see what he could discover about my whereabouts and my welfare.

"The Vicomte said you'd told him about your angel when he saw you in Brittany so I saw no harm in telling Raoul you were staying with your good genius for a little while," Madame Valérius wrote. "I told him not to worry, that you are fine, which he'll see for himself at the masquerade ball on Fat Tuesday."

Later in my bedroom I sat at the small secretary with a blank sheet of writing paper and tried to find the words that would set things right with Raoul. Again. But after crumpling three false starts, I gave up. Nothing I wrote conveyed my genuine shock at the killing of my pet or my sincere alarm at the violence directed at me. And I'd made too many excuses already. In my absence, he'd blame the Phantom. Again. In my absence, he always believed the worst. Only when we were together, where he could see my eyes and hear my voice, did Raoul listen to reason. When I saw him at the masked ball, I would repeat the assurance I'd given him in Perros. In May, when the season ended at the Palais Garnier, I could look to the future and so could he. All of us could, including the Phantom.

Just before the start of Lent an event occurred which transfixed Paris and gave me my costume for the Mardi Gras ball. As he entered his eightieth year, Victor Hugo, France's greatest living writer – greatest, perhaps, of all time – received congratulations from a grateful nation as he sat all day in the open window of his house on Avenue d'Eylau while a birthday parade of 600,000 revelers marched past. At the breakfast table the next morning, I offered the Phantom highlights from the newspaper accounts while he filled our cups with hot chocolate. "His grandchildren joined him in the window. The marchers left flowers before his door – a vast mound. The parade took six hours. The lines stretched all the way down the Champs-Elysees and past the Luxor obelisk. The parade monitors wore cornflowers to honor Cosette from *Les Miserables*."

"Cosette?" The Phantom stared at the chocolate pot in his hand, now hovering above his empty cup. "She's not quite right. But definitely Hugo. Esmeralda, perhaps?" He looked at me, his head tilting to one side. "Like your Juliette, she lived in the Court of Miracles. And your greatest admirer is also a living gargoyle."

I folded the newspaper aside. "You equate yourself with Quasimodo?"

"The hunchback and I have certain similarities, you must admit." He shrugged, finally filling his cup. He raised it in a mock salute. "You'll look very fetching as a gypsy with bare shoulders and bright petticoats."

"A blonde gypsy?" I returned his salute with my own cup of chocolate. "With blue eyes?"

"Esmeralda wasn't really a gypsy either." He gave me a genuine grin. "But, if you insist, we'll get you a black wig."

The Phantom returned to Esmeralda late that night when, after a final practice that included running through all of Juliette's songs from fifteen scenes, we rode toward the Longchamp racetrack in his brougham. My hair hung loose around my shoulders, as Juliette's would for much of the opera. He pulled off one leather glove, lifted a strand of my hair and wrapped it around his hand. "No black wig for you. I refuse to let you hide this beauty."

As Gaston slowed the horses on the road behind the grandstand, I longed for the Phantom to continue winding my hair around his hand until he'd reeled me across the carriage and into his arms. For a timeless moment we remained frozen, poised on the brink, yearning to come together.

191

The carriage stopped with a small jerk, and an anguished voice shattered the night silence outside the brougham. "Christine!"

Gaston's whip cracked the horses into a gallop as something burst from a clump of bushes beside the road. I slid around on my seat to look out the rear window. In the middle of the moonlit road behind us stood Raoul.

"Your sailor boy's gotten a bit frantic." I turned back and faced the Phantom, who'd dropped my lock of hair and relaxed against the leather bench. "Perhaps the time has come for you to see more of the Vicomte de Chagny. With a chaperone, of course."

19

*T*HE PROSPECT of my first ball with the Phantom as my escort left me dizzy with excitement. All of Paris loved to dance, and public balls were a fixture of life for everyone, from the *canaille* to the *gratin*. In winter, Parisians danced indoors – ragpickers at a dance hall in the 5th arrondissement, artists at the casino in Montmartre and market women at Ragache's grand salon on Rue de Sèvre. In summer, dancers took to the streets – soldiers held their balls at the old city gates, students their wild bacchanal at Jardin Bullier, and shopgirls their Sunday afternoon dances in the courtyard of Moulin de la Galette. For a franc or two, working girls like Victorine could leave behind the drudgery of their lives for a few hours of swirling gaiety with gentlemen as eager to flirt as they. During Lent, the dancers hid their frivolity from the clergy at masked balls that began at midnight and reveled until dawn. Each year the most extravagant *bal masque* came first – the Fat Tuesday masquerade at the Palais Garnier – and was the only public ball that welcomed ladies because few cocottes could afford the 20 franc admission. Even so, Madame Valérius had always discouraged me from going. Until now.

On the afternoon of the ball, I sat on a tall stool beside the Phantom's piano, trying on the masks that Eugenie Savatier had sent along with my costume. As usual, the costumer had quickly pulled together a striking ensemble with a tight flowered bodice laced around a simple white blouse and a full black skirt tucked up on one side to reveal a petticoat striped in brilliant jewel tones. I needed only a glance at the mirror in my hand to know that the gold-sequined mask definitely wouldn't do for Esmeralda. "Only one of these works." I replaced the glitter with a black harlequin's mask and spun around to face the keyboard. "What do you think?"

The Phantom looked up from the composition on the music shelf, his finger still pointing to the measure under review and his pencil still clamped in his teeth. After a few second's study of my face, he nodded. Before I'd pulled off the harlequin mask, he turned back to writing the music which lately occupied more and more of his time.

From the vantage of my elevated seat I looked down upon his bent head and noticed for the first time in weeks his second-skin mask, a clear edge running straight across his forehead just below the line of his dark hair. When he sang, the Phantom preferred the supple freedom of a black satin mask, but at all other times, in public and in private, he wore that rigid second skin. After the catastrophic wounds of the Great War, masks like the Phantom's became more commonplace, and not long ago I saw a story about them in *Le Figaro*'s weekend supplement. Sculptors fashion the masks of copper thin as a calling card that's painted to match the skin tone and held in place with earpieces, like spectacles. I thought, "Earpieces? No wonder his hair was always a little too long and shaggy." But on that long ago day of my first ball my thoughts had turned to another of the Phantom's masks. While he worked on his composition, I slid off my stool and walked to the pipe organ, trading the mirror in my hand for the small gilt frame laying on the console. His first mask. "We won't speak of it. Never." So he'd decreed on the day we met. But in the five months since things between us had changed so much. I might never have the courage to question him about the second-skin mask, but perhaps I'd earned enough of his trust to ask about the one he'd framed under glass. And so I returned to my stool and waited.

Minutes passed. He worked with complete concentration, moving measure by measure through his composition, breaking it into pieces and testing each piece separately. I couldn't make sense of the fragments. Now and then he hummed a few bars – notes already on the page or those that should be? Sometimes he pounded out chord after chord – up a half step here, down a full octave there – but I couldn't tell whether he was testing a variation or if the chords came from the score itself. He took the pencil from his teeth to make corrections – several on this page, none on the next. Finally, after most of an hour had slipped by, he gathered the pages from the music shelf and placed them in a music folio on the table beside the piano. Only then did he seem to notice me. "Christine! You've been so quiet I thought you'd gone."

"I've been sitting here wondering about this." I lifted the gilt frame from my lap and offered it to him. "Anyone can see that you cherish this mask."

The Phantom didn't take the framed mask but instead looked at me for a long moment. "Lecadre had brought the circus back to France. We were performing in market towns on the outskirts of Paris." He finally took the frame from my hand. "One afternoon the magician came to my wagon. 'Tonight we have business in the city,' he told me. 'Get into your evening clothes.'"

"He waved a scrap of black in his hand." The Phantom mimicked the gesture with the frame he now held. "'And wear this.' So I did."

He gripped the frame with both hands, staring down at it, rubbing a thumb over the glass. "This mask changed everything. People still looked. I remember a girl selling flowers, standing on a corner surrounded by tin containers of dahlias and zinnias and asters. She looked at me twice, but I read only curiosity in her eyes. Most people who noticed the mask were indifferent."

His gaze returned to me, his dark eyes wide with remembered wonder behind the second-skin mask. "No one drew back in horror. No one shouted a curse before crossing the street to avoid me. No one nudged a neighbor or jabbed a finger to point me out. I stood in the crush of opera goers queuing outside the theater on Rue le Peletier, pulled off my glove to touch the satin covering my cheek and decided this mask was a miracle."

How I longed for the sleek simplicity of the Phantom's miraculous mask that night at the ball. Red Death's bare-bone skull attracted the notice of everyone at the Palais Garnier. That night the

Phantom welcomed their stares. With his broad shoulders and narrow waist, he cut a fine figure in his form-fitting doublet and breeches of satin the color of blood. The costume attracted the reveler's attention, but his death's head mask spurred them to action. As soon as the attendant took our cloaks, the Phantom drew me into a promenade and the guests fell away before us. Under the brilliant chandeliers in the grand foyer, the fragrant and glittering sea of silk and velvet and lace parted at the sight of his frightful mask as we strolled the length of parquet floor. In the mirrored rotunda beneath the auditorium where the dancers whirled around the mosaic floor, guests loitering on the edge of the dance ducked behind the red marble columns or turned to face the niches lining the wall as we approached.

People recoiled everywhere we went, but the Phantom made no remark. Instead he inclined his head toward mine and kept up a steady commentary as we paraded through the *bal masque*. "There's a Quasimodo to match you. Shall we hail him and see if he asks you to dance?" Together we counted the most popular costumes – Napoleon I and Henri IV for the men, Marie Antoinette and Madame de Pompadour for the women. "Queens and whores but not a single saint," he marveled. "Why no Jeanne d'Arc, redeemer of France, or Genevieve, savior of Paris? Because women refuse to wear armor or sackcloth to a ball?" By the time we finished our circuit of the ballroom, a genuine smile had replaced the one I'd pasted on when we began, and I stopped worrying about his motives for wearing the ghoulish costume. Perhaps Red Death meant that the anger and pain in his past still tormented the Phantom. Or perhaps the choice signified nothing. Esmeralda ended her days on a gibbet, after all, but that didn't imply anything about my state of mind.

The Phantom guided me back up the marble steps of the grand staircase and into the grand foyer where we stood together by one of the doors to the smoking loggia overlooking the Place de l'Opéra. That's where Raoul found us a few minutes later. I recognized him immediately, despite his mask and the beard glued to his chin. The dagger at his waist and the sword on the hip of his simple costume from another age suggested a man of action, so I took a wild guess. A great explorer?

"Welcome, Jacques Cartier, founder of New France." I held out my hand. His blue eyes gleamed with appreciation as he took it. "Many thanks, Esmeralda, queen of the gypsies." Rather than raise my hand to his lips, Raoul erupted with laughter and I soon joined him. When our giddiness subsided, I turned to the Phantom, who'd remained silent and still during our outburst. "Maestro, I'd like you to meet Raoul, the Vicomte de Chagny." I turned back to Raoul. "Raoul, this is my teacher."

Side by side at last. For a long moment, neither man spoke. Each held his ground and stared at the other while I studied them both. Could two men be more different? Their choice of costumes told that tale. Foreboding Red Death embodied the gloom of life's end and swashbuckling Cartier the optimism of life's journey. Such different men and yet I was powerfully drawn to both. With his intensity and obsession, the Phantom thrilled me, but the precarious bond between us left me feeling vulnerable. With his confidence and tenderness, Raoul soothed me, and the constancy of our affection made me feel safe. Still, I feared both the tedium of the sanctuary Raoul offered and the recklessness of the passion the Phantom inspired.

At last the Phantom broke the silence. "Christine tells me you're her oldest friend and serve the Republic as a naval officer." He inclined his head slightly. "On both counts you have my esteem."

Raoul answered the Phantom's praise with a brisk bow. "Thank you, monsieur."

The Phantom turned his gaze upon me. "Although she hasn't said anything yet, I suspect Christine is eager to dance."

Raoul seemed taken aback by the Phantom's offer, but I wasn't. I grabbed his arm and gave a little tug. "Thank you, Raoul. I'd love to dance."

After another chilly exchange of niceties with the Phantom, Raoul took my arm like a proper escort and steered me toward the grand staircase. After we'd taken a few steps, I burst out with my news. "You'll never guess what's happened! He's lifted our restrictions. We're free to see each other wherever and whenever we want."

Again we laughed, like children released from an onerous duty. We danced that way too, struggling to contain our vitality for a stately minuet and almost vibrating with impatience as we waited for the other couples during a quadrille. Only the livelier dances satisfied us, the polkas, waltzes and mazurkas, but we also remained on the floor for the pas de gras and polonaise. We both knew it was wrong for me to abandon my escort and for Raoul to monopolize my time. But I wanted to dance and Raoul wanted to be with me. And so we defied convention to continue gliding and twirling around the rotunda floor.

The Phantom finally put an end to our dancing interlude when he appeared in the ballroom and claimed a spot by one of the marble columns near the platform that held the small orchestra. I lifted my hand from Raoul's shoulder as I spun past, signaling to the Phantom my imminent return. "I'm afraid this mazurka will have to be our last dance." I smiled up at Raoul. "I can't remember a more enjoyable evening."

Raoul sent a hard look in the Phantom's direction and I braced myself for another reproach. Instead his stormy eyes cleared and he returned my smile. "The first of many, I hope."

By the time I reached the Phantom a tall Cardinal Richelieu and a plump Pierrot had joined him. Although masks concealed their features, when Richelieu spoke I recognized the manager Poligny and knew the clown had to be his partner, Debienne. "You must see reason." The cardinal's whine held an angry edge. "These men are very influential and they wield great power."

The Phantom stiffened. "Artistic decisions in this opera house are mine alone. As a result of your toadying the Jockey Club now dictates the membership of the corps de ballet, but I will not allow such idiocy to harm my opera company."

The confrontation had drawn the attention of people nearby, including Carlotta, who stood a dozen feet away among a knot of admirers and watched us over the lacey edge of her open fan. But the blare of the nearby orchestra prevented the voices of the Phantom and the managers from carrying.

Pierrot spread his hands wide. "La Carlotta's friends—"

The Phantom cut him off with a hiss. "Carlotta must go. She not only lacks talent but has revealed a viciousness that I will not tolerate. You saw what she did to Mlle. Daaé's dressing room." He reached for my hand and drew me close beside him. "Let me make the choice before you perfectly clear: either Carlotta goes, or I do."

Richelieu raised his clasped hands like a penitent offering up a prayer. "But maestro—"

The Phantom leaned toward the manager until they stood almost nose to nose. At the moment he spoke, the orchestra fell silent and everyone standing nearby heard his words. "I repeat: Either she goes. Or I do."

Richelieu backed quickly away and the fat clown waddled after him. The Phantom slipped his arm through mine and leaned down to whisper in my ear. "This will be another waltz. Shall we dance?"

Without waiting for my reply, the Phantom stepped onto the mosaic floor, drawing me along with him. His arm came around me, pulling me close, and as the music began, he spun me into the waltz. In his arms I forgot all about Raoul and the managers and Carlotta's viciousness. I closed my eyes, giving myself up to the dance, and the heat of his touch drove away memories his ghastly mask. At that moment all I could think about was the nearness of him and my fervent desire that dawn would never come.

20

*A*FTER THE MASQUERADE, the Phantom vanished from my life as suddenly as he'd arrived in it. He took me home from the Fat Tuesday ball after one wonderful waltz. I sat opposite him as we rode the few short blocks from the Palais Garnier. Dawn remained hours away, and the city still pulsed with Mardi Gras excitement. When Gaston halted the horses beside my apartment building on Rue Notre Dame des Victoires, the clamor of distant revelry penetrated the carriage. A joyful shriek. An eruption of laughter. A bellowed song. By the glow of the streetlamp flooding into the carriage I saw that the Phantom had removed the awful skull and now wore a black satin mask.

I sat forward on the seat, gathering my velvet evening cloak in one fist. "Thank you for taking me. I had a marvelous time."

He intercepted the hand I reached toward the door. "Stay a moment." He gave my fingers a gentle squeeze before releasing my hand.

I sank back against the leather seat. "Of course."

"Our lessons are at an end. You're quite pre-pared to replace Carlotta in *La Juive*. And with Juliette you're ready to join Maestro Chénier and rehearse with the other principal singers." He shook his head gently. "I won't ask my diva to answer to two masters."

The Phantom's words should have delighted me. He'd said out loud what I already knew in my heart. We'd completed the transformation of my voice, which now surpassed those of all the other sopra-nos at the Palais Garnier. I'd become his prima donna. I should have been elated at our achieve-ment but instead dread soured my stomach. The beginning of my new career mattered less than the ending of our private lessons.

"You won't see me for a few weeks." His smile did nothing to dispel the chill settling over me at his words. "I'll be locked in my house finishing my composition."

Though I ached inside, I did my best to inject a bright tone into my voice. "The one you've been working on? You haven't told me anything about it."

"It's a concerto. For organ. The history of my life told in music." He gave me a careless shrug, but I'd seen for myself how much the piece gripped him. "I put it aside two years ago because I didn't know how it would end."

I tilted my head and smiled back at him. "And you do now?"

Behind the black satin mask, his eyes glowed. "I think so."

I widened my smile. "What do you call it?"

He let out a quick bark of laughter. "Don Juan Triumphant."

I raised my arms as if playing an invisible violin. "That Don Juan?"

He laughed again. "Yes."

That laughter, once so rare, reminded me of the new side of the Phantom that I'd discovered since Christmas – the happy man. He couldn't hide his excitement about his concerto. And I wouldn't begrudge him the solitude he needed to finish the piece. He'd invited me into his life before and would do so again. I felt certain of that when we finally said goodnight.

Late that afternoon Raoul came to the flat. After returning from church with a smudge of Lenten ashes on her brow, Madame Valérius had taken to her bed for her daily nap so I received him alone. Victorine brought in a tray of tea and madeleines, and then returned to her soupmaking in the kitchen. While I poured the tea, Raoul studied the framed photographs of my father and Professor Valérius on the marble mantelpiece. When he finally sat down, he looked forlorn.

I placed a cookie on the saucer and handed him a brimming cup. "The pictures of Papa and the Professor have made you sad."

Raoul took the cup and saucer but didn't drink. The next moment he set both down on the table between us. "Christine–"

Interrupting himself, Raoul leaped to his feet and bolted around the table to join me on the velvet settee. "Last night I thought I might soon have my heart's desire."

After I set down my own tea cup, he grabbed my hands. "You were happy to be with me. And you were glad that we're now free to see each other."

"I was very happy to be with you." Mystified by his intention, I frowned. "And I'm looking forward to spending more time with you."

Raoul's grip on my hands tightened. "When your teacher came into the ballroom, everything changed. He draws you like a magnet. I saw it with my own eyes. Can you resist him? Do you even want to?"

His words shocked me, and I tried to draw away. But Raoul clung to my hands. I stopped struggling against him. "What did you see?"

"I watched from across the ballroom." His blue eyes lacked their usual animation, chased away by misery and confusion. "He reached for your hand, and you were mesmerized. He led you onto the dance floor, and your face was radiant. He took you into his arms for the waltz and your eyes closed with ecstasy."

I swallowed a bubble of panic as Raoul's eyes darkened with despair. "The ball began like a dream, filling me with hope. But it turned into a nightmare when I realized that you're under some kind of spell. Today my hope is gone."

My heart lurched at his sorrow. "My poor Raoul. I'm not spellbound. I've no voice lessons scheduled and he's locked himself away to finish a composition, so I have plenty of free time to spend with you."

I leaned my face against his, forehead touching forehead. "You've forgotten what I told you in Perros. There is no nefarious plot. And in May the promise I made to him expires."

A hopeful note entered his voice. "And when it expires? What then?"

"When the Palais Garnier season ends, I can look to the future." I pressed a light kiss against his lips. "And you can, too."

As always, Raoul believed me face to face. I understood his frequent need for reassurance. In his years at the naval academy and the long voyage around the world, he'd clung to his memory of me, a lonely sailor far from home romanticizing an adolescent crush into true love. He'd returned to Paris to watch his fantasy dissolved by reality and, as a result, now distrusted himself. Yet since Raoul's return his sailor's daydreams had come true. I did love him in some way. And I accepted the truth of his next words. "Don't you forget what I said in Perros. I love you, Christine."

Raoul's native optimism quickly resurfaced, and we spent a pleasant hour scheduling outings that would amuse us both. That evening Victorine and I didn't leave for the theater until the last possible moment. *Les Pêcheurs de Perles* had returned to the schedule, and I needed only a few minutes to get into my costume and join the chorus. Not until I'd slid under my duvet in my bedroom beneath the eaves did I allow myself to think about my spurt of panic at hearing Raoul's fears.

Mesmerized. Radiant. Ecstatic. That's how Raoul described my response to my teacher's touch. Had the Phantom seen me the same way? Is that why he ended our lessons so abruptly? Had he pushed me away after the ball because I'd shown so clearly when we danced just how close to him I truly wanted to be? Despite the chill air of a March midnight, my cheeks burned. In the darkness, old doubts reclaimed me. His hesitation before returning my embrace at Perros. The woman who sometimes joined him in Box 5. His open contempt for everyone and everything that lived above the ground. To escape my bleak meditation, I deliberately turned my thoughts to Raoul, soothing myself with happier memories that finally carried me into the refuge of sleep.

For the next few weeks, Raoul had me to himself. I heard nothing from the Phantom and, freed from the obligation of voice lessons, discovered many empty hours in even the busiest week. Raoul eagerly filled them with merry outings that also amused my chaperones, Madame Valérius and Victorine. He'd returned from sea with a long list of amusements – horse races, champagne fêtes, boating parties, boulevard promenades, private dinners – and proved as good as his word.

In her last years, Madame Valérius liked to regale dinner guests with memories of our first meal at Lapérouse on Quai des Grand Augustins. Raoul had booked one of the small private dining rooms, which included a small table and a large couch because most guests came for a feast of love as well as food. "Three diners, Raoul told them, and we arrived to find the staff peeking out from every nook and cranny, all agog to catch a glimpse of a scandalous trio, only to find two young people and a creaking widow with a cane." Over time, she honed her story to perfection, repeating the tale word for word and then turning bright eyes on Raoul, to whom she granted the parting shot. "Still," he'd sigh in mock apology, "you must admit that you've never had a better chocolate soufflé."

Such simple kindnesses explained why, day by day, Raoul won more of my heart. Other suitors might have resented always having a chaperone in tow, but Raoul genuinely liked mine and treated them with courtesy and patience. As a maid, Victorine wasn't an appropriate companion for dinner, but he made sure to reward her sweet tooth whenever she accompanied me. She especially liked Café Tortoni, preferring a seat inside near the marble bar whose shining zinc counter cast a reflecting glitter across the carefully arranged glasses – tall goblets for champagne, small balloons for brandy, squat tumblers for vin ordinaire and sturdy mugs for beer. She always ordered a dish of Italian ice flavored with rum and topped with chopped almonds and glacé cherries.

Victorine's appetite wasn't the only way Raoul indulged her. One fine Sunday afternoon in late March, he took us to the Louvre to show me Joseph Vernet's paintings of French seaports, "Marseille. Toulon. Bordeaux. Rochefort," Victorine grumbled. "Harbor after harbor. Didn't this fellow get bored? I certainly am." Raoul laughed and guided us across the hall to one of the long galleries devoted to French painting, where Victorine took the lead in viewing the work of Charles Lebrun, Nicholas Poussin, Jacques-Louis David and other masters. When we reached the end of the gallery, she groaned. "*The Rape of the Sabine Women. Alexander entering Babylon. The Raising of Lazarus. Brutus condemning his sons to death.* Must the picture always be from the Bible or ancient history? Do none of these artists see anything worth painting in our world?" Raoul surprised me by agreeing with Victorine and promising to take us to an exhibition of just such art opening soon on the Boulevard des Capucines. "You've surely seen Monsieur Degas at the opera? He's one of the organizers."

A few days after the opening of the show of artists rejected by the Salon, Raoul escorted us to the makeshift gallery in a flat behind Nadar's atelier, five badly-lit rooms with low ceilings and too much furniture. As we dodged among a platoon of rickety chairs with rush seats, I recognized the hand of Degas in a half dozen canvases and admired the family scenes captured by two women painters who'd defied the conventions of the day to develop their talent in art. But a picture painted by a Paris stockbroker had grabbed most of the attention, a nude with a bulging belly seated on an unmade bed and sewing. Raoul let us study the canvas in silence for a few moments before he pulled out a newspaper clipping to share the critic's judgment. "He calls it a vehement expression of reality: 'This is not the smooth, even skin that the other artists produce; here is skin beneath which the blood flows.'" Victorine bent toward the painting, perhaps intent on finding the pulse throbbing beneath the skin, while Raoul continued. "'Here is a girl of our days, a girl who doesn't pose for an audience, a girl who is neither lascivious nor affected, who is simply occupied with mending her clothes." At that Victorine sniffed with disdain. "A lot that fellow knows. She'll be blind soon enough from sewing with her back to the light. And whoever heard of doing your mending bare naked?" Raoul and I shared a smile before he launched into a patient explanation of the painter's intent.

What a shock to learn that Raoul had a taste for rebellious painters! That afternoon I realized for the first time that he and the Phantom were not complete opposites. They shared a similar independence of mind. In truth, Raoul's friendship with me and kindness to my chaperones demonstrated that as well. Few French aristocrats acknowledged the petit bourgeoisie and even fewer noticed the serving class. But no matter the outing, if we were driving in his carriage with Madame Valérius through the Bois de Boulogne or promenading with Victorine along the grand boulevards, Raoul behaved toward us exactly as he behaved to the aristocrats we met along the way.

The only drawback to our new freedom came in the columns of Paris newspapers. The announcement of my coming debut as Juliette had revived the interest of journalists, whose spies sighted us whenever Raoul and I went out together. Day after day our names appeared in one newspaper or another. Not that we were singled out. The names of dozens of other people also appeared in the gossip columns, but I was unnerved by the attention all the same. And I couldn't help wondering if publicity wasn't exactly what the Phantom intended when he lifted the restrictions that had kept our friendship private? But I pushed that thought away and concentrated instead on the pleasures of freedom. With Raoul I could appear in public without the heavy veiling I wore on my outings with the Phantom. With Raoul I strolled anywhere I pleased in the brilliant light of early spring. With Raoul I lived above the ground.

One day, after rehearsing Juliette with the other soloists, I returned to my dressing room just as Victorine headed off for another tittle-tattle with Madame Giry. "What does she have to say these days about the opera ghost?"

Victorine paused in the doorway. "Nothing at all. He hasn't been to his box for weeks."

After the door closed behind her, I crossed to my vanity and sat down to freshen up before Raoul arrived. Thanks to the opera's craftsmen, no trace remained of Carlotta's vandalism. The walls had been repainted, the wardrobe refinished and the vanity's marble top replaced. When I'd made it clear to everyone – the Phantom, Raoul and the managers – that Papageno could not be replaced, they'd removed the pedestal that had held the canary's cage. But none of that mattered. Despite the careful restoration, I would never again feel truly at home in my dressing room.

The door banged open behind me. "Wait till you see!" Victorine darted to my side, a newspaper clenched in her fist. "Is it true? Oh, please say it's true!"

She offered me the newspaper – *Le Petit Journal* – and pointed to an item in a popular social column: "An April debut and a title in June: Swedish nightingale Christine Daaé plays Juliette next month in the Palais Garnier's first staging of Gounod's masterpiece and becomes a vicomtesse in June. A little bird tells us that she's accepted Raoul de Chagny, whose title is among the oldest in France."

I let the newspaper fall to the floor. "It's rubbish." I sighed and shook my head. "Another bit of viciousness from a little bird named Carlotta. Her influential patrons failed to persuade the managers to cast her as Juliette. Now she's hoping they'll see the error by suggesting I'm leaving the stage. But it's rubbish. All of it."

Victorine scooped up the newspaper and smoothed it against her apron. "Carlotta's not herself lately. They say she cries a lot. They say she may be drinking."

I looked up at her. "When did this start?"

Victorine shrugged. "A while ago. Around Christmas."

Before I could inquire further, Raoul rapped on the door. Victorine let him in and then scurried down the hall to meet Madame Giry as he took a seat on the sofa. The item in *Le Petit Journal* didn't bother him. He tossed the newspaper aside with a smile. "If I didn't have to wait until May to speak about the future, it might have been true."

I paced the room, my arms folded across my waist. "Your brother would never approve."

Raoul slouched down on the couch and stretched out his legs to block my path. "I don't need his permission. I have some money of my own, and I have a profession."

Faced with the blockade of his crossed ankles, I stopped and stared down at him without speaking. I found it hard to believe that a man with one of the oldest titles in France would marry an opera girl.

He patted the empty sofa cushion beside him, inviting me to sit. "Sometimes I think Philippe's a fool. His pride has made has him miserable."

I dropped onto the couch, perching on the edge of the cushion.

"Philippe loves Sorelli, but he won't marry her. And what's it gotten him? Misery!" Raoul snaked an arm around my waist and drew me against him. "I won't let that happen to me."

21

NEVER BEFORE had I visited the house by the lake without an invitation. The Phantom gave me a key to the hidden gate on Rue Scribe for only one purpose: voice lessons. For weeks after the Fat Tuesday ball I'd hoped my teacher would summon me, but I heard nothing from him. Even as I enjoyed Raoul's company, I longed to confront the Phantom with my suspicion that his sudden approval of our friendship was part of a publicity campaign. Like the picture postcards. Like my "disappearance." Like the newspaper report of my mysterious companion. Despite longing to see the Phantom and to know the truth, I couldn't bring myself to invade his privacy. I didn't want to make him angry. And I couldn't bear it if he rejected me. But a disturbing incident overcame my misgivings.

One day after another arduous rehearsal of *Roméo et Juliette*, I walked back to our flat on Rue Notre Dame des Victoires to find a horse-drawn hearse pulled up at the curb before the building, a grand vehicle with polished brass, gleaming black paint and glass windows etched with a filigree of flowers. Alarmed by the sight, I quickened my pace, but a shout from the undertaker stopped me when I reached the stoop. "Mlle. Daaé?"

I spun around to find him leaning down from his tall seat with an ivory envelope held out in his hand. After a moment's hesitation, I stepped to the curb and accepted it. The undertaker tipped his stovepipe hat before starting the team of horses with a twitch of his whip.

As the hearse rolled away, I tore open the envelope, halfway hoping to find another invitation to perform for a charity or endorse a face cream, even though the macabre courier suggested that this must be a darker missive. Still, the venom contained in the undertaker's envelope shocked me. Not a poison pen letter exactly – that implies coherence. More like a riddle, except the clues proved utterly incomprehensible. Only one phrase made sense: "the boatman on Garnier's Styx." To me, that meant the Phantom.

I hurried back to the opera in the falling dusk. No queues wound away from the ticket windows because that evening the stage was dark, but late shoppers and early revelers, omnibuses and carriages, thronged the square outside the Palais Garnier. I threaded through them and turned into Rue Scribe, loitering for a few minutes beside the carriage ramp of the Emperor's Pavilion, waiting for empty sidewalks so I could slip unnoticed into the alcove that hid the Phantom's gate. The noise of the city subsided as I descended the narrow ramped passage and disappeared completely when I rounded the corner halfway down, leaving only the quiet hiss of the gas lamps to break the silence. What if he wasn't home? As I neared the doorway, his pipe organ answered my question with a fearsome sob.

I stopped walking and listened, soon realizing that I'd heard the despairing elegy once before, on my first visit to the house by the lake. I sidled as close to the door as I dared and then lowered myself to the stone floor. If this was the Phantom's concerto – the history of his life told in music – I wanted to hear every note.

The Phantom built his concerto on a foundation of melody almost childlike in its simplicity and yet filled with such sorrow that my heart ached. This was his childhood, punctuated momentarily by a stab of fear or a flight of joy, but always lonely and always sad. In the passageway outside his door, I hugged my knees against my chest, weighed down by the story his music told of an unwanted little boy.

Just when I thought I couldn't bear to hear any more, a new theme emerged in the Phantom's concerto, a quiet thread of bright counterpoint, distant and barely heard but still a sharp contrast to the boy's dark melody. The new theme deepened as it grew louder, growing in complexity until it burst forth as a sacred hymn that overwhelmed the boy's song. Soeur Adeline. The Phantom's Angel of Music. The burden of the music lightened and I smiled, glorying in the angelic choir that completed the first movement of the Phantom's concerto.

But even holy women die, and with the old nun's passing, the boy was once again alone as the second movement began. The greater intricacy of his melody now bespoke youth and a higher octave suggested a lessening of sorrow. Again a new theme arose in the distance, a boisterous and rollicking tune that grew in intensity as the youth's melody diminished until the magician Lecadre and his circus took over the concerto. Soon a grim new motif wound through the carnival air – Red Death and his *Dies Irae*. As always, Red Death disturbed me, and I stared at the glowing gas in the lamp beside the Phantom's door, burning away the image of a ghoulish skull that arose in my mind. I wanted Lecadre's circus back but was even happier when the notes of the *Requiem* dissolved into the youth's melody as it reappeared, stronger and more confident, to conclude the second movement.

The Phantom I knew appeared in the concerto's third movement, a man in full – gifted, determined and assured. His melody advanced with the steady, marching rhythm of work. Brief passages of opera – *Rigoletto, Fidelio, Idomeneo* – drifted through like daydreams while under it all ran a hushed but lively folk dance. I recognized myself immediately, and my heart swelled to know that in the history of his life told in music, the Phantom had given me a place equal to Soeur Adeline and the magician Lecadre. Perhaps one day he'd also offer me the perfect truth he'd shown them and face me without his mask.

I rested my head on the arms I'd crossed atop my upraised knees and closed my eyes, letting the music that told my part in his story wash over me. All of it was there. The cautious early days when he first spoke to me. The kindheartedness that marked our growing friendship. The dedication of the teacher and the student. The clashes that followed Raoul's arrival. The elation of our shared success. Measure by measure our individual strains of melody became less separate, ending the third movement with a harmonious blend.

Most concertos contain only three movements, but the Phantom's finished with a short and passionate fourth that culminated with that intoxicating blended theme and an operatic reprise that left me in tears. Variations on themes from Gounod's *Roméo et Juliette* formed a backdrop for our newly-blended melody, which played out in twin lines an octave apart. As the melody built toward a crescendo, one passage from the doomed lovers' wedding night duet emerged as the dominating reprise. Over and over again, as the Phantom played those notes, in my mind I heard the opera's lyric: "Fate chains me to you forever."

I didn't wait for the Phantom to finish his concerto. I couldn't. Not after he'd made plain in his music what he'd never been able to say in words. He loved me and wanted me to be with him always. I rose to my feet and reached for the bronze handle, thumbing the latch and pushing open the door. I entered the house by the lake unobserved by the Phantom, who sat with his back to me on the bench of the pipe organ across the room. Fresh tears flowed each time I heard the lovers' refrain – "Fate chains me to you forever!" I wiped the tears from my cheeks as I crept toward him. His hands skipped over the quartet of keyboards and his feet danced on the pedal board as the concerto surged toward climax. I stopped a few feet behind the Phantom to let the final thunderous crest of his music break over me.

In the silence that followed, he turned from the console of the pipe organ, showing no surprise to find me standing nearby. I stretched my hands toward him. "Your prima donna wept tonight."

The next instant the Phantom was at my side, raising my hands to his kiss.

"Of course I recognized Soeur Adeline and Lecadre." His touch made me smile. "I feel like I know them both now."

I hummed the leitmotif from the third movement. He smiled down at me. "Christine's song."

"I'm honored to be included in your concerto, but I'm not their equal. With Soeur Adeline and Lecadre you had perfect truth, but between us there is always a mask." I reached up to touch his second-skin mask, and the metal cheek warmed my finger tips. "Won't you let me see the truth?"

Under my hand, the Phantom turned to stone. He didn't answer; he didn't move; he didn't even breathe. Lifeless, except for the dark eyes that searched mine. I didn't flinch from his gaze and in those depths read a rapid sequence of emotion – surprise, fear, hope, acquiescence, resolve – that told me I'd won.

He took a ragged breath and turned his back to me. Raising his hands to his head, one on each side, he slid his fingers under the fringe of dark hair. As easily as a near-sighted man removes his spectacles, the Phantom removed his face, the only one I'd ever known. He placed the second-skin mask face up on the console of his pipe organ, the blank expression hauntingly familiar, and then he turned back to me.

The face the Phantom hid from the world didn't shock me. I already knew the worst. He'd told me one cold night in the Bois de Boulogne. At the sight of his face, children threw rocks and women

218

screamed and men turned away. I didn't recoil from the sight of the Phantom's mangled face because I already knew and loved the man behind the mask. Instead, I went up on my toes, balancing my hands on his broad shoulders as I pressed a kiss against his gargoyle brow, against his misshapen temple, against his cavernous cheek.

The Phantom's face didn't shock me, but my kisses shocked him. Under my hands, a tremble ran through his shoulders. Then his eyes blazed with the same joyous wonder they'd held the night of my debut when he cried, "You are the one!" He caught me with one arm, lifting me off my toes and circling my waist to pull me against him. With the other hand, he clasped the back of my head, running his fingers into my hair as he lowered his mouth to mine. At last! His lips seared mine, finally demanding what I'd long been eager to give. At last! The thought reverberated through my mind again and again, chiming like a bell. At last! A kiss beyond anything I'd imagined, deep and rousing, melting the bones inside my flesh and igniting the blood coursing through my veins. I clung to him, pressing against the hard wall of his chest and the firm length of his thighs, kneading my fingers into the warm flesh of his neck. At last! At last! I'd wanted that kiss, needed that kiss, for such a long time, and now that I'd finally tasted passion in the arms of my Phantom, what I wanted, what I needed, was for our embrace to go on forever.

Later that night I curled against him on the library's velvet settee, resting my head in the hollow where his neck met his shoulder, while he told me at last about the full horror of his childhood. His father was a brute, uncouth and uneducated but clever, a stone mason who turned a trade into a business by building his own brick factory near Rouen. As he prospered, the mason decided his new affluence entitled him to a higher station in life, including marriage to a better sort of woman than the common jades of his acquaintance. For his bride, he chose the daughter of a prosperous innkeeper, a pretty dark-haired girl with a dreamy air who spoke little but listened patiently whenever the mason saw her in the inn's public room. Her father's eagerness for the marriage fed the mason's vanity and not until irrevocable vows had been exchanged did he discover the truth. His bride's patience and silence were the outward manifestation of a religious mania and the dreamy air that so attracted him was the earliest bud of the madness that soon claimed her mind. The mockery that was his marriage soured the mason on life and permanent embitterment followed the birth of their hideous son, rejected by his mother as marked by Satan. After hiring a wet nurse to make sure the brat didn't starve, the mason escaped the horror of his home life by submerging himself in business.

The madwoman became the unwanted boy's keeper when he was weaned. With slaps and pinches and screams she soon taught the toddler her highest law – never to show his face to his mother. In her presence, the unwanted boy wore a bag over his head at all times, a hot and smelly hood with slits to see through, a rough cord tightened around his thin neck and a smiling face crudely painted on the outside. The mason didn't object because everyone knew such freaks of nature were imbeciles. Often, when she could no longer bear the sight of the bag's painted face, the madwoman locked her son in the dark root cellar beneath the kitchen. Long before he was old enough to safely wander free, she pushed the little boy out of the house every morning, telling him not to return until dark. On just such a day, the boy with the devil's face met Soeur Adeline. The nun's interest prompted the mason to reassess the capabilities of his son and begin teaching the sturdy boy his trade, for which the child proved to have a gift.

"When Lecadre's circus came to Rouen soon after Adeline died, I discovered that the world did have a place for freaks of nature like me." The Phantom's tone remained even and matter of fact, with no hint of self pity. "A few weeks after I joined his troupe, I became Red Death."

No words of comfort or consolation could balance such abuse, so I didn't offer any. Instead I twined my fingers through his and let silence spin out as I sat in the circle of his arm. His confession cemented our love and, for now, that was enough. Later we'd have time to talk more about his childhood and decide whether the hours he'd spent in the root cellar as a child had made the choice to live underground easier for the man. Still, I wanted to complete his story. I gave his fingers a quick squeeze. "Where are your parents now? Do you know?"

"Gone. Long ago." He pulled me closer. "She filled her pockets with rocks and waded into the Seine. He fell from a scaffold on the grand staircase soon after I arrived at the Palais Garnier."

I needed a few seconds to master my surprise. "So you were reunited with your father here at the opera?"

The Phantom's laughter rang harsh in my ears. "Only for work, cherie. He had no family feeling, and neither did I."

I snuggled against him, pressing my lips against the warm pulse in his neck. "And the house where you were born?"

"Empty. Gathering dust." He lifted our twined hands and brushed his lips across my knuckles. "I have no need of it."

Thus the Phantom completed for me the outline of his life, a story told fully in music but thus far only sketched in words. For now, that was enough. In May, when the Palais Garnier season ended, when we could finally look to the future, we would have all the time we needed to resurrect his painful past in full before we finally laid that tortured history to rest for all time.

22

*F*OR THE SUPERSTITIOUS, three is a number fraught with significance. Optimists believe good fortune arrives in threes. Third time lucky, they exclaim. Pessimists believe bad luck descends in threes. Three on a match, they warn. I've sometimes wished to share such beliefs because life would be so simple, but I can't. All these years later I look back on three events that happened next at the Palais Garnier unsure whether, in the end, they delivered good or evil. Yet I'm certain each marked an essential and irreversible step to everything that followed. With each step, the press erupted with a new round of speculation, fanning the curiosity of their readers with wild allegations until the journalists had whipped up in the entire populace a frenzied obsession with the Paris opera.

Carlotta started it all, stunning the opera company at the Palais Garnier by cancelling her contract, shuttering her small house on Rue du Faubourg St. Honoré and leaving Paris, apparently for good. Her abrupt departure left a juicy mystery upon which the newspapers eagerly gnawed.

Two days later I contributed a second mystery by taking over Carlotta's role in *La Juive* and receiving thunderous applause as Rachel. The newspapers wasted few lines of type speculating on why the maestro had dispensed with Carlotta's longtime understudy because my performance spoke for itself. Instead the journalists zeroed in on that triumph, ruminating on the deeper mystery of how I managed to master a challenging new role in a mere forty-eight hours.

Through his pawns in the manager's suite and on the conductor's podium, the Phantom delivered a third mystery by breaking with tradition to order the Palais Garnier's doors locked during rehearsals, excluding all visitors, even those as well-known as Edgar Degas and as well-connected as Philippe de Chagny. Since only *Roméo et Juliette* remained in rehearsal, the new fury of conjecture centered on the final production of the season, an opera which offered its own odd trio of firsts. The first performance of Gounod's masterpiece at the Palais Garnier. The first starring role for the company's new soprano. The first new prima donna since the opera moved into the theater seven years earlier. With so many mysteries to choose from, the columnists and critics acted like a pack of jackals who'd torn apart their prey, leaving each with a choice morsel to savor slowly and thoroughly. Day in and day out the journalists hashed and rehashed anything to do with the Palais Garnier, from the freshest gossip to the stalest rumor, but the publicity no longer troubled me. By removing his mask, the Phantom had banished my last doubt.

The Phantom's lockout began two weeks before the premiere of *Roméo et Juliette*, when the entire cast – principals, chorus and dancers – came together to rehearse after mastering their parts during weeks of separate practice. Maestro Chénier stood near the prompter's box while Eugenie Savatier, the costumer, barked orders at center stage. "Capulets, stage left. Montagues, stage right." The jewels in her rings sparkled as she sorted the cast, waving each arrival toward one of the rolling carts of costumes on either side of the stage apron She gave me a harried smile. "Juliette. Stage left."

I crossed the boards and stood beside Pierre Lantin, the baritone who played Capulet. "Hello, father."

"Hello, daughter." Lantin pointed to the un-painted backdrops closing off most of the stage and the dust covers draping the wardrobe carts. "The set is a secret, even from us. As are our costumes. And guards at the doors! I watched them turn a half dozen gentlemen away this morning, including your young friend de Chagny."

Among the Montagues across the way, Meg Giry reached for the muslin that covered the costumes only to have a wardrobe assistant slap away her hand, much to the amusement of many of the Capulets milling around us. Little Giry raised a hand to return the slap, but a glare from the cos-tumer froze her mid-swipe. Then Mercier, the régisseur, took his place beside Eugenie Savatier, clapping his hands and shouting for quiet as Maestro Chénier joined them at center stage.

"Today you learn our great secret, one that's been carefully kept by a handful of us for many months." The maestro surveyed the company arrayed before him, turning oh-so-slowly on his heel to cast his stern gaze on each of us in turn.

The grim faces of the companions standing on either side of him underscored the gravity of his words. "If you value your career, you also will remain silent. If you fail to keep our secret, your job will be forfeit."

No one spoke, not even Carolus Fonta, the irrepressible tenor whose good-natured quips often brought peace just as everyone girded for war. Instead, my Roméo remained silent at the center of his Montagues, exchanging a wary frown with La Sorelli, who stood at his side. After the silence stretched to a minute or more, Maestro Chénier nodded at the régisseur, who flung up arm to signal a flyman to raise the blank backdrops that blocked the set from our view.

As the flats rose into the fly tower, a ragged bit of old France appeared before us. Downstage, squalid half-timbered houses framed a wide lopsided square, ancient walls sinking into the earth under sagging gap-tiled roofs, their upper stories jettied ominously over the street below and their faded shutters askew beside filthy windows with glass cracked or missing altogether. Upstage, the square sloped uphill and funneled into a crooked lane that rose sharply before disappearing into the darkness at the back of the stage. The dingy square boasted a trio of cooking hearths, complete with roasting spits and cauldron tripods, scattered across broken pavement awash with rubbish, everything from bloody bandages and castoff crutches to empty wine bottles and fly-specked bowls.

"Behold, the *cour des miracles*." The maestro spread his arms wide. "There'll be nothing quaint about our city of thieves. We're taking our cue from

Monsieur Hugo, who called the court of miracles a hideous wart on the face of Paris, a sewer and a monstrous hive." He clasped his hands behind his back and stepped into the shabby square. "A republic of rogues who elected their own king. He'll replace our duke. And in place of feuding families, we'll have rival clans – the beggars of Capulet and the thieves of Montague."

At a nod from Eugenie Savatier, the wardrobe assistants guarding the costume carts removed the dust sheets and began handing out clothing to the members of the rival clans. I already had my costume so I stood off to one side, watching the rest of the company. A few wandered into the set for a closer look. Weeks earlier, the Phantom had revealed the opera's setting to me, and I'd skimmed Hugo's *Notre Dame de Paris* to familiarize myself with the place and time. Still, I'd never imagined a slum as real as the one on the Palais Garnier stage. Most members of the cast stood about in knots of two or three, heads bending close as a dozen hushed conversations combined into one agitated drone.

A wail from Little Giry silenced them all. "This is an insult!" She held her costume at arm's length as if it crawled with vermin, suspending it from her fingertips, the bodice crudely patched and the uneven hem pocked with burn holes. "Why would anyone pay good money to see us dressed like this?"

The maestro turned on her with a growl, his black hair flying out as he spun. "How little you value our talents to suggest that costume alone attracts patrons to this theater."

In the face of Maestro Chénier's fury, Giry gaped, her cheeks flaming, until Sorelli stepped forward, sliding an arm around the girl's slumped shoulders. "The child wonders, as we all do, why our beautiful opera should be set among these wretched hovels?"

"A fair question. Perhaps Mlle. Daaé will answer it for us?" Something unreadable glinted in Maestro Chénier's gray eyes, but his smile reassured me. "Of all of us, the risk to her career is greatest because Juliette will be her debut."

"I have a friend who says opera is always the same – a king or a bishop, a palace or a cathedral, history or the Bible. Just the other day at the Louvre, Victorine wondered why France's great artists never see anything worth painting in our world?" I looked from the maestro to Sorelli, who regarded me coolly. Beside her, Little Giry clutched her costume to her breast and glowered at me. "My parents were peasants. Had I been born in France, I'd be one of the *canaille*, the kind of rabble who inhabited the court of miracles."

"All those people out there—" I swung an arm toward the auditorium, pointing to the empty boxes in the grand tier. "They think the *canaille* are nothing more than animals. This opera will show them they're wrong. This opera will show the *gratin* that people everywhere, whether born high or born low, all people feel love and fear, courage and grief, loyalty and despair. Some of us are born to wear silk and some of us are born to wear rags, but underneath we're all the same."

"*Brava!*" Carolus Fonta marched across the stage and stopped before me. He thumped a clenched fist against his chest, holding it above his heart. "Prima donna, I salute you. Only a true diva dares to defy convention." He dropped to his knees, his arms spread in surrender. "I will follow you anywhere!"

I gently cuffed the tenor's ear and smiled down at him, grateful for his rescue in more ways than one. Not only had he saved me from an awkward moment, he'd also very publicly confirmed my new status as the leading lady of the Palais Garnier stage.

He grinned back at me and bounced to his feet, addressing the entire cast. "I myself was born to the *bianti* and, before the discovery of my musical genius, was the best pickpocket in Napoli. By opening night, my thieving Montagues will be *verisimo*!"

Before opening night arrived, springtime came to Paris. Mild breezes blew away the leaden skies of winter to reveal a heavenly vault of robin's egg blue. The tree branches arching overhead suddenly bore a lacey fringe of fresh green, and at the park surrounding Tour St. Jacques the shrubs showed swelling buds that soon burst into flower. With the change in the weather, Raoul became restless, longing to escape the confines of the city with its endless and enervating round of social events. He spoke wistfully of the freedom we'd known in Perros as children and excitedly of the challenges he'd face in Antarctica a few months hence. And like all the other gentlemen who'd grown used to visiting their opera girls anytime they pleased, Raoul chafed under the prohibition on backstage visitors.

One beautiful spring evening, to take his mind off his troubles, I led Raoul to the rooftop of the Palais Garnier. Not the zinc and lead roof presided over by Guméry's sculptures of Harmony and Poetry but the soaring peak of the proscenium wall where Apollo raised his golden lyre over Paris. The setting sun gilded the clouds drifting above and the river flowing below, casting a warm and mellow light across the city from the dome of the Pantheon high above the Left Bank and the ancient towers of Notre Dame to the immense switching yard at Gare St. Lazare and the sturdy foundation for the new basilica rising on the heights of Montmartre.

I folded my arms and leaned back against Apollo's sun-warmed pediment. "I love it up here."

"Who wouldn't?" He anchored an elbow against the stone beside my head. Even the spectacular view hadn't improved his mood. "And I suppose that technically you haven't actually brought me backstage."

"Can you keep a secret?" Without waiting for him to answer, I blurted out the truth. "We're recreating the court of miracles with the beggars all Capulets and the thieves all Montagues!"

He let out a whoop. "What a marvelous idea! Imagine the surprise – the audience won't know whether to be outraged or inspired."

I studied the toes of my slippers peeping out from under the hem of my dress. "Which will you be?"

"Inspired." He lifted my chin until our eyes met. "It's a new world, and I like it. My life at sea taught me to judge men by their actions, not the circumstance of their birth. The old ways are going, and it's folly to cling to them. Look at Philippe. He's in love with Sorelli, but he won't marry her. Is it any wonder she turns from him?"

230

He stroked the line of my jaw, and I turned my cheek into his caress. "Christine, I've loved you since we were children. Through all those years of separation, my love for you never wavered. And it never will."

"Not now, Raoul." I pressed my lips against his hand before drawing away. "In May—"

"'—there'll be time to talk about the future.'" He groaned. "*Merde*! I hate that month almost as much as I long for its arrival."

Philippe had engaged Raoul for the evening so I sent him back the way we came while I remained on the rooftop, suspended between the city and the stars. At the bottom of the stairs on the flytower gable, he stopped to wave before setting off along the length of the roof above the stage. Was it only a few days ago that I'd been torn between Raoul and the Phantom, and the conflicting futures they might offer me? The Phantom would make me a star with a public life devoted to art. Raoul would make me a wife with a private life devoted to family. From childhood, an only child and then an orphan, I'd dreamed of both – the soaring beauty of song and the enduring refuge of love. But now I'd made my choice. When Raoul reached the door that opened onto an administration building staircase, he waved again and I answered with a lifted hand just before he disappeared from sight.

"Didn't I tell you you'd have Paris at your feet?"

I whirled around to face the Phantom, who stood below me on the gable stairs opposite the ones Raoul had taken. "Where did you come from?"

He climbed the last few steps and joined me on the peak of the roof with the bronze Apollo towering over our heads. "The stage isn't the only part of this building riddled with traps. And all of them open at my command."

My cheeks burned. "How long were you listening?"

"Long enough to hear you confide our secret to your sailor boy." Before I could apologize, he pressed a fingertip against my lips. "I'm glad you did because it led him to reveal himself. The Vicomte de Chagny really does love you, Christine, and he will marry you."

I searched the dark eyes behind the placid, second-skin mask but found them unreadable in the half-light of dusk. "That's no longer possible. We both know that."

He turned to follow the streak of brightly lit windows as a train pulled out of Gare St. Lazare, the sound of its whistle faint and reedy as it reached us. I wanted to press him for affirmation but couldn't seem to find the words. His merely echoed the ones I'd said to Raoul. "We'll speak of it in May."

23

THE PHANTOM'S assault on grand opera began with a violent tableau and a procession of miracles. Led by the orchestra's brass, the overture's ominous theme underscored the sinister image confronting the audience when the curtains parted. On a stage as dark as night, a single spotlight stage right captured two pairs of men – the first crouching over a rough sack spilling a bounty of pewter at their feet and the second ragged beggars toting the crutch of the lame and the white stick of the blind. As the orchestra spun two competing melodies into a whirlwind of confrontation, the Montague thieves drew their daggers and the Capulet beggars brandished their staffs. Then all four froze in place for a few seconds before the spotlight went dark, imprinting their clash like a photograph. As darkness erased the tableau, the rest of the stage slowly lit, revealing the flickering hearths of the *cour des miracles* and the crooked lane beyond, now clogged with humanity moving toward the fires. A legless cripple rode a wooden bowl, swinging forward on his hands. A palsied knot of a man, foaming at the mouth, staggered in next. A one-armed veteran, still wearing his rusty sword, limped behind. Other tattered men and women emerged from side streets and cellar holes, ignoring the miracles occurring at the spot where the lane reached the square. The legless man levered out of the bowl and stood on sturdy legs. The convulsive man spit a chunk of soap from his mouth and straightened his spine. The maimed veteran unbound his hidden wrist and flexed his second hand. Miraculously hale, the beggars' chorus gathered around the fires to sing a hymnal prologue that set the scene and sketched the plot of the opera.

On opening night, I stood alone in a curtain portal on the stage left wing as *Roméo et Juliette* began. That night the audience's agitation surpassed anything in my experience, and no wonder. Day after day the newspapers had flogged their Palais Garnier mysteries, inciting the kind of feverish anticipation once reserved for a coronation or an execution. The babble in the auditorium invaded every corner of the building, and the structure itself seemed to vibrate with expectation. Behind the closed curtain, I had to imagine what was happening in the hall. The audience quieted noticeably – the lighting of the footlights? They settled a bit more – Maestro Chénier's arrival in the pit? Still, a wisp of murmur ran through the house, penetrating the grand drape of the proscenium, a hushed but distinct rustle until the orchestra buried it with music. When the curtain opened, I could hear the audience again, a quiet buzz running under the overture. And then moans of dismay at the squalid set and pitiable beggars. Gasps of surprise at the first miracle. And mutters of anger when the choral prologue swapped Paris for Verona, broken pavement for palace thresholds, and rival underworld clans for feuding aristocratic families. Outrage, just as the Phantom had predicted. And he counted on the strength of my performance to silence their indignation.

The orchestra swung into the lively music for the Act I beggar's ball and Capulet's ragged flock donned masks and finery – colorful ribbons and brass earrings for the women, clean neckcloths and rakish hats for the men. I patted the sapphire skirt covering my thigh, counting down the four minutes before my entrance and wondering when Pierre Lantin would appear. The baritone slipped into the portal and took my arm thirty seconds before our cue. We stepped onto the stage and the audience groaned to see even the beggars' king and his daughter garbed in tattered finery. Then Lantin launched into Capulet's welcome, and I had a little more than two minutes before my first song with its two passages of demanding coloratura. When the orchestra fell silent, leaving only the plucked notes of a harp, I began to sing – a few measures with words before a burst of rapid high notes of elaborate ornamentation that took me to the top of my range. More melody with words, backed first by woodwinds and later by violins, and then another longer round of coloratura. Altogether barely more than a minute of song, all of it sung through a brilliant smile while I pranced among the assembled beggars, accepting their good wishes. And after I finished, a few hoorahs, a smattering of claps, and a quieter audience than when I'd begun. Another of the Phantom's predictions appeared to be coming true.

Less than three minutes later, I left the stage on the arm of my suitor, Paris, played by a talented baritone who'd been raised from the chorus to test his readiness for stardom. As I exited, Roméo appeared from the opposite side of the boards, but I didn't linger long enough to see him. Deep in the wings, Victorine waited with a hairbrush and the lace mask I'd wear for my waltz in the next scene. Behind me, the audience sent up another grumble of complaint, but I didn't pause to find out why. The twilit backstage seemed to have been invaded by a flight of owls that again and again called out "who?" as I searched for my maid. By the time Victorine had tied on my mask and I'd scurried back toward the stage, the crowd had quieted again during Roméo's passionate first sight of an offstage Juliette – "I never saw true beauty till this night!" I never heard Carolus Fonta in better voice! He'd made my job that much easier, but I had no chance to thank Roméo or even see him. The tenor exited stage left just before I entered from stage right.

I crossed the boards to a crumbling well that now stood downstage, pursued by a mezzo-soprano from the chorus playing Juliette's nurse. In the sordid square behind us, the beggar's ball continued as an illusion delivered by the Phantom's magic lantern, the dancing couples and drunken revelers projected onto a diaphanous screen. In this scene Gounod captured the generational conflict of women – elders urging marriage, youngsters preferring freedom. Juliette longed to return to the ball, a fact the Phantom chose to illustrate by having me waltz while singing her *valse arriette* with its challenging coloratura. How hard we'd worked on this scene – me full of doubt, he full of certainty – and once again his prediction came true. Not only did the dancing help my song, supplying an emotional boost that made it easy for me to hit the highest notes, but Juliette's waltz also enthralled the audience. Approving whispers began before I reached the frills and curlicues of the final cadenza. At the end, when each note emerged pitch-perfect and strong, the audience cheered.

As opera etiquette required, I held my pose and basked in the ovation, thrilled beyond measure because it was all coming true. What my father had wished for. What I had worked for. What the Phantom had predicted.

As the applause died away, I turned to follow Juliette's nurse offstage, knowing that Carolus Fonta's Roméo would appear out of the darkness beyond the well.

Instead the Phantom stepped into the light and reached for my hand. "By heaven, stay."

His touch electrified me. In that instant I became lovestruck Juliette, mirroring her reaction to her first sight of Roméo with the genuine surprise, apprehension and delight I felt at finding the Phantom on stage.

"Adorable angel." The Phantom fully unleashed the expressive power of his rich, smooth voice and became Roméo, passionate, magnetic, and absolutely riveting.

Our flirtatious duet charmed the audience. No one seemed to mind that a mysterious stranger had replaced the famed tenor listed in the program. No one seemed to notice that Juliette and Roméo had failed to unmask as the plot demanded. Our desire, so real and volatile, completely captured the audience, who saw past all of their misgivings to recognize the extraordinary performance unfolding on the stage. The hall remained utterly silent as the Phantom teased for a kiss. And the audience sighed as one when Juliette finally granted Roméo's wish.

Act I ended with Juliette's terrified lament at her fatal love, a tormented premonition that I carried with me offstage. Suddenly Juliette's story seemed to be my own, with Raoul playing the role of Paris and my love for the Phantom as doomed as her passion for Roméo.

Victorine met me in my dressing room, her eyes glowing with excitement as she babbled on and on, recounting the consternation on both sides of the stage with the mysterious tenor playing Roméo, providing a list of the famous and infamous who'd turned out for the performance, describing the glittering scene in the grand tier when she'd checked on the comfort of Madame Valérius in the de Chagny box.

"Only one seat empty in the entire theater." She slipped the blue dress over my upraised arms, hiding me inside the voluminous skirt. "Such a surprise! Madame Giry says the ghost's box is empty tonight!"

I bit my lower lip against the laughter that threatened to escape in a fountain of hysteria. How Victorine would shriek if I told her the truth – the opera ghost had abandoned his box for center stage!

She helped me into a filmy white nightgown and carefully tied the satin ribbon laced under my breasts. Victorine didn't expect a reply from me. She'd learned by now that I welcomed her chatter but had no taste for conversation between acts. And so she prattled on, filling my dressing room with talk that provided a useful distraction from the fear that my love story would end as unhappily as Juliette's.

My apprehension only grew when I returned to the stage for Act II, where the Capulet's small walled garden had replaced the *cour des miracles*. Juliette wouldn't appear on her balcony until eight minutes into the scene, but I didn't want to miss a moment of the Phantom's *cavatina* – "Arise sun! Appear! Appear! Pure and charming star!" – under her darkened window. I found an empty portal near the ladder to Juliette's balcony as a peaceful harp began the dulcet melody symbolizing the sweet sanctuary of love. Right on cue, the Phantom emerged from the shadows and vaulted to the top of the garden wall, still wearing his black satin mask. The audience greeted his appearance with absolute silence as did the backstage cast and crew. Who had become a question for another time. At that moment, all anyone cared about was his performance. What they heard was the voice of an angel – beautifully pure, emotionally vivid, powerful and at ease at the top of his range. As Roméo, the Phantom epitomized the lovesick swain.

Yet soon after I appeared on Juliette's balcony I realized that the Phantom wasn't acting. Eyes truly are the windows of the soul, and faced always with his masks, I'd come to know his eyes better than I knew my own. That night I beheld a new *tristesse* in those dark depths, not the bitter melancholy of an outcast but the profound sorrow of loss. And though I knew every word of the libretto of *Roméo et Juliette*, I heard it anew that night, with lines that took on fresh meaning from the genuine desolation I read in the Phantom's eyes.

Under Juliette's balcony, Roméo yearned to be anyone but a Montague, the blood-feud foes of his beloved Capulet. "To have your love, let me be reborn as anyone but myself." From his eyes, I knew the Phantom sang those words not as the lovesick boy he played but as the anguished man he was. He'd risked losing my love by removing his mask, but now, somehow, even the perfect truth between us was no longer enough.

When Juliette suggested solving their dilemma by defying the feud with marriage, Roméo fell on his knees to underscore his bottomless need. "Banish the night. Be the dawn for my heart and for my eyes." From the Phantom's eyes, I knew he sang those words not as the hopeful suitor he played but as the rescued recluse he had been. His concerto proved that I had freed him from his solitude, but now, somehow, our love was no longer enough.

I longed to follow the Phantom off the stage between acts and make him explain the heartache clouding his dark eyes. But fulfilling his dream was more important than relieving my dread. So I channeled my foreboding into my part, making Juliette as real as the Phantom's Roméo as fate, choice and chance curdled their romance into tragedy when the king of the rogues banished Roméo for accidentally killing Juliette's cousin.

Neither of us needed to feign bittersweet melancholy as Act IV opened in Juliette's bedroom in the early morning hours of their wedding night. The curtain parted to reveal me reclining upon Juliette's bed and the Phantom seated on the floor beside me. The orchestra swelled with a tender melody that suggested our new intimacy and our imminent parting. When Juliette's loving caresses failed to make Roméo forget his sorrow and remorse, she forgave him again, reminding her husband, "He hated you, and I love you!"

The Phantom rose onto his knees, clasping my hands between his. "Say it again." Hope surged through me at the naked yearning in his voice and the frank adoration in his eyes. "Say it again, that word so sweet."

As I reaffirmed my love, he stood and pulled me to my feet. As I repeated the vow again, he drew me into his arms and cradled me against his chest, both of us facing the audience for our wedding night duet. In his concerto, the Phantom symbolized our love in a passionate refrain borrowed from Gounod with a lyric that could be a blessing or a curse: "Fate chains me to you forever." Yet that night my heart hammered each time we sang another lyric: "*À toi, toujours à toi!*"

The first time, I leaned my back into the Phantom and wrapped his arms across my chest. "Yours, always yours!"

For the reprise, I faced him with our joined hands between us. "Yours, always yours!"

To finish the duet, I melted into his embrace, gazing into his eyes and raising my lips toward his. "Yours, always yours!"

The audience didn't wait for our kiss before erupting into tumultuous applause. But the kiss never came. As the Phantom lowered his lips toward mine, a metallic shriek cut through the thunder of the audience and orchestra.

The Phantom threw back his head, and I followed his gaze to the huge gas-lit chandelier glowing dimly against the muses of Lenepveu's painted ceiling. The massive light, with tiers of crystal pendants, frosted globes and gilt lyres, had been raised to the ceiling to allow the highest boxes a clear view of the stage. A shudder ran through the elaborate wedding cake of glass and fire high above us, trembling crystal and flickering flame. With a ratcheting clang that resounded through the theater, the hoist failed.

As the enormous light plunged toward the stage, the Phantom dragged me into its path. On the boards near the prompter's box, his foot beat a rapid tattoo. The trap opened beneath us, and we fell into the darkness under the stage.

24

*T*HE PHANTOM cushioned my fall with his own body. Still, the impact and the darkness left me momentarily stunned and blind. His arms came around my waist like a vise, hauling me deeper into the gloom as the chandelier shattered against the stage above. A shower of splintered glass and blazing sparks fell through the shaft of light left by the open trap. The screaming panic enveloping the auditorium overhead penetrated our refuge as well, but only for a few seconds before the asbestos fire curtain thudded down, sealing the stage.

"Fire!" Eyes wide with terror, the prompter stumbled down the steps from his box and scrambled away into the darkness. "Fire!"

With a groan, the Phantom climbed to his feet and hoisted me from the floor. He tugged my hand. "Come."

I staggered after him as he threaded between the steel pillars supporting the riveted girders that held up the stage, dodging around the machinery used to raise and lower performers and sets through the traps. My heart pounded in counterpoint to the drumbeat of running feet – a galloping herd on the boards above our heads, a solo patter in the gloom under the stage. My ears rang with the barrage of fear erupting through the Palais Garnier, screams and shouts and sobs, as one word echoed through the vast building – fire! *FIRE*! **FIRE**! – and one thought gripped inhabitants and visitors alike: escape! In the auditorium, they ran: glittering ladies and distinguished gentlemen running from their boxes; barmen, ushers and boxkeepers running from the auditorium corridor; boot cleaners, cloak-room attendants and ticket takers running from the vestibule below. Back stage, they ran: carpenters and gasmen running from workrooms in the base-ment; scene shifters and dressers running from their posts in the wings; singers and dancers running from dressing rooms behind the stage. And beneath the stage, the Phantom and I running through a dark maze of pillars. Then, up ahead, the sweet deliverance of an iron staircase spiraling up through a spill of light from above.

I lurched toward it, but the Phantom growled, jerking me through the puddle of light and into the darkness beyond. "No. This way."

He led me to a stone staircase that returned us to his underground world far below the roaring panic engulfing the Palais Garnier. At the bottom, he lit one of his lanterns and guided me back to the hideaway where I first heard his voice, the out-of-the-way niche where I'd tried to hide my tears. On the stone floor, shrouded by a tarp, lay another cause for crying. The Phantom folded aside the canvas at one end, revealing the frozen grimace and sightless eyes of the Comte de Chagny.

"Philippe!" I reeled away from the body. "What's happened to him?"

"He dueled Fonta." The Phantom tugged the tarp far enough to show the blood staining the impeccable shirt front of Raoul's brother. "And learned too late that the tenor spoke the truth when he claimed *bianti* birth."

Fear stabbed me. "And Carolus?"

"A flesh wound." The Phantom shrugged. "Sorelli is tending to him. Little Giry dressed for her part in the Act IV ballet."

I'm ashamed to admit the thrill of satisfaction that coursed through me when I learned that the chandelier's fall had robbed Meg Giry of her solo debut. Even with the theater aflame above my head and Raoul's brother dead at my feet, for a moment spite outweighed my fear and my grief. "Giry dressed for Sorelli's part, and you replaced Carolus as Roméo."

The Phantom smiled at me across Philippe's body. "I couldn't let the Comte de Chagny's death rob us of our opening night."

"Poor Philippe."

"He was a fool. He allowed his pride to overrule his passion." The Phantom lowered the tarp over that ghastly face. "Had he followed his heart and made Sorelli his comtesse, he'd still be alive and surely fathered his own vicomte to take your sailor boy's title. Instead, Raoul will choose the next Comtesse de Chagny."

The Phantom left me no time to think about the implications of that statement. He grabbed my hand and spun the tale of Philippe's death forward as we retraced the steps of my first journey through his underground world. "The fire in the auditorium will be doused quickly, and then the *pompiers* will search the whole building to make sure it hasn't spread. They'll find the body."

Those words stopped me, but he continued for a few steps down the spiral stairs leading to the lake before realizing that I no longer followed. He climbed back to me, taking up position on the step below the one I stood upon. "That will give them even more reason to probe deeply, and eventually they'll find the house by the lake. When they do, I'll become the chief suspect."

"Then you will tell them the truth." I placed my hands on his shoulders and searched his dark eyes, looking for reassurance but finding only sorrow. "Won't you?"

"And end the career of the finest tenor of the age?" He met my gaze without flinching. "Dueling may not be a serious crime in France, but killing an aristocrat still is. I'll take the blame. My work here is done." He turned his head and pressed a quick kiss against my hand. "They'll be coming soon. We must hurry."

The urgency of his words disarmed me, momentarily silencing my defiance. Silently I followed him down the spiral stairs to the small landing beside the lake. The lamp that had cast a blue glow on my first visit had gone dark, no doubt extinguished by a stagehand with the quick wits to shut off the gas. But the light of the Phantom's lantern showed the same small rowboat tied to the familiar iron ring.

He hung the lantern in the bow of the boat and took my hand to steady me as I stepped into the stern. As he rowed across the dark water, I fought against the dread souring my belly by rehearsing my arguments in my mind. We loved each other –

he could not deny that. And our performance proved we were a truly exceptional musical team. The time had come for him to abandon his man-made cavern and rejoin the world above the sidewalks. If we stood together, neither of us would ever again stand alone or apart.

With a brush of his hand, a click and a whir, the door opened in the blank stone wall. He preceded me with the lantern into the darkness beyond and went straight for the tall candelabrum standing beside the piano. He lit all nine candles, carried in a high stool from his workroom and patted the seat. "Wait here."

The Phantom lifted the lantern and disappeared into his bedroom, leaving me alone in the silent room with only flickering candles for company. Without the glow of burning gas, the bronze tor-chieres in their wall brackets looked like iron insects. The darkness erased the Phantom's beautiful paintings, leaving only a procession of black rectangles decorating the pale stone walls. The walls themselves might have been made of ice because the warm, mellow tones had vanished as well. Nothing had really changed – there stood the organ upon which he'd played his concerto, there his workroom scattered with brushes, jars of paint and tiny models, there his library shelves overflowing with books – and yet every inch of it now as drained of reality as an empty stage set. At that moment I understood that the fault lay in me, in the distant vision of my eyes struggling to memorize for all the days to come the beloved details of a place I was seeing for the last time.

The Phantom returned without the lantern. He'd replaced Roméo's black satin with his own second-skin mask, his doublet with his own evening clothes, and carried an overcoat and hat for himself and a velvet cloak for me.

"You're leaving me." As soon as the words were out I realized my arguments would be futile. He'd made up his mind before Philippe's duel, days before when he'd stood in the shadow of Apollo's lyre and overheard Raoul declare his love for me. Still, I had to ask. "Why?"

"Tonight I've given you everything I can." He tossed the garments on top of the piano and came to stand before me. "If you sing for a thousand years, you'll never have a night of greater triumph."

He bent down to brush his lips across mine. "I have given you something Raoul never could – tonight's triumph. And he will give you things I never can – children and a home in the world."

I leaned into him, pressing my face against the soft wool of his coat and wrapping my arms around his waist, struggling to accept the fact that the Phantom's love for me didn't outweigh his contempt for mankind and his fear of passing on his deformity. For an endless moment, he stroked my hair, gentling me with his touch. Then he cupped a hand under my chin and raised it until our eyes met. "Until today, Raoul wanted you. But after tonight, he'll need you even more."

"And what about you?" I choked on the words, fighting against tears. "What about your wants? What about your needs?"

"Tonight, with your help, I achieved my dream." He traced my lips with his thumb. "Now I'll have to find another. In Raoul you've already found yours."

Through a blur of tears, I saw the desolation return to his eyes. Behind the impassive features of his second-skin mask, anguish dulled those dark eyes.

"Promise me you'll be happy." He slipped his arms around me and clutched me against his chest. "He'll make you happy if you let him. Promise me you'll let him." His arms tightened, crushing me against him. "Promise me."

Beyond the Phantom's hidden gate, pandemonium had overtaken the sidewalks and pavement of Rue Scribe and the opera square. Gendarmes massed along the curbs to hold back the surging crowd – opera patrons in bedraggled finery, *flâneurs* with excited eyes, waiters from nearby cafes, prostitutes who'd abandoned their street lamps. In the rank of fire engines drawn up before the Palais Garnier, the massive draft horses stood in their harnesses, stamping their hooves and snorting as the *pompiers* rolled up the hoses that crisscrossed the steps of the theater. I seized the Phantom's arm and held it tight as he plowed through the throng, clearing a path with a sharp elbow and a lowered shoulder.

"There he is." As he reached the leading edge of the crowd, the Phantom pulled me to his side and pointed at a knot of men milling just outside the theater's gaping doors. "There."

Raoul stood to one side, shaking off the hands of two men in uniform who tried, again and again, to guide him away from the entrance. "No!" His bellow carried over the excited hubbub of the crowd. "Not until I find her! Where is she? Christine!"

"He doesn't know." The Phantom leaned down until the brim of his hat touched the top of my hood, creating a private space for us within that seething mass. "They haven't told him yet. But any moment they will. He needs you now. Go to him."

I turned back to the Palais Garnier. On the other side of the entrance, a few meters from Raoul, a tall man wearing a bureaucrat's sober derby stepped away from a knot of men who'd been eyeing Raoul from afar.

The Phantom's arm snaked around my shoulders and gave me a quick squeeze. "Go to him." His hand slipped to the small of my back and nudged me forward. "Now."

I took a step toward the line of gendarmes then spun back to face the Phantom. The brim of his hat shadowed his eyes but not the sad smile on his lips. "You promised."

"Raoul!" Singing technique gave my voice the volume I needed to cut through the roar of the crowd and stage presence the authority to clear the gendarmes blocking my path. "Raoul!" I swept the back the hood that covered my hair. "I'm here!"

He bolted down the stairs and met me halfway up, throwing his arms around me to draw me into a tight embrace. "Christine! You're alive! Oh, thank heaven, you're alive."

Raoul lifted me off my feet and spun slow ecstatic circles on the steps of the Paris opera, around and around and around. I clung to him, holding fast to my future, but couldn't stop myself from searching the crowd for the Phantom who would forever own my past. One moment he was there – a tall, broad-shouldered man whose pale impassive face drew not a single second glance from the goggling mob surrounding him – and the next he'd disappeared into the gawking horde.

The man with the derby descended the steps toward us. "Pardonnez-moi, Vicomte." He swiped the hat from his head and held it over his heart. "If I could have a word—"

Slowly, reluctantly, Raoul lowered me to the ground, one arm gripped around my waist to hold me tight to his side. "Very well, monsieur. What is it?"

A quartet of men crossed the square and paused below us to resettle on their shoulders a small boat, a flat-bottom punt of the sort used upon shallow waters, before carrying it up the steps and into the marbled halls of the Palais Garnier.

25

I NEVER SAW the Phantom again.

In the first nightmarish days that followed the chandelier's fall I didn't try to. Within hours, I'd been forced out of my home by the siege of a ravenous press and the need of my grieving Raoul. With Madame Valérius upstairs to chaperone and Victorine below stairs to ease the burden of my arrival amidst their mourning, I agreed to Raoul's urgent request and moved across the river to the Hôtel de Chagny in the Faubourg St. Germain. There a platoon of footmen kept the journalists at bay while Raoul himself dealt with the parade of officials who made it past Philippe's butler. Politely but firmly he turned them all away. In the face of the young comte's obvious anguish, the police inspectors, ministry bureaucrats and opera managers found it impossible to press their cases and were soon murmuring apologies as they backed out the door. In the next few weeks I emerged from the velvet cocoon of Raoul's home only once, to attend a private funeral mass for Philippe. Then I returned to St. Germain while Raoul went alone to see his brother laid in the family crypt at Cimetière du Père-Lachaise. Of us all, only Victorine went about the city freely, and many days passed before I asked her to help me find the Phantom.

I didn't go out, but the world came to me in the pages of the newspapers that arrived each day and in the stories Victorine brought back from her visits to my dressing room at the Palais Garnier and our apartment in Rue des Notre Dames des Victoires. The opera stage was dark, of course, but while repairs were made Poligny and Debienne scrambled to rescue what was left of their season. Three days after the chandelier's fall, the managers summoned the company and crew back to the opera house. Victorine went in my place, carrying my letter withdrawing from the company. She returned home to describe the manager's blustering about "breach of contract," but I was far more interested in what else she might report.

For seventy-two hours officials at the Préfecture de Police, Paris fire brigade and Hôtel de Ville had spoken with one voice: The incident at the Palais Garnier remained under investigation. And so for seventy-two hours the newspapers had printed nothing but rumors. About a strange dwelling place beside the forgotten lake in the opera's cellar. About a scandalous truth whitewashed by the tale that Philippe was the sole fatality of the tragic mishap. About earlier opera mishaps – a stagehand's suicide, a horse gone missing, a dressing room defiled – all orchestrated by a single evildoer. Rumors that would help transform a hidden home into a sinister lair and a solitary genius into a murderous monster.

Victorine returned from the Palais Garnier with hard facts. That the house by the lake had indeed been found and judged to be the dwelling place of the opera ghost. That the costume sketches, models of sets and annotated opera scores discovered there suggested a profound influence by the opera ghost on the Palais Garnier's productions. That set designer Achille Meril and costumer Eugenie Savatier greeted that suggestion with scorn while Maestro Chénier merely shrugged and continued to study the score of an organ concerto found in the ghost's home. Hard facts the managers found most unwelcome and ample reason to recast their secret impresario into a public scapegoat.

Victorine soon emptied my dressing room and the small apartment that had been our home ever since Madame Valérius brought me back to Paris to enroll in the opera's singing school. But I sent our maid to the Palais Garnier again to inquire in the shops and cafés along Rue Scribe and nearby streets, particularly those in the vicinity of the Emperor's Pavilion, about a servant couple named Gaston and Martine. He drove a handsome carriage often pulled by a mismatched team that included an old white horse, and her vinaigrette was reputed to be the best in Paris. Victorine's inquiries proved fruitless. She found no trace of the Phantom's servants nor his coach and team.

For several months I considered hiring a private detective to continue the search but ultimately decided against it. I couldn't risk leading the authorities to the man they believed responsible for Philippe's death. I couldn't risk providing a means to blackmail the future Comtesse de Chagny. And I couldn't risk breaking my promise to be happy with

Raoul. As my wedding day drew near, I gave up trying to find the Phantom.

He wasn't the only thing I lost on the night the chandelier fell. What exquisite irony that lost to me also was the boy I'd loved since childhood. Raoul held me close beside him on the steps of the opera that night while the police inspector informed him of Philippe's death. For a moment he remained silent, his only reaction the rapid blinking of his eyes and the tightened circle of his arm around my waist. Only later, when we were alone in his brother's carriage, did Raoul free his emotions. I held him in my arms while he wept like a child with gulping sobs, shuddering shoulders and copious tears. When that first storm of grief had passed, the boy I loved had vanished, never to reappear. From that moment on, Raoul inhabited his new role as Comte de Chagny, wielding all the authority of that ancient title to protect me – to protect *us* – from the prying questions and scandalous suspicions of journalists and policemen.

Philippe wasn't the only thing Raoul lost on the night the chandelier fell. His dreams of Antarctic adventure, his naval career – those vanished as well. Raoul gave up both without complaint. Honor and duty demanded no less. Before my eyes, he became a man, one I admired immediately and eventually came to love even more than the boy I'd lost. As the days of mourning passed, I prayed that I would find a way to live up to Raoul's example and embrace what honor and duty demanded of me.

From the first, our marriage was happy. After losing so much, one of Raoul's wishes had at last come true. And I had promised. As the months passed, I showed the world a happy face, but in

private, when I was absolutely alone, I often brooded, sifting through my memories to solve the riddles
in my past. One puzzle loomed especially large: the
suicide of Joseph Buquet. Despite the rumors of
the day, I knew the Phantom hadn't murdered the
scene shifter. Nor had he sabotaged the chandelier.
But, imagining the worst, novelist Gaston Leroux
blamed the opera ghost for both. Yet no one knew
why Buquet had killed himself. I came to blame
Carlotta for his death. In hindsight, the enmity
between them seemed too pronounced, too extravagant, simply too much. They were hiding something. Undoubtedly a love affair. However
improbable that sounds, one need not be French to
acknowledge that between men and women that is
always the fundamental question. For proof I had
only Victorine's assertion that Carlotta began
drinking and changed utterly at the time of Buquet's death. The mystery of that was easily explained: guilt or grief. In the end, only one riddle
remained unsolved: I still didn't know my Phantom's name.

Eighteen months after the chandelier fell I finally set off in search of him. I was carrying my first
child, and Raoul and I had returned early to Paris
to begin modernizing the old children's wing at the
Hôtel de Chagny, leaving Madame Valérius and
Victorine in Brittany to enjoy the fine autumn
weather. Most of the *gratin* remained in the country
until November, freeing us from the duty to enter-
tain and be entertained. A few days after our arrival, when Raoul left for the Touraine to sort out a
problem at the de Chagny estate, I stayed behind in
Paris. One morning I slipped out early, took a cab
across the Seine to the Gare St. Lazare and rode

the train to Rouen where I could hire a carriage to take me to the village where the Phantom had been born.

For much of the way, the railroad followed the river, making wide loops through a countryside gripped with the frenzy of the harvest. On the roads, wagon after wagon passed, laden with fruit or vegetables bound for a cannery, while flotillas of barges piled with produce clogged the Seine. I'd left Paris on impulse. I had no plan, and as the train clattered toward Normandy, I refused to develop one. I told myself I only wanted to know his name and didn't allow my thoughts to stray any further. His name, his name, his name. The words echoed in my mind in time with the clack-clack, clack-clack, clack-clack of the train rolling along the tracks toward his birthplace. I would have only to ask because he would be remembered.

We rounded a bend and Rouen came into view, thrusting upward on both sides of the river, the great bronze spire of the cathedral rising above the many squat Gothic steeples in the old city and across the water the tall brick chimney of the La Foudre mill towering over dozens of smaller stacks belching black smoke into the clear autumn sky. The trip to the Phantom's village didn't take long, carrying me up a long hill leading out of the river valley and through a small forest of pines. The carriage driver dropped me in the market square, promising to return in two hours. Across the square a café drowsed in the mid-morning sun. When I turned in that direction, the waiter who'd been lounging with a fistful of brioche in the café door crammed the bread into his mouth and brushed the crumbs from his hands, a gleam of curiosity lighting his eyes. I inclined my head in his direction but walked past without speaking. Not him.

At the post office a few doors away, I stopped in front of the notice board, pretending to read a bulletin posted there while actually peering through the window to study the thin-lipped woman behind the grille. She glanced up, caught me staring and gave me an inquisitive smile. Not her.

And so it went throughout the Phantom's village. At the sight of me, the butcher paused, his cleaver hanging over a side of beef. The chamber maid stopped scrubbing the window, leaving her rag to drip soapy water on the windowsill. The tobacconist looked away from his match, almost lighting his customer's moustache instead of his cigar. I'd been in Paris so long I'd forgotten country ways, the intense curiosity that greeted any stranger and the habit of minding your neighbor's business. Given the least encouragement, any one of them would be eager to talk. To answer. And to pry.

As I walked on, I felt their eyes following me, and the weight of their curiosity prickled my skin. Suddenly I could no longer bear the heat of the sun and the glare of the street. I passed the church and escaped through an iron gate into the graveyard.

I paused just inside the wall, momentarily blinded by the heavy shade cast by a towering chestnut tree. I closed my eyes and let the cool and quiet air soothe my burning cheeks. When I opened them again, my gaze traveled the full length of the cemetery. There in the distance, glowing like a living heart, stood a large bouquet of red roses that drew me across the grass to a simple stone chiseled with a single name: Adeline.

"Roses. Always roses. Always red." As he stepped out from behind an imposing mausoleum, the groundskeeper bobbed his head and his white hair fluffed out like the down of a dandelion. "Every week fresh. Winter, summer, year in, year out, red roses."

I tilted my head. "A devoted husband? A loving child?"

"Not that one." He let the wooden handle of his rake rest against his shoulder and spread his hands wide. "She came from the convent. A nun."

I smiled, inviting him to continue.

"No roses when her grave was fresh. I should know. I opened it myself." He shook his head and stared down at the vase standing before Soeur Adeline's stone. "Then one day Père Joseph tells me she's to have roses every week, red ones only. Says I'll be paid for my trouble by an *avocat* in Paris whose client wishes to remain anonymous."

He turned his gaze back to me and lifted his shoulders into a shrug. "That was ten years ago, and the money still arrives as regular as sunrise and sunset."

I nodded slowly. Another one I could ask, the likeliest of all. Yet still I didn't speak. Instead, I faced Soeur Adeline's grave, bowed my head and raised my hand to cross myself. As I'd hoped, the groundskeeper backed away, retreating behind another mausoleum.

Before I completed the cross, it happened. Somewhere deep inside me, a bubble. I froze. Startled. Delighted. My child. And Raoul's. Then a flutter. Stronger. Robust. Our ever-exuberant son somersaulting into his mother's consciousness for the first time. I lowered my hand to my belly, which had barely begun to swell, and a wave of longing washed over me. How this would thrill Raoul!

The antics within me subsided, and once again I made the sign of the cross. I offered a prayer of thanksgiving for the kindly nun and a prayer of safekeeping for the man she'd rescued. Then I walked across the shadowed graveyard, stepped through the iron gate into the September dazzle of the provincial street and lifted my face to the sun.

The de Chagny Letters

Paris, October 1, 1929

Yesterday I buried my mother, and this morning our attorney delivered her memoir to me. He hurried through the rest of our business, undoubtedly sensing my eagerness to open the folio that lay on the desk between us. To be in her company again, to hear her voice and know her thoughts, if only through a web of words inked on a page, was indeed my dearest wish. When the door closed behind him I settled into my armchair before the fire and began to read. To say I was surprised by her story scarcely describes the roiling emotions that swept me in the hours that followed.

I was not in France when Gaston Leroux published his novel, having followed my father into naval service and been posted to Indochina. When I returned from Hai-Phong in 1912, the gossip stirred up by his book had been eclipsed by new uproars, fresh sensations in the endless parade of spectacles that now comprise the whole of our shared public life. And, of course, in our private life, among our family and our friends, the subject of Leroux and his story never arose.

I spoke with Mother about the Phantom of the Paris opera only once in the late autumn of 1925. She had received an invitation from an impudent columnist to be his guest at the premier of the American film of the story starring the actor Lon Chaney and asked me to convey her regrets in the firmest possible way. I offered to arrange a private screening in the ballroom for the family, but she dismissed my suggestion out of hand. I now believe she must have slipped away one afternoon by herself to see the film. In the winter that followed her habits of a lifetime changed, the afternoons devoted to music gave way for a sudden interest in writing. I remember coming into her boudoir one day to find her at her desk – again – and asking the nature of this new project. "I'm writing my memoirs," she answered. "How wonderful," I replied. "May I read them?" She turned to me with a brilliant smile. "Certainly. After I'm safely in my grave." Our exchange ended in laughter, and we never spoke of the Phantom or her writing again.

Mother wrote her memoir to prove that the Phantom was a gifted man, not a frightening monster. In that she clearly succeeded. But I find myself more concerned with the other man in her memoir, the one who cared for her for thirty-seven years until the great flu pandemic took him from us eleven years ago.

Mother and Father were wonderful parents who left me with a treasure of priceless memories that will warm me all the days of my life. He adored her. No one who saw them together or heard him when they were apart could ever doubt that. She was by inclination less showy with her feelings but that her affection for Father was real and lasting and deep I have no doubt. Still, somehow reading her memoir feels like losing him all over again. My father's loss remains too fresh, his memory and his reputation too dear, for me to welcome the re-examination called for by this book. To have my parents' private lives become the latest spectacle exposed before the public is more than I can bear. So I will seal this letter inside an envelope addressed to my son, tuck it behind the last page of the memoir and return the folio to our attorney to safeguard in his vault until I, too, am safely in my grave.

Philippe de Chagny

Paris, April 30, 1940

I lay the blame for my last bloody nose at the feet of Grandmère's Phantom. Of course she saw the American film! Didn't I take her? Didn't she swear me to secrecy and insist I pull the brim of my hat low over my face while she hid her own behind a chic veil? Little did I know then that she and I were reenacting history, obscuring our identities and waiting until the house lights darkened before slipping into our cinema box just as she and the Phantom had so many years before. I was just sixteen and eager to defy anyone and everything except for Grandmère, my beloved companion in many adventures that would have left my parents aghast. A few days later a *sallop* at my school taunted me about the film so I clobbered him, beating him thoroughly to uphold Grandmère's honor and earning a bashed nose for my trouble.

Thus does history repeat itself and yet again to-day – another de Chagny safely in his grave and the Germans on the march. How I would love to launch the spectacle my father so dreaded and see Grandmère's last wish honored! What a pleasure on such a grim day to hear her voice in my head as I read her words and discovered her passionate secret! Instead I will add a letter of my own to her charming folio and hope that one day, when peace returns to Europe, I can finally fulfill her last wish. If I do not survive, Edmund will see to it. If, God forbid, my brother was also lost, the duty will fall to my sister Garance.

Raoul de Chagny

Paris, December 31, 1989

My father did not survive the war. He died in battle in Tunisia in 1943 as did his brother Edmund the following year at Monte Cassino in Italy. Their sister, Garance, was among 35 resisters executed by the Germans near the Bois de Boulogne's great waterfall on the day before the Free French liberated Paris. Thus, as the last de Chagny, I inherited the duty to fulfill my great-grandmother's wish.

Her memoir came to me when I turned twenty-one in 1958. I was then a student at the Paris conservatory, sharing both her name and her talent. Imagine my delight to read the story of another gifted, young soprano intent on conquering Parisian opera and of the maestro who honed her voice to stardom. He, especially, intrigued me with his tireless absorption in his art and his discerning formula for success. I returned to the memoir time and again during those early years: "To achieve greatness, you must put aside worldly things. To sustain that greatness, you will need to turn your back on society, whose celebrations of your brilliance will eventually drain the vitality from your art." The career which followed owed much to his wisdom. That he was a genius is unquestionable, and yet I wondered how he could remain so utterly unknown?

To answer that question I spent hours in the national library on rue de Richelieu, reading contemporary newspaper and magazine accounts of his last infamous season at the Paris opera with its string of surprises great and small for a company and an audience unwilling to be part of the musical vanguard. I found dozens of accounts of my great-grandmother's debut as Juliette, when her Phantom played Roméo, but discovered none that discussed the substance of their performances or his daring staging. Beyond a mention here and a line or two there, what happened on stage that evening had been completely overshadowed by the night's famous disasters – the fallen chandelier and death of Philippe de Chagny. And so, in time, the Phantom's revolutionary production was completely and inexcusably forgotten.

Yet another generation has passed but her story – and his – remains untold. Heeding his advice, I allowed nothing to distract me from my career – not a man, not my great-grandmother's wish, not our need to vindicate her Phantom. There would be time enough for all of that when I had conquered Paris and Milan and London and New York – every opera stage in world. But as I rose to the first rank in my art, so did an English composer who conquered the world of musical theater, culminating in 1986 with an operetta based on Gaston Leroux's classic novel. I had planned to publish my great-grandmother's memoir when I retired from the stage, but the phenomenal popularity of Andrew Lloyd Weber's show forces me to delay. After three decades in the spotlight, I've earned a respite from the blinding glare of the paparazzi. When the Englishman's musical has safely closed, my great-grandmother's wish will at last be fulfilled. However, if by some unlikely chance his show outlives me, the attorneys will see to it after I'm safely in my grave.

Christine de Chagny

French soprano dies in Paris at 72;
de Chagny seen as "last true diva"

January 30, 2009 – French soprano Christine de Chagny, whose quicksilver voice earned her admirers around the world, died yesterday at her Paris home after a brief illness. She was 72.

Miss de Chagny specialized in roles created by French composers and her interpretation of the tragic heroine of Gounod's *Roméo et Juliette* remains the standard for the part. In her most unforgettable performance, de Chagny played Juliette as the princess of the beggars of the mythical court of miracles as depicted in Victor Hugo's *Notre Dame de Paris*.

Her French repertoire also included roles from Meyerbeer's *Robert le diable*, Berlioz's *Les Troyens*, Gounod's *Faust* and Bizet's *Carmen*, but her full repertoire included roles sung in a half-dozen languages and she performed at every important opera house in the world. In addition, Miss de Chagny released numerous solo recordings throughout her career and won acclaim for several concert tours. When she retired from the stage in 1989 at the age of 52, critics pronounced her opera's "last true diva."

Although her name was linked in the press over the years with a Hollywood mogul, a Greek shipping magnate and a French Formula One driver, Miss de Chagny never married and was the last member of an aristocratic family whose nobility dated back to the 14th century.

A spokesman for the estate said Miss de Chagny's instructions call for the sale of her historic home in Paris, extensive estates in the Touraine and Brittany, and a collection of Impressionist paintings assembled by her great-grandparents that museum curators say is the finest remaining in private hands. The spokesman said the proceeds will underwrite two new charities which will bear her name: one to provide medical intervention for children born with severe facial deformities and the other to offer free musical education to indigent children who show exceptional promise.

About the Author

Anstance Tamplin is a pseudonym of Beth Quinn Barnard. Writing as Elizabeth Quinn, she is the author of *Alliances, Any Day Now, Blood Feud,* and the Lauren Maxwell mysteries: *Murder Most Grizzly, A Wolf in Death's Clothing, Lamb to the Slaughter and Killer Whale.*

Made in the USA
Lexington, KY
26 September 2011